The Bend Sinister

The Bend Sinister

A Mystery

by

T. J. Doyle

Brunswick

Copyright © 1998 by T. J. Doyle

All rights reserved under International and Pan-American Copyright Conventions. No part of this book may be reproduced in any form or by any means, electronic or mechanical, including photocopying or by any informational storage or retrieval systems, without written permission from the author and the publisher, except by a reviewer who may quote brief passages in a review.

Library of Congress Cataloging-in-Publication Data

Doyle, T. J., 1930–
    The bend sinister : a mystery /T. J. Doyle. -- 1st ed.
       p.   c.m.
    ISBN 1-55618-174-4 (alk. paper)
    I. Title.
PS3554.O977B4   1998
813'. 54--dc21   98–26424
                                                           CIP

First Edition
Published in the United States of America
by

Brunswick Publishing Corporation
1386 Lawrenceville Plank Road
Lawrenceville, Virginia 23868
1-800-336-7154

To Peggy Wood Doyle, my wife, best friend, editor, confidant and collaborator, without whose patience, encouragement, endless reviews and suggestions, this work could *never* have been completed.

Historical Prologue

Constantinople—1204 A.D.

Claudia stood by the casement and watched as the dawn's first rays pinked the blue crested hills to the east of the city. She was momentarily lost in the beauty of the sight; in her thirty-six years she had beheld but few dawns and then, most unwillingly. Through the billowing smoke, still fed by subsiding fires, she could see the walls of Constantinople. Beyond these walls smoke curled over the Golden Horn and the more distant Bosporus' calm waters. I have no time for day dreams, she thought and within her belly the small snake of anxiety writhed again. In an uncharacteristic moment of weakness, Claudia wished herself walking in the safety of those pink tinged hills.

I delayed my departure too long—why didn't I leave with the others? After the Pretender had been slain the Franks cut Byzantium open like a ripe melon. Betrayed from within by apathy and cowardice, the city lay helpless. She watched with disdain when the first plunderers came the day before, ungainly German bumpkins who could not imagine Byzantium's splendor. Claudia dismissed them with a silver goblet apiece, for which they gratefully thanked her. But I underestimated them, she chided herself bitterly. I know men, she thought—I should have realized that the character of the pillage would change. We can buy these barbarians off with trinkets for a while but soon they would find wine and distorted with drink, the young Franks would realize that they could do as they wished. Then the brutalities will begin. She was well aware that men muzzled by drink and seized by the blood-lust were capable of felonies they would never have dreamed of in the past.

They came four times yesterday and at each appearance they were more threatening. Claudia continued to give them her valuables until she had nothing left—nothing but the casket. That still lay secure in its repository in the wall.

An unemotional woman, acquainted with the cruelties of her time and with a profound understanding of men, Claudia knew intuitively that her survival depended on living through this night. At dawn, sick with the excesses of wine and slaughter, the Franks would slink trembling to a guilty sleep. Satan comes with the night and would clutch the city but he would leave at dawn, traveling westward, following the dark shadows.

I have always had the ability to calculate, Claudia thought, to see opportunities that others might miss. Slowly the plan formulated and, with her young daughter Hilaria, she grimly set to the destruction of their large and imposing home that would have satisfied the most violent Frank. With her own slim hands she smashed the glass cabinets, broke crystal and ceramic goblets and ewers, tore down drapes, and overturned furniture. She grasped the heavy iron bar that secured the main door to the house and with a feat of strength that amazed even herself, smashed the lock and splintered the wooden door, leaving it gaping open. In the atrium she lit a fire of burnables she collected, singeing the door itself, charring the lintel and blackening the outside facia. Leaning exhausted against the door she was satisfied—the building looked gutted and raped.

"Come," she said curtly to Hilaria and they went to the second floor. Together they pushed and inched a large, heavy wardrobe cupboard to the staircase and tumbled it down so that it blocked the stairs, not an insurmountable but a discouraging obstacle. She extracted the casket from its repository. It was a magnificent piece of workmanship, eighteen inches by twelve by ten inches, inlaid with gold and encrusted with jewels. It bore no crosses or religious symbols and was clearly of Asian origin—and worth a King's ransom.

Claudia toyed with the idea of prizing off the jewels for her planned trip but decided against it. Women would be trying to buy their lives and virtue throughout the city with glass beads—anyone looking at the stones in this magnificent box would know they were real. No one sets glass in gold . . .

They hid behind the heavy timbered door of a small storeroom on the second floor. Claudia set the golden casket on a nearby shelf and stood by the window while the fifteen year old Hilaria remained with her back against the opposite wall.

Her instincts were correct—Satan did come with the night! The air was filled with the raucous laughter of unrestrained men that gradually deteriorated into manic growls—and with other, terrifying screams. The red glow of fires began to show and this was what Claudia feared most, to be driven into the streets by fire.

Her precise and controlled mind turned to the casket. If the Crusaders came steeped in dangerous blood-lust she must douse these flames of passion and quickly replace them with others—avarice or lust. The casket represented more wealth, more innate power, than these barbarians could conceive of. If after seeing the box some embers of passion remained, Claudia could quench them with the gifts of her body, for she had long ago traded away her virtue.

Looking dispassionately across the room, she measured Hilaria, sitting on the floor with her back against the wall, her knees up with her elbows resting upon them. The girl was staring blankly into space. She would age to womanhood before this was over, Claudia thought grimly. There was little affection between the handsome mother and the pretty daughter. Claudia had never forgiven Hilaria for her gender.

Passions were ebbing in the street below. As she predicted, young callow boys were beginning to look upon the vileness of their crimes in the uncompromising light of day and were stealing off to try to forget through sleep.

She had planned her next moves carefully. They would put the casket in a wicker basket and take it to The Golden Horn where Lucius had a small boat—if it was still afloat, and if Lucius was still alive. At mid-morning, the safest time, they would cross the Bosporus to the east and hide in the hill house until all this was over.

She heard a sound! Tense and alert Claudia turned. The heavy footfalls were of a mailed man on the floor below! She waited breathlessly. Hilaria had also heard and had risen, pressing her back against the wall. The feet thumped up the staircase. Claudia strained intently to hear them descend again but instead the cupboard crashed down! The steps were louder in the hallway and the closed door rattled as it was attempted, filling the room with a terrifying sound. There was silence before the body crashed against the heavy timbers again and again.

Claudia walked across the room and stood in its center before the door. She hoped it was a Venetian rather than a Frank. Venetians were sly and thought ahead. The Franks thought of nothing but the present.

The door splintered and crashed aside. Through the aperture stepped a tall mailed figure with the white mantle and red cross of the Crusader. His brownish, blond hair was encased in a steel helmet and he carried a large, double-edged sword. His blue eyes looked at the calm and prepossessed figure of Claudia standing before him.

Appraising the Frank with the certainty of a woman who had evaluated men all her life, Claudia calmly walked to the shelf where the casket reposed. She picked it up, turned and proffered it to the startled intruder. Taking the casket and turning, he saw Hilaria pressed against the wall. He then returned his gaze to appraise Claudia. She knew that look well. Slowly undoing her dress down the front, she dropped it from her shoulders until it caught at her elbows to show she was naked beneath the gown. He placed the casket on a small table by the door.

It happened so quickly that Claudia and Hilaria screamed at the same instant. With his back half turned, the blade flashed in a downward, then upward arc! Claudia staggered for a step and then dropped like a stone! Hilaria watched petrified as blood sprinkled across the wall in a diagonal track, low at the left and upward toward the right!

The cold blue eyes turned on Hilaria. He approached the trembling girl who stood on her toes, her slim back, shoulders and the palms of her hands pressed flat against the uncompromising wall, her head turned at a slight angle. She watched the large hand approach and grasp the bodice of her dress at the neckline and begin to methodically tear it down.

Chapter I

Wexford, Ireland—1995

It was freezing cold in the silvery sunlight. For the Irish, after shivering all winter in the damp and the cold, this was a fine spring day, but I could feel the chill creeping up my legs. I took another sip from the tumbler of Bushmills.

"Are you sure?" I asked again, nodding toward the glass.

"It's too early for drink," Sarah Grey replied with a gesture as if to brush away the nonexistent hair. She looked across the small round table, her eyes furtive beneath the dark brows, trying to size me up.

We were sitting in what the Irish laughingly call a "sidewalk cafe" in Wexford the morning after my arrival at Shannon. It would have been grand if I were an Eskimo. The proprietor didn't bat an eye when I ordered Bushmills rather than morning coffee, in fact he seemed impressed with my good sense. I had called Sarah Grey in Dublin and she had driven down in an ancient, beat-up Volkswagen.

She was pretty despite her efforts to hide it. I guess I'm an old-fashioned Virginian but I like a girl to look like a girl. She was wearing an old military jacket that could have parachuted in with the 82nd on D-Day, a pair of ceremonial jeans appropriately sliced up to show she had flesh underneath and heavy flat shoes. You couldn't tell how she was put together. And her hair, ash blonde and cut close to her head, defeated any discipline or form. Her nice green eyes were carefully hidden behind large round glasses with a very narrow black rim. Her voice was attractive in the lilting way the Irish speak.

"Someone's trying to kill me," she said at last, awkwardly lighting the third cigarette since we sat down but the words caught in her throat, as if saying them gave them a frightening credence. I stood pat; a big part of my job is evaluating clients and the best prod is silence. Nature abhors a vacuum and silence is the ultimate vacuum. People unconsciously try to fill it with talk and usually tell me all kinds of things about themselves that they regret later on.

As with most of us, perception is reality. I didn't know whether Sarah Grey was in mortal danger or not but she thought she was. She puffed on the cigarette a few times and snubbed it out with the pile of other dead soldiers in the ash tray. Her hand trembled.

"I know it sounds melodramatic but I do have this," she held up her right wrist encased in the soiled plaster cast. I still didn't say anything. I guess I had a questioning look, so she answered my unspoken query.

"I know, you can break yer wrist yanking too hard on the handle of a slot machine but that didn't happen to me; someone tried to run me down with a lorry."

I took another sip of Bushmills and she was getting mad. That was good; angry people really opened up.

"Och—I don't know why I'm wastin' me time with you!" she lilted in exasperation and lit another cigarette.

"If I were them I'd wait," I said at last.

"What do you mean?"

"In two or three months you'll smoke yourself to death."

"I've been tryin' to give it up," she said bitterly, "but what's the use. If someone is tryin' to kill one, one might as well enjoy one's small vices."

Good point, I thought. Living on borrowed time you may as well enjoy what you can.

"Anyway that's why I've hired you and Miss Benedict—you are art detectives after all . . ."

I guess I smiled at that.

"You think this is all a bloody joke, don't you, Peete?" She was really sore now; her green eyes were flashing and color rose in her cheeks.

"Sorry," I said. "I don't mean to seem calloused. I was tickled at what you said, not your predicament. Dr. Charlotte Montaigne Benedict would go ballistic at being called a 'detective.'"

"Really? Well I don't find it amusin'. You use the deductive process to solve problems—to find things. That sounds like a detective to me."

"I don't know. So do doctors and lawyers and engineers—use the deductive process with problems. That doesn't make them detectives—that makes them doctors or lawyers or engineers."

"Well I don't care about Benedict's reactions."

"You better start caring about them. If we take this on it could be very important to your sanity—and mine."

"If—what do you mean, 'if'?"

"That's right, Miss Grey. It's a very definite 'if.'"

She bridled now and there was real fire in her eyes. "You're tellin' me that you've flown all th' way to Ireland and you might not take it on?"

"That's right. I have Miss Benedict's authorization to reject clients, but not accept them. Only she does that. Suppose you tell me about it, then we'll see where we go from there."

"I told you about George Fowler in my letter..."

The letter had come a week or so ago. Most of our work comes by direct referral to Miz Charlotte herself, generally from insurance companies or museum foundations, but we do get inquiries from the great unwashed—the lady from Oshgosh who finds an oddity in old Aunt Tilly's trunk in the attic, and so forth. The letter from Sarah Grey seemed unsophisticated. Either she was a graduate student reading History at Trinity College and the victim of some strange events, or she was something else—and very shifty indeed.

The letter talked directly, but with some literary flourish (which I thought very Irishy) about opening an old tomb at the site of the Monastery of St. Camillus and uncovering something rare and possibly quite valuable historically and maybe financially. She had been involved in the effort on a part-time basis (owing to class commitments at Trinity) and had been compiling and editing the notes of George Fowler who was working at the site. She knew a good deal about the events surrounding the discovery. Fowler was working as an assistant to Professor Alfred Steiner of Markham College, a small place in South Carolina. All she said was that Fowler met with an accident and the "box" had disappeared.

"Yeah, he's the guy from the dig who was killed," I replied.

"George Fowler was very excited about th' casket—in fact he was positively gloating about it."

" 'Casket?' What do you mean, a coffin?"

"No, no—just a box about eighteen inches by twelve inches by ten inches. It was stored in the tomb, you see, and..."

"Wait a minute," I said, holding up my hand, "let's start at the beginning. How did you, George Fowler and Steiner get involved in this?"

"Fowler was sending me notes, for his thesis..."

"No, no—further back, at the beginning."

She lit another cigarette and immediately snubbed it out.

"I'm reading History at Trinity. I don't have a lot of money, almost no one in Ireland does. So I started workin' th' genealogy thing on the side."

"Genealogy?"

"You know, all those rich Yanks findin' their roots. It's pathetic. Most Americans don't know th' names of their great-grandparents. Then they start wonderin'. They find th' name of a parish, or a village, and they want to know all about it. That's how I got to know of Lacy."

"Lacy?"

"Aloysius Lacy of New York. Rich as a bloody baron, he is. A contractor, he says. He wanted to find out about his family; they had immigrated early—about 1820."

"You've met him?"

"Aye, I did. He visited about three months ago. He had written th' Historical Society here in Wexford an' they passed him on to me. I couldn't find out very much. He had no names you see. I was near givin' it up when I came across something that I thought might be of interest."

"That being?"

"I was thrashing about for a thesis meself, tryin' out different ideas, you know, and I thought of something on the development of the Mafia."

"The Mafia!"

"Those criminal organizations of Sicily are very ancient. The extortion has been goin' on fer centuries. I wanted to see if there was a historical root, you see."

"What the hell would that have to do with Aloysius Lacy?"

"Well there was Count Odo deLacy an' the Bend Sinister."

I held up my hand and took another gulp of the Bushmills. "Now look . . ." I started.

"Are you wantin' to hear or not?"

I shrugged. "Try and ease up on the fairy tales."

"I know. I told Lacy it didn't mean anything—that th' deLacys were a huge family, that he might not really be related at all. But it tickled his imagination."

"All right, I'll bite. Who is Count Odo deLacy? Is he real or did you make him up along with the banshees and leprechauns?"

"Oh, he was real. It was his tomb, you see."

"I thought he was in Sicily?"

"He was. You know how the Normans exploded on the scene during th' Eleventh, Twelfth and Thirteenth Centuries. It was remarkable. In th' ninth century they were Viking raiders with a foothold in northern France. In two hundred years one was th' King of England and another th' King of th' Two Sicilies."

"Spare me the history lesson; what about deLacy?"

"He was born in 1167, here in Ireland."

"In Ireland?"

"He was born on th' wrong side of th' blanket—a bastard by birth and, apparently a bastard by nature. His father was one of those wild Norman knights sent over by Henry II. He left Ireland around 1190. No one knows why. In any event he went to Sicily. Then he went on th' Fourth Crusade."

"To Constantinople?"

"Yes."

"How did you uncover all of this?"

"From various sources. The Normans kept close track on things an' people—for tax purposes, y'know. Governments don't bloody change much, do they? Then Count Odo was mentioned both by the Byzantine Emperor's niece, Anna Comnena, and more frequently in th' chronicles of Geoffery de Villehardouin, th' Chief of Staff to th' Count of Champagne. He kept extensive records of th' Fourth Crusade and I guess deLacy was a thorn in everybody's side.

"You know th' Crusaders sacked and burned Constantinople for a three day period granted by th' leadership. All th' loot was supposed to be collected and then meted out later, as th' leadership saw fit. But Odo deLacy had gotten his hands on somethin' grand and he refused to give it up. There was a great to-do about it but Odo was very much feared. He brought it back with him."

"What was it?"

"It was a golden casket, encrusted with jewels, but no one knew what was in it."

"He went back to Sicily?"

"Yes—an' he founded an order of soldier monks, the Friars of th' Bend Sinister."

"The Bend Sinister?"

"The sign of illegitimate birth on th' coat of arms. They were all bastards. It was a very small order, you see. An' they were nothin' more than a band of extortionists."

"But Odo finally came back here?"

"Aye, I get th' impression that Odo deLacy had to keep on th' move. He came back to Ireland and, I guess, more devilment. He was confined to th' Monastery of St. Camillus."

"Confined?"

"By Royal decree. He died around 1220. But he was not to be found in th' remains of th' basilica. I went to th' ruins, you see. I had contacted Father Courtney, the local pastor in whose parish th' monastery ruins are located and he's very interested in historical matters. We went over th' ruins but could find no trace of deLacy in th' chapel. I thought perhaps he had been put into th' ground—a suicide or somethin' and not buried in consecrated earth."

"But you did find him?"

"Aye, by accident. I had written to Lacy in New York about Count Odo. I was very honest, I swear, I explained th' size of th' family, how they were all over England as well as Ireland. But I thought he might be interested...."

"And cough up a few more bucks for further investigation?"

"Yes," she flashed again. "An' why not, I'll be askin'? As long as no one was deceivin' him, why not? It's easy fer you, Mr. David Peete, dressed in yer fine suits with yer Bally shoes to be very superior about money. I could live a year on Aloysius Lacy's pocket change—dreamin' about his ancestors!"

"His ancestors? You don't even know if Odo had issue."

"He probably had bastards all over th' county. He was th' type. I explained all that to Lacy."

"Did you explain the mathematical sequence of direct parentage? The 2, 4, 8, 16, 32, 64, 128, etc.? Did you explain to him that going back to the year 1000 A.D. his direct parent lineage would be nearly a half million people?"

"Sure an' he was a grand contractor, wasn't he? Makin' pots of money? He'd know his numbers. He'd know he was chasin' one small rhizome of th' whole tree!"

She lapsed into silence; her conscience was eating at her. I think, deep down, she felt she had done something tawdry or dishonest.

"I wouldn't worry about Lacy," I said, trying to soothe her. "What about the tomb?"

"It wasn't in th' floor of th' chapel where you would expect, him bein' an Abbot an' all. He was over in back of th' bakery. I don't know why. We knew there was a tomb there, you see. Th' steps to th' entry had been filled in but you could see an old marker, an exposed an' worn stone tablet. It couldn't be read, but you could make out somethin' in Latin. I thought it said that someone named 'Alexander' was buried there. So I never paid attention to it.

"I wrote to Lacy an' told him we were findin' nothing. I said there were other graves about, like this 'Alexander' person, but I wasn't hopeful. He wrote back an' said he was comin'. An' come he did—in January . . . a small weasel of a man with great ears. Out at th' ruins he said he wanted me to continue— to leave 'no stone unturned'.

"It was his money, so, why not? I fiddled about for a while and finally thought I'd have a look at this Alexander person. I thought there might be others entombed with him. So I had th' entryway dug out . . ."

"How did you do that?"

"I hired Muldoon, a laborer recommended by Father Hugh."

"The local parish priest?"

"Aye. He was interested in th' ruins. Father Hugh was helpful, spent most of his free time with us."

"Were you there when Muldoon dug out the entryway?"

"Oh, yes. I wouldn't let him do that unsupervised. You never know what you might find—and Saints in Heaven, what we did find! When we reached th' doorway to th' tomb, we found a skeleton—of a woman, curled up in the corner by th' door!"

Chapter II

Saints preserve us, the Irish! I put my head down on the back of my hand on the table and held up my other hand.

"No—stop, wait a minute. . . ." I gasped.

"It's true! You can ask Father Hugh. I presume you'll believe a man of th' cloth?"

"I'm not sure I'll believe anyone in Ireland," I tweaked her. She said something under her breath.

"So you found the crypt?" I asked at last.

"We still didn't know it then. When we uncovered th' door slab there was faint Latin writing cut into th' stone. Again we couldn't read it but Father Hugh thought it was an interdiction."

"A Church interdiction?"

"Aye, that's what we thought, and it made some sense. The bones by the entry slab, you see, it was as if she had been interred there. The excavation material had been clean earth, very little stone in it and no rubble at all. And there was somethin' else."

"There was a stake through her heart?" I asked, warming to the topic. This was getting hokier by the minute.

"No, but her neck had been broken . . ."

"So you opened the tomb," I marched on resolutely, waiting for the eerie howl of the banshee.

"No, there's th' Irish government and th' Church. Father Hugh an' I did a great deal of jawing about what to do. There were questions of propriety, of religion, of possible national treasures—and of my qualifications." She toyed with the cigarette packet. "I'm only a graduate student, after all. . . ."

"So you went back to Lacy?"

"Yes," she said. "No authorities knew what we were about—not th' government or th' Bishop. The Irish are capable of discussin' these questions fer a hundred years and still gettin' nowhere. I called Lacy an' he talked to Father Hugh. He got Father Hugh to agree to a 'preliminary look' by well-qualified people. If anythin' turned up, then we'd go to th' proper authorities. That's how Lacy hired Steiner an' Fowler."

"It seems like a lot of people just to open a grave."

She was silent for a moment, as if thinking back to the time at the tomb. She shook herself a bit and continued. "A grand boondoggle it was. Steiner marched about like Brian Boru with his hands behind his back holdin' his brelly an' makin' grand statements about this an' that. He was in a 'supervisory' capacity, you see. That means you don't do any of th' bloody work, you say profound things, an' make yer headquarters in th' nearest pub with yer backside by th' fire.

"Fowler was to do th' work, or rather see to Muldoon doin' it. I was about as needful as a midwife at a calving."

"What was Fowler like?"

I sensed her retreating warily behind her defenses.

"He was all right. . . ."

"Tell me about him."

"He was free and easy—always ready with th' cheeky joke an' th' repartee but he had a face like a choirboy—so innocent lookin' an' sweet. He couldn't stand Steiner, I can tell you that. Steiner was Fowler's mentor for his Doctoral thesis and Steiner was th' one with th' grand reputation. Steiner had no sense of humor at all, you see, an' Fowler was continually havin' him on."

"Did that make Steiner angry?"

"I don't know—Fowler was very clever, you see, like I said he could say things with th' face of an angel. He seemed to disconcert Steiner; he couldn't keep up with it. Steiner was th' perfect foil, he was so pompous—so full of his own importance."

"How did you get on with Fowler?"

Again I sensed an evasion.

"An' what's this got to do with anythin' I'd like to be knowin'?" She was getting angry again.

"I don't know, maybe nothing."

"Fowler seemed to know his business. . . ."

"So he came on to you. Is that bad? You were both young. What's wrong with a little romance while searching out the roots of history?"

"Och, to his way of thinkin' women were only good fer one thing an' th' grandest way to discuss archeology an' history was between th' sheets!" She said this bitterly, as if it was more a reflection on her scholarship than her virtue. She lit another cigarette with a dry cough.

"So you didn't appreciate his advances?"

"He was a randy goat in rut so I left . . . there was my schoolwork of course, an' I had no desire to stand about an' be insulted. But I did want to keep me hand in th' project. After all, it was my discovery—the tomb, I mean. So I would come when I had a chance or anythin' important was to be happenin' . . . an' I agreed to transcribe Fowler's notes.

"I made sure I was there when th' crypt was opened. Of course Steiner was there also so there was a great deal of 'mumbo jumbo.'"

"And it was deLacy's tomb?"

"Oh yes. Inside was a sarcophagus with th' prone stone figure, his ankles crossed to show he'd been on a crusade."

She jabbed out her cigarette with vehemence.

"There was a stone tablet in Latin. I copied it down an' took it back to Trinity to translate. It was an interdiction against disturbin' th' tomb. I wondered how Aloysius Lacy would be feelin' about that! An' then there was th' other thing. . . ." she said with satisfaction.

"What was that?"

"We found a reliquary. At the foot of th' sarcophagus was a niche—again with an interdiction not to open it an' this presented a problem. We were on Church lands. Father Hugh had been very nervous about th' business from th' start and he was in a blue funk now. He said that it couldn't be opened without Church permission. He had a great to-do with Steiner. It was finally agreed that Father Hugh would go to th' Bishop."

"But the reliquary was opened?"

"Oh yes. Everyone left after Father Hugh agreed to go to th' Bishop. I went back to Trinity, Steiner carried his backside back to th' pub fire, but George Fowler opened th' reliquary that night. . . . Inside was a sealed box."

". . . golden and crusted with jewels?" I asked. Maybe she thought I just fell off the pumpkin truck.

"No—old battered bronze. That night he wrote a detailed description of th' box which he forwarded to me by letter. That was the last I heard of him—alive."

She hugged herself as if she was cold.

"He didn't open the box?"

"I don't know. Not at th' time of his letter apparently. He said it was sealed an' he wanted to be very careful. He was thinkin' about tryin' to get it x-rayed."

"And then?" I asked, waiting for the big finale.

"He just dropped out of sight. No one could find him. He hadn't checked out of his hotel, but he was gone. There was the very devil to pay at th' crypt. Father Hugh was really upset and Steiner was huffing and puffing about. Actually I think that Steiner was terrified—it was all his responsibility, you see—an' now th' project was goin' to hell an' Steiner's reputation would be followin' it. He accused me of bein' in collusion with Fowler. Then suddenly, Fowler was back."

"I thought you said the letter with the notes was the last you heard from him?" I pounced; I figured I had her.

"Aye, that's true. Downey, th' desk clerk in th' hotel, saw him on th' 12th of April, about three weeks ago. But I never saw or heard from him, and Steiner claims he didn't either. Then he was gone again. We thought he had run off until they found his body."

"What happened to him?"

"He had drowned in th' Slaney."

She took out another cigarette and then put it back with a petulant sigh.

"What was th' coroner's verdict?"

"Death by misadventure—he had been dead drunk."

"And the box?"

"It's gone," she shrugged, her owl-like eyes staring at me.

"You have no idea?"

"None."

I had that old uncomfortable feeling. What did I really know about Sarah Grey other than she was studying for an advanced degree at Trinity and wasn't above taking rich Yanks for a bit of a ride? Only what she told me and that sounded like a complete farrago—a lost crusader's tomb, a mysterious order of monks, a strange box, interdictions—all the characteristics of an elaborate scam.

On top of that my conscience was pinching. I had spent a dull winter at Avalon, reading about Dr. Dorphmann's latest finds at Troy and sparring with Miss Benedict during her usual fits of pique. This trip was a boondoggle. Going to Ireland in May appealed to me after the long winter hibernation. Why not dehibernate in Hibernia?

I didn't expect a damned thing to come from Sarah Grey's letter, but I was intrigued by the little liar (that's what I thought she was) and figured since I was here, I'd play the game and see how good she really was. The idea was, of course, that we'd stumble on the famous box during our travels and it would contain some rare, and very bogus, treasure. Benedict never interfered with my spending her money in this way; she was realist enough to know one good find would compensate for many wild goose chases, and she was gambler enough to have a fling. Also, after uncovering the mare's nest, she'd have sufficient substance to needle me for months.

"Let's drive up to the tomb," I said at last.

"There's nothing up there."

"I'd like to talk to Father Courtney."

"He won't be knowin' any more that I do."

"Not necessarily, most people see things differently."

"I'd prefer you wouldn't be botherin' Father Hugh. He's got enough troubles as it is." She began to get edgy again.

"Oh, and why is that?"

"Father Hugh has great problems with the' Bishop, and th' parish. Bein' a priest is not easy, especially today. He's had a hard time of it . . . sent forth as a missionary he was—to America, no less—somewhere in Florida. It was th' ruination of him."

"Did the natives try to eat him?"

She bridled and slammed her fists on the table top. "You're

like th' rest, but tis true! The Church is very different there. All types of freedoms an' questions bein' allowed. An' Vatican II, th' Americans took th' bit in their teeth with Vatican II!

"Then he was called back. A great blow, it was. He wanted to stay in America with his fine car an' fine house and freedom. Of course I've never been to America but it must be very grand.

"He crossed th' Bishop some way an' was sent out here to St. Brendan's—to Siberia. Th' parishioners don't care for him, he's too liberal."

We had walked to my Mercedes under the chill silvery sky. A brisk wind was shaking the limbs of the budding trees.

"Is this yer car, now? Isn't it grand? You could have rented a Ford a lot cheaper."

"A Mercedes is safer."

"Och, there's not many cars here, it's very safe."

"I could hit a sheep; sheep can be dangerous—I hear that they charge when they're wounded."

She climbed in and snuggled her trim behind into the soft leather. She was enjoying this and I wondered just what she'd be willing to do for "grand" things.

People are victims of their training. I had been carefully taught that in life threatening things can happen too fast for the cool application of logic, but good training can trigger automatic responses that operate below the level of reason. For nine years I had been honed by training to a razor's edge and now, some reactions just came naturally. Pulling out of the parking lot of the hotel where I was staying, I noticed the Morris Minor behind us. It was no big deal but it registered in some deep corner of my brain, a random fact catalogued and stored for future reference. It came from years of being conditioned to watch my rear. As we slid out on the road toward Carlow, the Morris was behind a lorry but still there. I said nothing to Sarah Grey.

"Why do you think that someone tried to hurt you?"

"It was a narrow lane in Dublin, the street where I live. I was walkin' home from th' tram stop an' passed a parked lorry at th' end of th' street. I paid no mind and walked on. Then I heard th' roar of th' engine and it was comin' down on me in th' narrow way—full tilt, it was! I just barely managed to throw meself into a doorway...."

"Maybe he was drunk?"

"I don't think so. He didn't have his lights on, you see. At any rate I've been afraid to go back there since."

She pointed out the gravelled roadway that led to St. Camillus' ruins. I checked the rearview mirror. The Morris had made the turn.

Chapter III

The Monastery of St. Camillus sat astride a rocky perch in those bald hills that lie to the North and West of Wexford. A few crumbling walls of the enclave remained and the narrow entry road followed the natural lines of the hillside in a steep, meandering ascent, ending in a small gravelled parking lot. Smiling inwardly as we approached, I watched a large tour bus disgorge its whelp of garishly dressed American tourists.

Nosing the Mercedes into a spot next to the bus I took a small OD bag from the back seat that had, among other things, my collapsible binoculars and a flashlight. Sarah Grey's green eyes watched me probingly.

"What's that for?"

"Bird-watching—I might see something interesting." I started to follow the jabbering crowd to the ruins of the old basilica.

"Wait, th' tomb is this way. . . ."

"Let's see the basilica first."

Standing amid the crowd on the stone floor of the old church as the Irish tour guide droned on, I spotted the Morris parked by the side of the entry road and took a quick peek. He was by the roadway, looking down, his coarse features frowning. A big man with heavy brows, dark curly hair and a blue chin, he was obviously trying desperately to locate us on the monastery grounds. Sarah again looked questioningly at the binoculars.

"What are you looking at?"

"I think I saw a yellow-breasted sapsucker."

I felt reasonably safe with the tourists about and Sarah led me to the tomb which was cordoned and signed as "off limits." Located some distance to the side, away from the basilica on the peak of a small mound, what remained of the old bakery was in much better shape with much of the masonry walls still standing. Buried deep within the womb of the hill the slotted openings of the stone kilns gaped back at me.

"These ovens were used for th' baking of bread until not too long ago. The tomb is at the back," she informed me. As we circled the old ruin I saw that "Mr. Bluejaw" had located us and seemed content just to watch.

The tomb, butted against the warm kilns that conveniently kept it dry over the ages, was in excellent shape. The stone staircase had been excavated with a mound of clean earth deposited by the steps. Sarah had been right; there was no rubble.

Taking a flashlight from my bag, I held it to the side of the door panel. Squinting at the shadows I could read the Latinized "Alexander" but could make out nothing further.

"Th' woman's remains were found huddled in th' corner, by th' door slab."

"You think she had been hanged?"

"I don't know—her neck had been broken. . . ."

Not normally given to flights of fancy, I felt a chill. Maybe the old tomb stirred some deep atavism, maybe it was Ireland with its wee people and folklore. After that, however, the tomb itself was anticlimactic.

Set near the back wall, barely visible in the faint light, lay the sarcophagus with the recumbent figure cut into the top. The reliquary was merely an empty recess at the foot.

"So the box was here?"

"Aye—as you can see, there's the stone cover."

I looked down at the Latin interdiction. It didn't say much, just that it was not to be opened.

"When we first saw it, before Father Hugh came down on him, Steiner did a great deal of posturing. He wanted photographers present at th' opening and a grand hoopla. Fowler was furious. If th' box was anything, Steiner would be hoggin' all th' glory. There'd be none left fer others."

"Wait, go over that again."

"Fowler found th' reliquary, callin' to us, sayin', 'Look at this!' or some such words. We could all see it was important, but Steiner stopped everyone. 'Don't touch it,' he said, 'this must be recorded!'

"An' Father Hugh was joinin' in. 'Don't touch it,' he said, 'it's Church property.' Then he an' Steiner had a fine donnybrook."

"I don't get it. Why was Father Hugh so upset?"

We had left the close, stale air of the crypt for the tinny sunlight at the top of the entry steps. The brisk wind ruffled her close-cropped hair. The green eyes were pensive behind the black rims of her glasses.

"Father Hugh is a bit of . . . well, a rebel, you see. I told you that he didn't get on with th' Bishop. He was tryin' th' new ways but he was caught in-between. The old ladies in their shawls wanted none o' that. Religion had held Ireland together for centuries—through hard times, I'll tell you! Anyway Father Hugh had a great fallin' out with th' Bishop and he was sent out here —to St. Brendan's.

"He has a keen interest in history an' researchin' th' old monastery grounds gave him a fine diversion. A great help he was, as amateurs often are. They have that pristine motivation that's jaded in th' rest of us after a bit.

"He never told th' Bishop about th' search fer Count Odo. He should have perhaps, but th' Bishop is an old stick, an' that would have been th' end of that.

"I'm sure he thought findin' th' tomb would have made a difference. It might improve th' attraction of th' monastery for th' tourists an' bring in some more money. Lord knows, folks here could use a bit of that!

"Then we found th' interdiction an' the reliquary an' things changed for him. It wasn't just a tomb anymore, but maybe somethin' else. Now he would have to go to th' Bishop and it would all come out—not only allowin' th' diggin', but bein' a part of it.

"Th' interdiction really upset him. We could tell what it was; a solemn pronouncement by Holy Mother Church regardin' th' tomb. Even if th' Bishop was willin' to go ahead—which would be like Easter in January—the question might have to go to Rome."

"So Father Hugh went up the chain?"

"He was goin'. He hadn't last time I saw him—wrestlin' with himself, you know. He forbade anyone to touch anything."

"And Steiner?"

"Och, there were great pompous speeches about what he was goin' to do an' th' grand mucky-mucks he knew in Rome an' whatnot."

The tourists gathered by the bus and I ushered her silently to the car while she talked. Caution seemed best; I didn't want to be caught on a deserted hillside with Mr. Bluejaw.

"Let's go talk to Father Hugh."

"I wish you wouldn't Mr. Peete. He's got enough troubles right now an' I can tell you everythin'."

"As I said, we all see things a little differently. I'll try not to ruffle him. After all, he wants the box back, even if it's just to put it back and seal the tomb again."

She lay back silently against the cushions. Adjusting the side mirror, I could see the Morris still at its same location. As the last of the tourist stragglers clambered aboard, the diesel rumbled and the bus started to move. I waited until the timing was just right and gunned the Mercedes in front of the bus and shot down the narrow lane toward the Carlow Road. Mr. Bluejaw bolted for his car while I hit the accelerator. The bus descended with stately dignity with the Morris caught at its rear.

Sarah directed me west on the Carlow Road to the small village of Ballyfaleen. I could see what she meant by the Bishop sending Father Courtney to Siberia. The meager street contained a row of ugly brown houses, a market and a disreputable looking Pub with "Courage" in bold letters in the window. A few cottages could be seen, the kind with roses and thatched roofs that seem so quaint to American tourists and are sheer hell to live in.

The stone church frowned on the village from a bleak mound at the other end of the street. Austere and old, but serviceable, I noticed the roof could do with some work.

"Th' Rectory's over there," Sarah said, pointing to a forlorn cottage also needing repairs. While not bustling with activity, there were people about. The Morris and Mr. Bluejaw weren't in sight, but I was willing to bet my skivvies he was around, somewhere.

Tugging the old-fashioned pull chord, a bell faintly tinkled inside the cottage. Sarah Grey was quiet, lost in some thought of her own and I looked at the dismal front yard. I was about to give it up when I heard a rustling from within. The door opened a crack and a pair of suspicious eyes peered out at me.

"Hello, Mrs. McGinty," Sarah said. "Would Father Hugh be about?"

The face of a middle-aged woman softened fractionally and the door opened a bit wider. "Och, Miss Grey—I dint see yer standin' there."

"Is Father Hugh about?" Sarah repeated.

"Och, now, and hasn't he gone to Dublin these past two days—to see th' Bishop, he is."

I seemed fated to find no one involved in this thing but Sarah Grey. Walking back to the Mercedes, I eyed the church.

"Let's take a look."

"Are you religious, now?" she muttered sourly, but she followed me.

We walked up the short stone steps to the heavy, weathered door and entered. Inside it was chill and damp. No stained glass here, just the cold metallic light filtering through yellowish glass to reveal the small nave with its rows of battered pews. The altar, of dark crusty wood, was mantled with tired linen that sagged from too many washings. The single red-globed altar light flickered, and Sarah Grey dipping her fingers in the holy water font, knelt in the back pew.

"Are you done?" she whispered hoarsely. I had the feeling she wasn't comfortable in church.

Sometimes I have a devil in me. Because she pressed me I was just ornery enough to take her arm for a slow transit of the place. We ambled down the side aisle, across the front and over to the confessional that stood on the left side. Then I saw them. The rusty, black confessional curtain hung down, but beneath, a pair of old but carefully polished boots protruded from the deep shadows into the faint yellowish light.

Chapter IV

I stood frozen and she looked first at my face, and then, following my line of vision, to the tips of the shoes. There was a small croak and her complexion assumed an even more ghastly pallor in the mordant light. A gentleman would have escorted a lady to some remote spot, shielding her from whatever reality lay behind that curtain—but I wanted to see her reaction. Either Sarah Grey was a consummate actress or she was genuinely shocked and frightened.

In the fright department I was beginning to feel a bit queasy myself. Pulling aside the curtain, we saw the priest sitting there, staring but not seeing. Father Hugh Courtney, who I assumed him to be, was a man about fifty with crisp curly hair that was once reddish but was now a burnished bronze. Running to weight over the years, he sat slumped to the side, his head and black beretta against the side wall, his plump, freckled hands resting on his lap. A faint, unpleasant odor emanated from the confessional box.

"Oh my God!" Sarah moaned, finding her tongue as she sank into the nearest pew, great tears rolling down her cheeks.

I steeled myself and unfortunately my silent predictions became reality. For the next few hours we enjoyed all the glories of Irish beadledom. The nearest phone was at McGinty's pub.

Besides the dead priest's housekeeper, apparently hundreds of McGintys lived under every stone hereabouts. Someone had to stay with the body and it would be better for an Irish person to call the Garda. So I sent her off while I did a little snooping.

I didn't move the body. Rigor mortus had passed and there were no marks on Father Hugh that I could see. While it all looked straightforward, I had a "pricking of my thumbs." Later I found Sarah Grey at the front door, her pretty face still with a greenish tinge. She didn't want to go in.

"I called th' Garda," she mumbled.

A quarter of an hour later a beefy constable named, of course, McGinty, came peddling over the hill on a bicycle. A ponderous man with a red face and ginger hair, he marched with elephantine resolution to the confessional. He said little beyond throat clearings and grunts.

"Th' Inspector must be told," he declared stentoriously and off he went to McGinty's pub for what I thought was a longer period than necessary to make a phone contact.

A little later a police car bumped over the hill, followed by an ancient Ford. A gigantic, cadaverous man unwound himself from behind the wheel. In his rusty black overcoat and hat he looked to me for all the world like an IRA "hit man." The illusion continued as he mounted the steps, a grim scowl on his skull-like face, but ended abruptly with a high-pitched voice and a tendency to pluck, like a chicken.

"Tisk, tisk, tisk . . . where is th' body please?"

A small, brisk man followed carrying a black Gladstone bag. At the confessional with a chorus of "My, mys" and "Saints presarve us," the clucking reached an absolute egg-laying crescendo.

The doctor, whose name was Brady, fussed about the body for some time and finally advanced toward us. "He's been gone above 24 hours," he said to the Inspector.

"Everyone thought he had gone to Dublin—to see th' Bishop," Sarah said in a husky voice.

"What happened?" I asked innocently.

Brady looked at me with his baggy blue eyes. "Sure an' it was his heart, man. I've been tellin' him these last years—stop th' spirits, get yer rest an' eat proper. . . ." Then Brady reddened at talking of the dead, and a man of the cloth, at that. ". . . not that he was a libertine or anything, mind you, but the state of his heart wasn't good."

"He must have been hearin' th' confessions," the inspector said.

"I wonder why the . . . the person who'd gone to him didn't go for help?" I asked, not knowing whether to call said person "sinner" or "shrivee."

"He was finished, an' th' one he shrove had left. Sometimes he'd sit there an' pray a bit. The church was probably empty when he was took," the Inspector said.

"Yes, that's probably it," the doctor said knowingly, "it would take him sudden-like. Tis a great shame in one so young."

So the wheels of officialdom ground on relentlessly. Their minds made up, they proceeded to reinforce each other's prejudices. I kept my mouth shut.

By noon we were released. The Morris was nowhere to be seen. Sitting for a moment, I thought about our next move.

"Have you got Fowler's notes?"

"No, they're in my flat in Dublin. As I told you I've not gone back there since th' lorry tried to run me down."

"You just left them there? Why didn't you bring them?"

She was silent for a moment. "I don't know you, Peete. Th' notes may be valuable an' they're th' only connection between Fowler, th' box an' meself."

"Well damn it, I'd like to see them. What kind of game is

this? It's okay for me to hike here from America, but you can't trust me to peek at the notes?"

"I notice you haven't said you're takin' it on," she snapped back, ". . . you an' Miss, 'High an' Mighty,' Benedict!"

"Well do I see the notes or do I drop you off at Whyte's Hotel in Wexford and head for the airport at Shannon?"

Again she sat silently for a moment. "Yer a great bully, Peete! All right, you can see them. . . ."

We drove northward to Dublin and into a drizzling rain as we picked our way through the streets to the quiet mews where Sarah had her flat.

"Where were you almost run down?" I asked as I parked.

She nodded her head over her shoulder. "I was comin' down th' road. Th' lorry was parked over there at th' entry. There were no cars parked here—you're not supposed to. I heard th' roarin' of th' engine behind me an' I threw meself into that doorway back there."

If it happened as she said, it sure seemed like a case of attempted vehicular homicide. The narrow carriageway was hardly wide enough for a truck. The streetlight, mounted on a wall bracket near the doorway, faintly lit the road but surely would show anyone walking there. We entered through another doorway further down the Mews.

The building, one of those dismal European affairs, was a couple of hundred years old and Lord knows its original purpose. We climbed the grungy staircase to the third floor and a wooden door with peeling brown paint.

She froze, dead still, at the landing. The lock had been forced and the door stood opened a crack.

Curiouser and curiouser, I thought. Pushing her aside, I slipped into the darkened room, my back against the wall next to the opening. A light switch nudged my back and I snapped it on. An old bedstead with worn blankets stood in the corner by the wardrobe. To the side a small kitchen space peeked from behind a lank curtain. A bookcase full of new and lovingly cared for books, an overstuffed chair and standing lamp placed before a small, blackened gas fireplace also greeted my eyes. You couldn't have hidden a gnat in the chilled, damp room.

She entered wide-eyed and nervous.

Was it a set-up? It's easy to jimmy a door and make believe there's been an intruder. "Is anything missing?" I asked, getting down to cases.

She walked to the kitchenette table where a typewriter and some paraphernalia were strewn. "They're gone!" she gasped.

"Fowler's notes?"

"Fowler's notes, th' carbons—everythin', even th' ribbon!"

Great, I thought, now the last link went poof. All I had was Sarah Grey, probably lying like a trooper. She sat down.

"What's happening?" she croaked. "First George Fowler, then Father Hugh—and now this?"

I was getting nowhere at very high speeds. Except for the untimely passing of Fowler and Father Hugh, I might have been tempted to head back to Avalon and the Benedictine needling. It was getting like the last act of Hamlet—and Sarah Grey was the only player left standing so I decided to deal what cards I held and see where it might lead.

"Who was the guy who was following us today?"

She blinked up at me as if I were a lunatic. "What guy?"

"Big, ugly, with a blue chin, wearing a dark overcoat and hat and driving a Morris Minor that I think, under the dirt, was cream colored."

She silently shook her head.

"No one you know?"

"No," she replied firmly, "are you sure?"

"Oh, I'm sure. He followed us to the monastery."

"Why would he follow us?"

'Why indeed. I don't think you should stay here."

She started to cry. Not the blubbery kind, just tears welling in her eyes and rolling down her cheeks. Her mouth was funny when she talked. "I want out of all this," she said in a chokey kind of voice. "I just want to forget th' whole business. Father Hugh . . ."

I wondered if she noticed anything at the church. "What about Father Hugh?"

"Somethin' was wrong. He was in th' confessional but he wasn't wearin' his stole . . ."

So she had noticed something.

"A priest always wears his stole during confession—he would never have gone there without it."

"I don't think you should stay here," I repeated.

"Where can I go?"

"Back to Whyte's Hotel with me. You can spend the night there. I want to call the U.S.A.—to Miss Benedict."

"I don't have th' money fer grand places like Whyte's."

"I'll take care of it."

"But what if Miss Benedict won't help?"

"Then we go to the Garda, tell them everything, and I wish you luck."

"You're a bastard, Peete . . ."

The ride from Dublin to Whyte's Hotel was without incident and we weren't followed. Sarah Grey wasn't talking. Maybe she was still contemplating my parentage, or maybe, if she was on the level, she was sitting there, worrying. The business about the missing stole was odd, but in Ireland who knows what the rules are?

"Tell me about Fowler," I pressed her. "Not the externals, what was he like?"

"He was impatient—impetuous even. When we found th' reliquary, I guess there was no holdin' him."

"How was he financially?"

Her mouth turned down at the edges. "He was an American."

"My God! The Irish still think the streets of New York are paved with gold."

"He wanted more," she said bitterly, "like most Yanks he always wanted more than he had."

"And, of course, the saintly Irish aren't a bit like that."

She ignored me. Then suddenly she began again. "He was a poor scholar," she said with definition. In Ireland being a scholar was serious business. "He hadn't th' interest or fascination with what he was doin'."

"How so?"

"I tasked him about it. Trapped, he said, back in th' late '70s, at th' university. His father wanted him to have a degree, so he took History because it was easy. After graduatin' he couldn't get a job. Nobody in commerce cared why th' Punic Wars were fought. So back to college he went an' took his Masters. He still couldn't get a job teachin' an' he bummed around fer a bit—livin' rough, as a waiter an' in th' construction.

"To get a teachin' job he needed his doctorate, so back to school he went again where Steiner found him. Steiner is—was his proctor, so he had Fowler jumpin' through th' hoops."

"But he didn't like what he was doing?"

"Och, no. All he did was complain about how he hadn't been counseled properly at th' university an' how th' world was all wrong fer not knowin' how grand an' wonderful George Fowler really was, an' how Steiner was a narrow-minded, pedantic, petty bastard—which indeed he is! You Americans make me fair sick, yer such crybabies."

"How did Steiner feel about Fowler?"

She shrugged her slim shoulders. "Beneath contempt; that's not unusual since Steiner feels that way about th' whole bloody world. He was goin' to drop Fowler before too long. Steiner measures everything by his own yardstick. 'What's in it fer me before I chuck it in th' dustbin.' Fowler's doctorate depended on Steiner an' Steiner used it like a whip. He even had Fowler carry his bags at th' airport! When we found th' reliquary they had words an' that was the first time that I saw Fowler overtly cross Steiner."

"What happened?"

"Nothin'—Steiner just told Fowler to shut up."

"Sounds like a delightful bunch."

"It was no larky expedition at th' tomb, I'll tell you that," she said bitterly.

"So Steiner wanted photographers at the opening of the reliquary?"

"Oh yes. It was easy to see how his mind was workin'. If it were an important find, it would be 'Steiner's discovery'. With his backside parked near th' fire, he was already dreamin' of his next book an' the History Chair at some grand university."

"So you think that Fowler took the box to get there first?"

"As I said, he was terribly impetuous. Maybe he was goin' to try to discredit Steiner."

"Why do you say that?"

She was silent for a moment, as if she was back there, at the tomb. . . . "Everything changed with that box. It was as if it had some evil of its own. Fowler took it despite his slavish relationship to Steiner—Father Hugh changed—even I changed. . . ."

"Oh God! The Irish!" I moaned.

Chapter V

The desk clerk at Whyte's Hotel eyed us suspiciously as Sarah bent over the register.

"You have a telephone call, Dr. Peete. From the U.S.A.— Dr. Benedict," he said with a sniff.

I thanked him and we entered the corridor to our rooms.

"I don't believe you're a doctor," Sarah sneered.

"Behave yourself or I'll have you committed."

Depositing her in her room, I put through a transatlantic call to Miz Charlotte in Virginia. The line was busy so I brushed my teeth. Brushing my teeth always sets me thinking and naturally my mind turned to Charlotte Montaigne Benedict and the screwy job I have at Avalon. As my sainted father was fond of saying: one man's (or woman's) ill fortune can be another man's jackpot. Miss Benedict had been wallowing in success for a few years and, like the man with a better mousetrap, the world was beating a path to the doorstep of her hermitage at Avalon.

I guess Miss Benedict would be described as an antiquarian. Although she'd never admit it, she's also a gigantic economic accident. Had she been born twenty-five years earlier she might have been a professor at some genteel seminary for young ladies and living on the edge of poverty.

In the 70s the economic scene changed, however. Investors

were always looking for places to stash excess profits but basic stuff like autos and steels were losing their pizzazz.

It started with paintings . . . Van Gogh's were suddenly selling at astronomical figures. It didn't stop there but spilled over into books, musical manuscripts, sculpture—anything that would appreciate. I even saw a Sotheby's catalogue with a Mickey Mantle baseball card listed at 12 to 15 thousand!

Miz Charlotte cashed in on this and since art fraud is as old as the pyramids, she saved some clients on big ticket items and built a world-wide reputation for herself. But success can also draw the wrong kind of notoriety. A while back she was inspecting a valuable object for an insurance company when some heavy-handed Neanderthals broke into her homestead in Virginia and stole said rather valuable object. But that wasn't the clincher. In the process she had been pushed around a bit. This shows the terrible inversion of the world sometimes; Miss Benedict was renowned for pushing others around (verbally, of course) and she was deeply traumatized by it all. She feels, with justification, that she's the equal of any man. The fact that in some biological arenas this is untrue really galls her.

At this point, she and I were unconsciously floating toward each other, like the Titanic and the iceberg.

I had spent nine years as a Navy SEAL doing all the wonderful things that the SEALS do—but it was like being a pro football player. What's great at twenty-one gets very old (and achy) at thirty. I was going to have to leave the SEALS program and I could see a grim line of logistic desk jobs waiting for me. On retiring from the Navy I wanted to teach so I had gone to school at night, taken my Masters in Art History and was bumbling on to my doctorate, looking wistfully toward the outside when the Panama business erupted. SEALS always get choice jobs in times like that and we were sent in to secure the airport. It got very messy. A few of my men were killed and I was wounded in an unfortunate spot where no SEAL should ever be wounded. It wasn't really everyone telling me I should wear my Purple Heart on the seat of my pants, it was just that I was scared of desk jobs.

So there I was. My main talent was sneaking around in the dark and doing unpleasant things. I went back to school and finished my doctorate—that way I figured I could do unpleasant things in the daylight. . . .

Frank Thorpe called me at the College of William and Mary and put me in touch with Miss Benedict. This stroke of good fortune, plus a glowing letter from Admiral Barnes got me an interview and ultimately my job with Miz Charlotte—and the beginning of our love-hate relationship. The idea of my looking as innocuous as I do but having a well-rounded spectrum of lethal talents won the day. Having a bodyguard with his doctorate appealed to her sense of humor and her ego. It does let her sleep soundly and if I don't jump smartly, she threatens to can me and get a Doberman pinscher.

There is one other thing—Charlotte Benedict is like a wraith resurrected from the Edwardian Age. Besides epitomizing the other values of that bygone era she has a life-long love of words and that means that profanity [save for that acceptable to the bard] is verboten. This is hard on some ex-SEALS and I've had to resort to antiquated argot as a substitute.

The bedside phone gargled in that European way. I picked up the receiver, without salutation, to the petulant piping voice of Charlotte Montaigne Benedict. "What in blazes are you up to, Peete?"

Miz Charlotte has a world-wide reputation for coming straight to the point in any discussion.

"Ah ha! You've discovered my empty seat in the inglenook."

"In Ireland, for Heaven's sake! And who is this idiot, Lacy, who keeps calling and threatening me with legal action?"

The great terrors of Miss Benedict's life are lawyers and litigation. She's afraid somebody will get his grubby little hands on her hard-earned, if not ill-gotten, gains.

"Aloysius Lacy from New York? Now that's interesting. I wonder how he got our number?"

"Well, what's going on?"

"Absolutely nothing. I've been chasing leprechauns and other wee creatures. I'll leave from Shannon tomorrow night."

"What did Sarah Grey say?"

Now that was typical. Miss Benedict likes to make believe that she doesn't know what's going on, that she couldn't understand why I was in Ireland, when it was obvious that she had read the file with Sarah Grey's letter and had it committed to memory.

"If there's anything here, I'm not going to find it. We're too late. Or, conversely, it could be a real sting."

"Tell me about it."

So I went through it, down to the last detail; the remains of the woman with the broken neck by the crypt door, the evil Count Odo, the Bend Sinister, Fowler, Steiner, Father Hugh, the infamous box, the interdictions, Mister Bluejaw and the various odd corpses as of this tally.

"It's like Carnarvon and the curse of King Tut," I concluded. ". . . and without the mysterious box, whatever that is, there's no trail—except for dead bodies. Meanwhile I miss Avalon in the Springtime, a-maying with the village lasses and all the thrilling stuff waiting for me in the minutes of the Royal Historical Society. I think I'll come home."

"You couldn't read the interdiction on the crypt door?"

"No, but that might be some kind of mix-up. They thought

that it might be the tomb of someone named Alexander. In any event this is all too rich for my blood."

"Fowler disappeared for seven days after taking the box?"

Miss Benedict loved to cross-examine people.

"That's right."

There was complete silence. I thought I had lost the connection. "Are you there or have you died from excitement?"

"Find out where he went."

This also was typical and I cursed myself for not handling her better. If I declare myself as doing something, nine times out of ten, Miz Charlotte will disagree to emphasize my lowly minion status. If things pan out she can preen herself and needle me about it. If it's a wild goose chase she can needle me about that. As you can see, needling me is a big part of Charlotte Montaigne Benedict's life. I mentally shrugged. It looked like I'd be playing "Twenty Questions" with Sarah Grey for a bit longer; tell me Sarah, is it bigger than a bread box?

I've found that ours is a territorial business. A foreigner could stumble around Ireland for months before coming up with a good lead on Fowler. Like fishing, when trying out a new pond, you need a few tips from a good guide. Fortunately, over the years Miss Benedict has developed contacts with people all over the world who are good at this sort of stuff. She pays fast and top dollar for services and gets attention when she needs it.

"Who have you got in Ireland?" I asked.

There was a pause while she went through her little black book—the one even I never get a peek at. "Liam Mullin, Dublin," she said and gave me the phone number.

"This will take a couple of days," I said tentatively.

"If you're going to do something, David, you should do it properly," she snapped and the line went dead.

My mind was made up; all I wanted was to leave Ireland,

Sarah Grey and her assorted bodies—forever. I didn't waste any time putting the call through to Dublin. A woman with a tired voice answered the phone. In the background there must have been sixteen howling children. When I asked for Mullin, she said to wait one.

"Mullin here," a gruff voice came on the line.

I identified myself and got a terse, "Oh yes," in response.

"I represent Charlotte Montaigne Benedict."

"Ah, well now, Dr. Peete, nice of you to call, sir—an' what might I be doin' fer you?" The Irish charm oozed through the instrument.

I told him I couldn't talk on the phone, which he judged to be most proper and correct, and made arrangements to see him at eleven that night at Whyte's Hotel.

I showered, put on a blue pin-striped suit and took Sarah to the dining room. She was still in her Palestinian terrorist camp uniform so I'm sure we made a striking couple. Eyebrows were raised in the small room and it was easy to see the thoughts that were a-flitting; rich American tourist treats "twinkie" to dinner incident to banging her later in upstairs room. The Irish still deplore this sort of thing.

While Sarah landed on the freshly caught salmon like a barracuda, I noticed Mr. Bluejaw in the corner looking for all the world like a traveling drummer passing through. I leaned toward Sarah.

"Relax and casually look around the room. Take a peek at the guy in the corner with the blue chin and a face like a squashed cabbage . . . easy now . . ."

She pulled it off pretty well.

"Do you know him?"

"Never clapped me eyes on him."

"He's the one who's been following us." This upset Sarah so

I continued my interrogation to let her know that I wasn't concerned.

"Where is Steiner?"

"Och, he's gone."

"Gone?"

"Back to America. Once th' box was lost and Fowler dead, he went home as quick as a schoolboy on holiday."

"He didn't go to the police—the Garda?"

She patted her hair nervously. "Like I said, he was upset. He was in charge after all, and any investigation would have made him look exactly what he was—an arrogant nincompoop . . ."

"Wait a minute. You find this box and you're all excited about it and Fowler cops it and disappears. Then he's drowned and the box is gone, and no one goes to the police? Why didn't you?"

She played a little with her wine glass. "It was Father Hugh. In a terrible state, he was, after th' box was taken. Of course we looked fer Fowler an' reported him gone missin' to th' Garda. When th' body was found Father Hugh identified him but we couldn't find th' bloody box anywhere.

"Father Hugh knew that he had to go to th' Bishop. He waited a bit, you know—to see if it would turn up. I was goin' to let the Church handle it."

"But Father Hugh never got to the Bishop."

"No."

"You didn't even call the police after the lorry tried to run you down?"

"I was frightened . . . I just froze . . ."

Chapter VI

After dinner we went to my room and waited for Mullin. Sarah was getting more nervous by the minute.

"I called Miss Benedict."

"Oh? An' what did she say?"

"She wants me to find out where Fowler went."

She wiped her mouth nervously. "I've been thinkin' on all this, Peete. Maybe you're right, maybe I should go to th' Garda an' tell them everythin'. I wanted to give Father Hugh a chance, but now—with him gone . . ."

"That's your decision, Miss Grey. You realize that there's little so far to excite the Garda. Those two at the church have already written off Father Hugh as a heart attack victim, as indeed it may well have been. The stole may mean absolutely nothing. You said he was under a strain and drank a bit? That could account for a little forgetfulness. All you've got is an old box that's missing. And you don't even know what's in it."

"Yer a big help!" she snapped.

"Of course you could tell them it's the curse of the Bend Sinister . . ."

She started to leave in a huff.

"Don't go, there's someone I'd like you to talk to."

All of a sudden her temper was unleashed; she was in a fine

Irish froth. "I'm not stayin' here to listen to th' sharp side of yer tongue. Yer nothin' but a little twit with yer eyeglasses an' yer knowin' ways an' yer fancy briefcase!"

"Why don't you sleep on it," I said calmly, cursing myself for needling her. "Tomorrow you can decide. Tonight you might need someone around—to keep an eye on you."

"You? If I need someone to look after me, I can find much better than th' likes of you! There's Michael O'Shea who stands six foot three and fifteen stone! He could pitch you through th' window with one hand!"

"I'm sure that Michael is a braw lad, and ferocious as they come—and maybe you can find him at 11 P.M. of a Friday night in some pub in Dublin—at, or under, the table."

She flashed angrier yet and I put up my hands. "Sorry—I have a bad tendency toward sarcasm, but think a bit. You're settled tonight. Like it or not, you've won me until morning."

There was an authoritative knock at the door.

"Oh my God—th' hotel manager!"

This was the first inkling I had that she was nervous at being in a man's hotel room. I forgot this was Ireland.

Mullin wasn't much to look at, but, as Sarah Grey so incisively put it, neither was I, and I've found that appearances count for very little. He was the short, tubby variety of Irishman with grayish hair peeking out from under his tweed cap, a red nose with jowls to match, bushy eyebrows above snapping blue eyes, and (for paying customers) a perpetual smile.

"Dr. Peete, is it?"

"That's right, Mr. Mullin. This is Sarah Grey."

Mullin looked at the girl with two bright red spots on her cheeks and her green eyes flashing. "Sure an' I'm not interruptin' anythin', am I?"

Like maybe a carnal attack, I thought. I ignored him and they both finally settled down; I explained to Mullin about George Fowler.

"He disappeared on th' night of the 4th of April, you say?"

"Or in the early morning of the 5th. He was seen again at his hotel on the 12th. The desk clerk saw him."

"An' then he disappeared again?"

"His body was found in the Slaney on the 14th."

"But no one saw him after the 12th?"

"He had gone into the water not long after he was seen, according to th' inquest," Sarah said sullenly.

Mullin went through the story again. Despite his unassuming appearance, he knew what he was about.

"Perhaps I'd best talk to this Father Hugh?" Mullin muttered.

"He's dead," Sarah said dully.

Mullin's reaction was swift. "Dead, you say. My, my—what's goin' on here, Dr. Peete?"

"The police think he had a heart attack."

"This is all very strange, Dr. Peete."

"You want out?"

"Oh, no—my goodness, no. I just like to know where I'm at, you see. Is there anything else?"

I couldn't blame Mullin. I would have felt pretty much the same if I had been wearing his hat. "We were followed today," I said, describing Mr. Bluejaw.

Mullin shook his head. "I don't know th' gentleman." The discussion didn't last much longer.

"This might take a bit of time, Dr. Peete. He could have gone anywhere in this broad land."

"Give me a call here each day around 10 P.M."

"And you can leave a message at my number if needs must."

We left it at that and Mullin swaggered out and down the hall. Sarah seemed scared, really scared.

"C'mon, let's have a look at your room," I said. We walked silently down the hall to the door and I entered first, snapping on the overhead light. I lifted her rough, canvas bag off the chair and sat. My little speech was all prepared. "Look, Miss Grey—Sarah. Why don't I call you Sarah and you call me David. Look, Sarah, I don't know what's going down here but two people are dead. Maybe that's all a coincidence, maybe there's a curse on the tomb, but I don't like coincidences or curses. I don't know who Mr. Bluejaw is, but he's in this hotel. So I'm proposing to slip back here and spend the night." I held up my hand. "Your virtue is safe, I promise."

She just nodded. She wasn't looking forward to spending the night alone. I took her key. "I'll be back in ten minutes." At the door, we had a loud conversation about meeting at 8 A.M. for breakfast. I did the talking, she did the grunting.

Back in my room, I changed into black trousers and a gray turtleneck. I took some time going back to her room—and made doubly sure that I wasn't observed. A few minutes later I opened the door and slipped in. "It's only me," I said softly.

It was really romantic. She bounced out of the bathroom wearing a huge terry-cloth robe with a towel wrapped around her head like a nun and looking God-awful. The way she used her gifts I'd say her chastity was safe as houses.

"What do we do now?'" she asked.

"You go to bed and turn out the light."

"You mean yer just goin' to sit here—in th' dark?"

"You're a big girl now, the dark can't hurt you. Try and get some sleep—you look like hell. Make believe I'm not here."

"You won't drop off?"

"Not a chance. If anyone's coming, I hope he'll come early so I can catch a few 'Zs' later."

We settled in the dark. The chair wasn't comfortable but, despite my brave words, I had to fight drowsiness. Sometime around 2 A.M. I heard a sound in the corridor. It wasn't my imagination, the girl stiffened in the bed.

"Lie still," I said softly.

I heard a credit card at work and the door opened. I could see his outline in the aperture. Whoever it was had killed the nearby hall lamps. Then the door quietly closed. Reaching over my shoulder, I snapped on the overhead.

As the room flooded with light, I walked over near Sarah, who was holding up the blanket and hiding everything but her big green eyes. Mr. Bluejaw was by the door. He wasn't happy.

"Hi, I was wondering when you'd get around to visiting."

He didn't improve on closer inspection. He stood around six-three and tipped it at 220 or so, but he was inclined toward fat. He struck me as long on muscle and long on stupid. He stood blinking, the wheels of his mind turning but without any great efficiency. He had all the earmarks of hired help.

Of course, all this appraising happened very fast. His mood changed from initial confusion to nascent anger. A brick-like color suffused his face above the blue jowls and on his receding forehead below the thinning black curls. "Yer a smart cove, ain't you?" he hissed. He was pure cockney, born well within the sound of the Bow bells. Judging from his teeth, he could use some dental work.

His face was like a book and I could almost see his ponderous thought process. There he was, mammoth and nasty, and there was I, standing five-nine in my stocking feet and a heroic 154 pounds, wringing wet. I was also wearing my thin-rimmed, black glasses that give me a scholarly look.

He smiled (I think) and produced a knife. It had a split handle and he whirled out a very nasty looking blade. I had to talk to this bozo and it was pretty obvious that there wouldn't be any discussions in his present frame of mind.

Karate is a combination of intense mental concentration combined with hours of practiced katos. When the moment comes, every bit of mental and physical energy has to be concentrated in the move.

He stepped forward on his left foot and I waited for his second stride—then I spun and kicked, removing his kneecap from its normal spot to a very painful new location on the side of his leg. He bellowed and I popped him on the way down. He went to sleep for a while.

"Saints preserve us!" Sarah Grey gasped.

Reaching for his wallet, I discovered our visitor was Algernon Duncan, with a London address.

"What are you, Peete? Some kind of intellectual gangster?"

I looked at Sarah, "This is great, it looks like I'm going to get to bed after all." Duncan's wallet was devoid of interest but he had a small black address book. Riffling through the pages, there was nothing until I got to the "S's." I found a listing for Alfred Sparrow with an address in Switzerland.

"Well, well," I muttered.

"What is it?"

"Things clear from positive blackness to dark murkiness."

Duncan moaned and rolled on his side, holding his knee.

"Welcome back," I said to him. "We'd like a few words."

"I ain't sayin' nuffink to you," he groaned.

"Sure you are—or else I start breaking all your other sundry parts one at a time. I bet by the time I get to your hips you'll be singing like Pavarotti."

I made a slight move in his direction and he shrank away.

He was really hurting and I wasn't enjoying this, so I was happy when he caved in.

"All right, damn you . . . all right . . ." he muttered.

"Now Algie . . . you don't mind my calling you, Algie? You work for good old Alfred Sparrow, right?"

"Yes," Algie said in a strangled voice.

"Doing what?" (For brevity I'll leave out the gasps, groans and gargles).

"We 'ad been associates before . . . 'e called me from Zurich an' tolt me to look up this cove, Fowler."

"To get rid of him?"

"What? Yer daft! 'e 'ad somethin' that Sparrow wanted. 'e wanted me to keep an eye on Fowler—'e dint trust 'im."

"Sparrow didn't trust Fowler?"

"Yes . . . but when I got 'ere, I couldn't find Fowler. 'e 'ad done a bunk."

"What did Sparrow want?"

Duncan tried to shrug and then flinched in pain. "Some kind of box. An old fing—I don't know what it were. Then Fowler were found in th' Slaney River. So I called Sparrow . . ."

"Then what?"

"Sparrow come. 'e's 'ere in Ireland, but first he tolt me to get rid of th' other one—Steiner. So I put th' fear of old Hornie in 'im . . . tolt 'im to keep 'is maw shut."

"And Father Courtney, did you shut his maw too?"

"Who? The priest today in Ballyfaleen? I know naught about 'im, nor does Mr. Sparrow . . . I were just followin' you." He seemed really surprised at the question.

"Sparrow never mentioned the priest?"

"No, Sparrow is just worried about th' box. 'e tolt me to follow Miss Bright-eyes 'ere. To find out if she 'ad it."

"What's in the box?"

"I don't know . . . an' if I were to come across it, I wasn't to open it. Mr. Sparrow made that very clear . . . I were to bring it straight to 'im . . ."

"What happened then?'

"I followed 'er," Duncan nodded toward Sarah, "to see if she 'ad th' bloody box."

"And you tried to run her down with a truck."

Again Algie was surprised. "Run 'er down wiv a truck? You're daft mate. Why would I do that? I just wanted to talk to 'er."

"I'll bet—and maybe whittle her ears off if she didn't give it to you."

I could see that Algie's elephantine mind was in motion again. A strange look captured his face, a look I interpreted to be the epitome of guile and craftiness.

"See 'ere, mate. There's no need fer all this grief between us. We could come to a understandin' in this matter."

"Grief? I haven't had any grief. Have you had any grief, Sarah?" I asked rhetorically.

"Look mate, we're men o' th' world, we are . . ."

"Uh oh, Sarah—we're being men of the world. You'd better put your hands over your pink little ears."

"Look you 'ere. You got th' box an' Sparrow wants it. I'm not sayin' 'e wouldn't take it if 'e 'ad th' chance, but 'e don't, do 'e? 'e'd come to a accommodation, wouldn't 'e?"

"I've as much as told you that we don't have the box."

"Come orf it, mate! You got me . . . dead to rights. I freely admit that. I dint know th' little bird 'ad lined up 'er own muscle. I took you fer th' intellectual type, I did. So I were wrong. No 'arm done—except to me . . . I think you should talk ter Mr. Sparrow. What 'arm can it do?"

As a matter of fact this seemed pretty good. Sparrow obviously knew what the damned thing was, which was more than Sarah Grey and I did, or, at least more than she was telling.

"Where is he?"

"'E's at Creame 'ouse outside Dublin, near Bray."

To show that I'm not completely without feeling, I helped Algie to his room and dropped him on his bed. Finding a bottle of good malt scotch, I thrust it into his eager paws. "Good night, baby," I muttered.

I arranged to meet Sarah at 9 A.M. for breakfast, then went back to my place and put another call through to Miss Benedict. Raphael, the black majordomo of Avalon who runs everything and everybody at Avalon (including Miz Charlotte and me) answered the phone. In a few moments she was on the line.

"Good heavens, Peete, you're not around the corner, you know! I'm trying to keep expenses down."

She always liked to start a conversation with a complaint.

"Sparrow's here," I said.

There was probably fifteen seconds of silence.

"I'm seeing him tomorrow," I added.

"Keep in touch."

Chapter VII

I met Alfred Sparrow a year ago in London where we spent a pleasant afternoon together. His position with Oskar Hammerschmidt was similar to mine with Charlotte Benedict. Miz Charlotte has a grudging admiration for Oskar Hammerschmidt and this is surprising, and, I might add reciprocated by the continentally urbane Oskar.

Professionals seem the same the world over. When I was finally capped with my doctorate, I thought I was joining a legion of high-minded truth-seekers. I didn't think that we'd get together occasionally like the prosaic lawyers, medical doctors and engineers to swap fibs.

The gathering was for a special exhibition of Hittite artifacts but that was bogus. It was a lame excuse for the "heavy hitters" of the world of antiquities to alternately impress and insult each other. Since this was my first visit as her assistant, Miss Benedict filled me in on the dramatis personae.

Oskar Hammerschmidt topped the list and, while I didn't know Miz Charlotte well at the time, I was surprised by her references to the dashing Oskar. She said that he had a profound sense of aesthetics and history and was a business man of the first water. After this glowing litany she added (almost parenthetically) that he was also a crook. Though Interpol suspected his sleek fingers were in a number of unsavory pies, ranging from art fraud on the grand scale to some remarkable art heists, Oskar had never been caught.

He sat like a spider on his mountain-top chalet in Switzerland, enjoying his objects d'art, a succession of semi-renowned tootsies who marched, single file, through his bedroom, his thirty dollar cigars and his thirty year old cognac. Meanwhile the peripatetic Alfie Sparrow did his leg work.

I introduced myself to Sparrow on entering the exhibit. After listening to protracted erudition by Miz Charlotte, Hammerschmidt and company for about ten minutes, Alfie and I retired to the nearest pub and spent a comfortable afternoon conversing, playing chess and drinking Guineses.

The intrusion of Sparrow into the affair changed things from hallucinations by Sarah Grey to something quite different. While Oskar and Miss Benedict might admire each other's virtues or skullduggery, neither was above doing the other in the eye. The tall and dashing Oskar, although close to sixty, didn't deny himself much in the pleasure department, and while his tastes usually ran to the Epicurean, what could be more delightful than to catch his archrival in some gigantic hoax. Maybe slippery little Sarah was part of this kind of gambit.

In spite of my active night, I woke early the next morning. With Algie's purloined key, I looked in on him as he snored like a big, ugly teddy bear, hugging the empty bottle. He was going to hate himself in a few hours.

At breakfast, Sarah looked fairly well rested. Dressed in a woolen sweater and tweed skirt, she no longer looked like a fugitive from a chain-gang. After our set-to last night she wasn't talking about the Garda now. She was also enjoying the "freebies," tying into the full Irish breakfast with certain shark-like qualities; as she masticated her prey, she was constantly on the lookout for more.

"Aren't you eatin' yer sausage?" she asked.

"That's not sausage, it's rolled suet. Sausage has spices an' stuff in it." That didn't stop her from putting it away, plus all the toast, rolls and bread within reach.

"Yer goin' to see this Sparrow person?" she asked with a mouth full of egg.

"Yeah, do you know Creame House?"

"Och—tis a grand place, it is. An old manor house converted fer th' tourists . . . out near Bray."

I didn't spend the afternoon with Alfie without getting to know something about him. The "old school tie" type, I figured he must be the black sheep of some well-off British family. Nearly sixty, he spoke with one of those fruity, south English accents where "been" becomes "bean" and so forth. I timed our arrival to "pop in" on him for lunch.

Everything worked like a charm. Some of the European hostelries can be very snooty but I was well-groomed, Sarah looked presentable and driving a Mercedes helped. We were greeted by a rooster-like doorman whose primary mission in life was to keep out the riffraff but I managed to convince him that Mr. Sparrow was an old chum and I wanted to surprise him. This and a well placed £5 note did the trick.

Alfie sat, in an aura of fastidiousness, by a tall narrow dining room window that strained sunlight down on his bald head accentuating the satchel-like pouches under his eyes. A helpless fish lay on the plate as he pursed his small, plump lips, holding the fork and fish knife between deft fingers, about to attack it like a surgeon removing a carbuncle.

"Well, I'll be dashed! Alfie, old chap!" I said with bonhomie.

Looking over his half-glasses, there was a flicker of both surprise and resentment. Shame on you, Alfie, I thought, you're losing the old stiff upper lip.

"Upon my soul, it's Dr. Peete, sit down—do, and have some lunch."

It was all very bright and chirpy. We were seated, the waiter was hailed with a flourish, the menu presented and Alfie leaned forward advising us confidentially on the bill of fare as if he were giving us the combination to Queen Elizabeth's safe.

I have an awful tendency to burp at tea parties. "I'm overwhelmed with all this hospitality, Alf. Do we keep up the 'gas and gaiters' while we eat, or can we talk business?"

He gave Sarah a pitying look that seemed to say—how could you associate with this lout? "Dr. Peete is so impetuous, my dear," he said instead. Pretty good for somebody who sent Algie Duncan to chop off her ears last night.

"Have you heard from Algie lately?" I asked innocently.

His mouth turned slightly downward at the corners. "I'm not sure I know . . ."

The waiter brought our order and Sarah and I set to enjoying it. I noticed that Sparrow wasn't touching his. "Gee, I hope I haven't put you off your feed, Alf. We met Algie—or more accurately, bumped into him last night—late. Had an accident, poor chap, but he'll be back to battery in a few weeks. He mentioned in passing that he was working for you."

Sparrow picked up his wine glass and went through the usual routine—smelling it, tasting it, rolling it around his tongue. I was waiting for him to gargle with it. "Ah, Peete, you always approach things like a cement lorry, with a great clashing of gears and roaring of the engine."

"Yeah, I know . . . I'm not cultured like you—and your friend, Algie."

That did it. It wasn't more than a slight narrowing of his eyes but I know when I pink someone. It was "a hit . . . a palpable hit." I wish I could stop doing it though, it always leads to perturbations.

"Very well, if you must ruin our lunch, I see no other course of action. I take it from this charade, Miss Grey, that you have possession of the casket?"

"Miss Grey has stipulated that I act as her agent in this matter, Alfie," I interrupted.

He turned his wary, blue eyed gaze toward me, removing his glasses and carefully polishing the lenses. "I see. I also presume, by your presence here, you're prepared to negotiate?"

"Yep, as I said to Miss Grey, in delicate matters like this it's always best to deal with the top man, but we're realists. Your man, Algie Duncan, wasn't much of a negotiator," I shrugged, "he didn't seem very flexible, you know what I mean?

"Of course Oskar never leaves his castle in Switzerland except for important things, like that Hittite stuff last year. So we'll give you a try, Alf. If you can't hack it we can fly to Switzerland and dicker directly with him. . . ."

Sparrow casually sipped his wine. Beneath his unruffled exterior he was desperately trying to get back in the game, but it was like chasing Jack Nicklaus with a four stroke lead on the last three holes. There was no joy in Alfie Sparrow. "Miss Benedict knows nothing of this?" he asked casually.

"C'mon, Alf—Benedict's a girl scout. She'd go straight to the Irish authorities and turn it in as a National Treasure. After she looked it over, of course."

"And you and Miss Grey are willing to negotiate for its . . . 'private sale'?"

"Why not? I'm here. Benedict's in Virginia playing with her pottery. You understand that it's got to be top dollar, Alf, don't try to play games with us. Kamaroff would be willing . . ."

"You've not talked to Kamaroff!" Sparrow's veneer cracked at that. Sergei Kamaroff was as big a crook as Hammerschmidt, and even nastier. Sparrow's reaction made me wonder if Sergei was also sniffing about somewhere.

"I'm not at liberty to disclose who my client contacts. All I can say is that we expect, and will get, top dollar for the sale."

If I wasn't sure before, I was certain now that this little game had definitely put Alfie off his feed. Buying something like the box rather than nicking it is bad enough, but bidding for it against another crook like Kamaroff is really the pits.

I was trying desperately to think of some way to get Sparrow to say what the damned thing was without letting on that we didn't know. It was like sitting in a poker game when you've got two pair and the other guy is standing pat and raising. Do you take another card or do you ride with what you have?

"Don't be blue, Alf. Just think about its resale value. Think about the sales pitch and the fascinated customers when you tell them about it coming back from Constantinople with the Fourth Crusade."

Sparrow's gaze bored into mine. It was like watching a fine Dresden figurine shatter before your eyes. His features changed from their urbane, polished set and his color rose. "You vermin, Peete—you have no idea what it is! You don't have the casket!" Rising, he stormed out of the room leaving Sarah and me staring at each other across the table.

I shrugged. "Better to have loved and lost . . . "

I started to leave but Sarah wasn't about to pass up an elegant lunch. Again she tucked in like a refugee at a relief camp which was ironic since Sparrow, at the beginning of the meal, had magnanimously insisted on putting it on his tab.

On the road back to Wexford, I did some recapitulating. The game was getting a lot more dicey. It was one thing to play with a Neanderthal like Algie Duncan, particularly when he didn't know we were on to him, but different to openly face someone of Sparrow's ilk. Even more uncomfortable was the thought that Sergei Kamaroff & Co. might be off somewhere lying in the weeds.

Kamaroff had also been at the London gathering and he was the kind that pulled the wings off flies. I'd heard that Sergei was the son of a Russian aristocrat who barely got out in 1918. He made Alfie Sparrow look like the White Rabbit by comparison. I had thrown out Kamaroff's name like a fisherman casts a new fly to impress the guy fishing next to him. He doesn't expect a strike from a great white shark. Just a hint of a screwball like Sergei in the wings complicated the game exponentially.

Suddenly I didn't like the hand we were holding at all. Sparrow correctly deduced that we didn't have the box. That meant we were just a nuisance but if the game was rich enough, nuisances might be eliminated—permanently. I had another uncomfortable thought. If Kamaroff was around, and Alfie, by some clever ploy, could convince him we had the box, that could remove Kamaroff from the game . . . and maybe Sarah and I, eternally. Those kind of ploys were Sparrow's stock in trade!

"You're very quiet," Sarah said as we whizzed south.

"I'm thinking."

"You didn't find out much from that Sparrow person."

"I found out enough—like we're up to out chins in kim chee."

"What do you mean?"

She was a client of sorts and I felt some obligation to level with her. "Okay, I'll lay it out. First of all, there's the business aspect. There's nothing going down here of any monetary value to Miss Benedict. She's tricky and a trial in many ways but she's honest. If we find the box it goes to the Irish Government. And we're not looking forward to paying your expenses either; all you've done so far is eat us out of house and home.

"Of course there are professional considerations that invested now can pay big bucks later. If it's a significant find and we unearth it and give it to the proper authorities (all with appropriate fanfare) that enhances her reputation. Her business depends on reputation.

"Okay, but Sparrow knows that we don't have the box and now we're a nuisance to him. I mean, we won't help him find the damned thing for Hammerschmidt, but we can hinder his finding it, or, worst of all, beat him to it.

"Then there's Kamaroff who's even less congenial than Sparrow. Sergei might just cut your throat for the fun of it.

"So maybe it's time to go to the Garda. Maybe with the weight of Miss Benedict behind us they'll take us seriously. . . ."

"So you want out? Is that it?"

"What do you mean, want out? Yesterday you said you were afraid someone wanted to snuff you. Now I'm agreeing with you."

"An' it will all stop if I go an' tell th' Garda? You think they're goin' to give me some big-footed policeman to squire me about? Fowler an' Father Hugh were murdered by someone smart enough to make it look accidental. If they had run me down with that lorry, what would my death have been? I'll tell you—a hit an' run!"

"What are you saying?"

She huddled down miserably in the seat. "That if you leave me now, I think I'm a dead person. . . ."

Chapter VIII

So that little ploy didn't work; Sarah wasn't going to the Garda. At Whyte's Hotel I called Mullin's Dublin number. He was out but I left word for an urgent contact. The next three hours were the pits; all kinds of bogeymen disturbed my peace of mind. Suppose Sparrow had other people checking on us and found out about my transatlantic calls to Dr. Benedict? Being a crook himself, he might figure that I was one too, but he knew that Miss Benedict wasn't. Contacting her twice in ten hours would convince him I had opened the thing up with her.

Finally, at 6 P.M., Mullin called back. "Are there developments, Dr. Peete?"

"You bet there are. I need a safe house and fast."

"I see, how fast?"

"Like yesterday."

He was silent for a moment. Thank God there was no Irish blather and questions. "On th' Arklow Road, near th' 40 kilometer mark is a pub called Fitzgerald's. Meet me in th' car park at 10 P.M."

"That's good—I'll also need hardware."

"Yer makin' me very nervous, Dr. Peete—this isn't wild America, y'know."

"At ten then," I rang off.

"In hidin', are we?" Sarah Grey said and sniffed.

I shrugged. "We're sitting ducks here. Does your car work?"

"My Volks?"

"Yes, unless you'd rather take the Alfa Romero."

"It works fine," she said sourly, the thought of sporting about in the Mercedes fading from her vision.

Our luck was holding. We left the hotel by the kitchen entry and made our way to the old Volkswagen that Sarah had left parked down by the river, near the statue of Commodore Barry. If Sparrow had anyone on our tail, they would be watching the Mercedes parked in the hotel lot.

With a few preliminary coughs and sputters the ancient wreck shuddered forward. It sounded like an old washing machine and with the pedal on the floor we clipped along at a rousing 50 mph.

We arrived late at Fitzgerald's. Being unfamiliar with the road, we didn't see the pub at first. Mullin was waiting with a small van. We didn't waste any time in conversation. "Just follow me, Dr. Peete. It tisn't too long."

I have a good sense of direction, honed sharp by all those night exercises in the SEALS, but I couldn't retrace the route we followed. Leaving the Arklow Road after a few miles we turned into the Wicklow Mountains and took some meandering country lanes and finally unpaved tracks that twisted through the bare, flinty hills deep into the countryside.

We stopped before a ramshackle building that looked ready to fall down and go to sleep—forever. Mullin pulled the van to the side and, opening the big leaf door, had us drive in while he waited with a flashlight.

"This way, Dr. Peete," he muttered and led us to an old stone cottage set in the side of the bleak hillside. It was cold and damp like everywhere in Ireland in May, but Mullin lit a lantern and a peat fire in the small hearth.

"I hope you won't mind livin' rough fer a bit, Dr. Peete?"

"We'll do fine, what is this place?"

"It's called the 'Back o' Beyond.'"

"You Irish have a way with words."

"I'll be back in a twinklin'."

After he went down to the van, I looked over our new castle. A few sticks of furniture were about, a rudimentary kitchen and on the other side of the fireplace, a small bedroom with a double bed. "Conveniences" were out in back.

Mullin made a couple of trips. The first with a carton of foodstuffs and two pretty good sleeping bags. On the second he carried back an old .22 rifle and a .38 Webley revolver with boxes of ammunition.

"I tried to get a larger bore rifle, Dr. Peete, but I couldn't lay me hands on one on short notice."

"This is fine. Whose land are we on?"

"The Slattery's have a farm just over th' hill an' in th' hollow. They're trustworthy folk an' can be findin' you anythin' you might need. Yer honeymooners, by th' bye, although knowin' Patrick Slattery, he'll not be buyin' that blarney."

We spent the next four days at 'Back o' Beyond' and it was really romantic. It rained, the roof leaked, the food was awful, sanitary facilities minimal and we slept in the same bed, Sarah in her sleeping bag and I in mine. She told me in disgust that I snored.

From a tactical standpoint, I could have kissed old Liam. I wondered how many naughty IRA lads had dossed down here during the "Troubles." Set in a bleak range of bald hills, without a tree in sight, nothing was alive but sheep. The visible access road meandered for miles following the broken terrain and to get here on foot at night would take Kit Carson, Indian Scout. We weren't going to have any unexpected visits.

The problem turned out to be internal, not external. After three days with Sarah Grey in this God-forsaken place, I was ready to strangle her and she was all for lacing my tea with arsenic. My professional protocols prohibit playing "patty-fingers" with clients but I must admit the thought never crossed my mind; I would rather romance Medusa. We were safe from Sparrow but I didn't know how long it would be before we did each other in.

On the 9th of May, Mullin returned and I greeted him like Livingston must have greeted Stanley. "An' how are you gettin' on?" he asked.

"Like dogs and cats—have you found anything?"

Actually Mullin had found a great deal. When he finally got himself settled by the peat fire his snapping blue eyes had a look of pure triumph. "Twas a long an' tortuous trail . . . ." With a beginning like this I knew that he was going to wax eloquent but what can you do with the Irish? "Yer friend, Mr. Fowler, was quite a boy-o. His brief sojourn in Wexford did not go without notice."

"Heavens . . ."

"Of an evenin' he spent quite a bit o' his time at a pub out on th' Arklow Road, McGee an' Bloomfield's—affectionately referred to by its habitués as 'Maggie's Bloomers.' "

"That sounds dire."

"Aye, yer right there, Dr. Peete. Tis a dire place noted fer its second-rate ale and (he looked blushingly at Sarah) its ladies of th' evening."

"That's Fowler all right," Sarah said.

"Well now, he could be found there on most evenings, and of course, bein' a rich Yank, his company was sought after. I spent some small amount of time with th' barmaid of th' establishment—a fine, strappin' girl named Maureen O'Brien.

"She led me to understand that Mr. Fowler became quite friendly with one of their regulars. Him bein' a certain Michael

Walsh, who, I'm sorry to be tellin' yer, is a sad example of Irish manhood."

"I'm shocked to hear it."

"An' well you should be, Dr. Peete, an' well you should be. There was considerable drinkin' an' consortin' with . . . with . . ."

"Ladies of the evening?"

"Exactly! This Michael Walsh I'm afraid is naught but a scoundrel an' yer friend, Fowler—well, if yer don't mind me sayin' so, he was spendin' money like a beggar on horseback ridin' to hell!"

"Deplorable. . . ."

"Aye, that it is. I thought it might be to our mutual interest to be lookin' up this rascal, Michael Walsh, an' see if he had any light to shed on th' sad events surroundin' Mr. Fowler's demise."

"Very prudent indeed."

"I'll be thankin' you fer that, Dr. Peete, but I'll also be tellin' yer that it was not easy. Th' man was a will-o-the-wisp, flittin' here an' there, willy-nilly like, wherever his evil intentions might take him. . . ."

"Evil intentions?"

"Aye, Dr. Peete, this Michael Walsh is a blackguard of th' first water. He has more than a passin' acquaintance with th' Garda. He's been before th' Magistrate fer brawlin' an' bein' light-fingered."

"So you hunted him down?" Hearing about it was almost as exhausting as tracing him.

"In a word, no; I've not clapped me eyes on the rogue as yet. After some considerable effort I tracked down his digs, only to find th' bird had flown."

"Did you find out where?"

"To th' Bahamas, no less . . ."

"The Bahamas!"

"Yes, Dr. Peete. Around th' 20th of April he seemed to come into extraordinary funds. He left his digs but had some baggage shipped out."

"What baggage?"

"A trunk with some clothin' an' personal effects."

I sat for a minute trying to digest this. It was the last thing I'd have expected. "To the Bahamas?" I asked in confusion.

"Aye, that's where he had gone. I took meself down to th' grand airport at Shannon. Fortunately, me wife's cousin's sister-in-law works there."

"It's great to have kin."

"Sure an' tis a grand thing. She, little Rosie McBride, did a little checkin' fer me . . ."

"And what did little Rosie find out?"

"That one Michael Walsh was manifested on British Airways flight 214 to Georgetown on th' 30th of April!"

"When did his trunk leave?"

"It was shipped on th' 20th."

"You better give me everything you've got on this Walsh."

"There's very little to find, Dr. Peete. I could work on it but you understand there are Michael Walshes spread all over Ireland. I did some checkin' with th' Garda (me Aunt Mary's postman's brother bein' with them) an' can tell he showed up in Dublin some two or three years ago, takin' up th' profession of cab driver.

"The Garda looked into some activities of his concernin' th' loss of baggage in his cab an' his habit of introducin' foreign visitors to 'interestin' ladies."

"He was pimping?"

"That was never proven, I'm afraid, but there was some speculation in that direction."

"How did he meet Fowler?"

"Well now, there's a bit o' speculation upon that point also. Maureen O'Brien, th' barmaid at Maggie's Bloomers, was not sure but was of th' opinion that Fowler had taken Walsh as a sort of tour guide, an' common interests led to th' bloomin' of amity between them."

"Fowler wanted to see all the historical sights?"

"Aye, and apparently Walsh knew where they all were. In any event their friendship grew an' they drank together near every night. Maggie's Bloomers was their favorite haunt."

"Why the Bahamas? Any lead on that?" I was still groping for an answer to that one.

"Not much, but Maureen O'Brien did hear Walsh holdin' forth on th' glories of tropical isles, warm sunshine, undressed ladies an' th' like. She said that he spoke like a man who'd seen, not just read about. In any event, it appears that one of Michael Walsh's great dreams was to leave th' cold an' damp of his native soil, an' cavort with dusky-skinned maidens in some heathen land. . . ."

"How degrading."

"That's what I thought, Dr. Peete. In any case that's where the trail of Michael Walsh leads—to Georgetown in th' Bahamas."

"So that's it?"

"Not quite." I felt a small surge in my belly. The poetic Liam Mullin was holding the best to last.

"Well?"

"When I had little Rosie McBride check on th' flights to th' Bahamas, I also had her look into any other manifests. Sure an' aren't th' computers grand things, Dr. Peete! She sat there with her fine brows knit an' her slim fingers clickin' at th' keyboard . . ."

"She found something?"

"Bless me if she didn't. She found that George Fowler, on an American passport, was manifested on th' Aer Lingus flight to Zurich on th' 7th of April!"

Chapter IX

Realistically Sparrow couldn't find us in six months unless he stumbled on the chink in our armor—Mullin, our only contact to the outside. Of course even if he did follow Mullin, the Back O' Beyond was practically impregnable.

Movement represented vulnerability but it had been five days since I last talked to Miz Charlotte. She'd be breathing fire by now so the three of us jumped into Mullin's van and went to the Arklow Post Office to make a transatlantic call.

Sarah and Liam stayed in the van, much to our Irish bombshell's displeasure; she wanted to pop into the pub for a quick dish of bangers and squeak. Fortunately, Miss Benedict hadn't wandered off and was waiting to hear from me.

When working for Miz Charlotte, one must be ready for mood swings. The "Grand Dame" sat on her lands and estates in Gloucester County, Virginia, USA, like Eleanor in the Aquitaine, and if every little thing in her fiefdom didn't go exactly as Her Highness wanted it, look out!

Her voice was low and weak, so I knew that I was in for the pained and long-suffering Benedict, the one I most hated. "Is that *really* you, Peete? I *hope* I haven't disturbed your golf, tennis, riding to the hounds and other crushingly *important* efforts that I *know* must be consuming you. . . ."

"Look I . . ."

"... I feel rather shabbily used, Peete. It might be different if I didn't pay you a truly royal stipend for your small efforts on my behalf. 'Keep in touch,' as I recall were my last words. A simple request, one might think. Not really *too* complicated, one opines—merely the lifting of a telephone instrument, as generally found at one's bedside at one's hotel. I have sat for days now with *my* telephone instrument within easy reach . . ."

"Okay, okay, I done wrong. I admit it. Do you listen or do I do penance for twenty-four hours and call you back tomorrow?"

"You hang up this phone and you're fired, David!"

"That's a hollow threat, you can't fire me and you know it. If you did you'd never find out what's going on and that would bug you. You're itching to know and I'm pressed for time. Do you want to hear it?"

There was a pregnant pause. "Do you have possession of Miss Grey?"

"What do you mean, 'have possession'? She's not a pair of socks, you know."

"You have access to her?"

"Sure I . . ."

"She must get in touch with this Aloysius Lacy person; his lawyer, Mr. Bernbaum keeps threatening litigation."

"So what? You haven't done anything to Lacy . . ."

"I've checked on this Bernbaum in New York. He's known as 'Banzai' Bernbaum up there; it's reputed he can make a litigation out of a gift to the Children's Hospital of the King's Daughters."

So that was it! Miz Charlotte was like a kid with an imaginary dragon under her bed. She was deathly afraid of the courts of law as places where *"truth and justice seldom reside."*

"Okay, I'll talk to Sarah Grey and see if she can call off Lacy and his ruffians. Now—do you want to hear?"

She wanted to hear so I gave her an update on the conflab

with Sparrow, the Kamaroff angle, Michael Walsh and the Bahamas.

"Is that all you know about Walsh?"

"All—right now . . . We could dig up some more, I guess."

"So Sparrow doesn't think it's just a fancy piece of goldsmithing . . ." she mused.

"It's not fancy now. If it's the box that Geoffery de Villehardouin mentioned it was faced with gold and jewels. This thing, according to Fowler's notes, unseen but relayed to me by Sarah Grey (if she's not a liar, but I think she is) has been stripped, probably by the wicked Count Odo himself."

"So it must be what's *in* the box."

"It looks that way. What do you want me to do? Check further into Walsh? That could take time and my movements are limited right now. I'm living in a swell place by the way. I was going to call you from the poolside with all the Irish lasses prancing around in their bikinis but it's so distracting . . ."

"You'd better come home."

It was my turn to pause. "There are loose ends here."

"Such as?"

"The girl—somebody may have tried to close her book once. I think our involvement is dangerous to her . . ."

"Ah ha! I thought you didn't care a fig about her. Under that phony crust you're all mush, Peete. Anyway, I definitely want you to bring her."

"Bring her? Look, your Majesty, I know that everyone is just dying to come to Avalon to pay homage to you on your fiefdom but folks just can't drop everything. They have obligations."

"Such as?"

"Well, her studies—earning a living. You know, mundane things that I tremble to mention in your august presence."

"Oh piffle, David. Hire her as a researcher, that will make the passport business easier."

"What about her academic schedule?"

"Good heavens, Peete, she can learn more from me in two weeks than she can in two years at some dingy university. Working for me can only enhance her academic standing." There's no arguing with that size of ego!

"What are you going to have her do? Oh, I get it—she can be the vestal virgin and keep the eternal flame at Avalon. Do you want me to check her qualifications? Like if she's a virgin? Otherwise . . ."

"She's the one who found the tomb, isn't she? Besides, I want to talk to her; you tend to complicate issues."

"Tell Dixie to get a lot of food in the larder."

We rang off.

Bouncing along the dirt roads in the van, we returned to the Back o' Beyond. "America, is it?" Sarah said with a toss of her head. It would have been more effective if her curls hadn't been executed. "And what am I? Baggage to be moved about? What about me school efforts? What about me friends—me family?"

"We'll hire you as a researcher and Dr. Benedict will write a letter to the Dean at Trinity. Your working for Charlotte Benedict for a quarter term won't hurt."

"An' me clothes? Am I to go with what I'm standin' in now?"

She reminded me of Eliza Doolittle when Henry Higgins offered her chocolates, afraid of his intentions, but with her greedy little soul contemplating America, where the paving blocks are of gold, or, knowing Sarah—food.

"Do you have a passport?"

"Sure an' what would th' likes of me be doin' with a passport? Visitin' th' Great Wall of China, maybe?"

"Me cousin Brendan's half-sister's nephew works in th' Foreign Office, if yer needin' a passport," Mullin said, his teeth clamped on his pipe. It must be great to be related to everyone in Ireland.

For the next six days, Sarah vacillated. Meanwhile we made a few trips to Carlow for passport pictures and to buy clothes. Mullin also paid the bill at Whyte's Hotel and for the Mercedes and I felt the security of the Back o' Beyond was being severely compromised.

On our last day, the 15th, I spotted them. I had taken to sitting on the front steps in good weather with my fold-up binoculars and, believe it or not, bird-watching (and among other things, the access road). Panning the hills, a flash of inappropriate color caught my eye on a rocky hillside near where the entry road twisted off in the distance.

Getting up casually, I drifted into the house to a window and propping the glasses on the sill, had another look. Some bozo was standing behind a tripod mounted telescope and he wasn't bird-watching!

"Sarah Grey looked up from the book she was reading, "What are you lookin' at?"

"We've got company," I replied and she dropped the book.

There's an old maxim of war that says always do the unexpected. I started by studying the terrain until I felt I knew it—very well. We were being observed, so let them observe. We took the Volks from the shed and stowed our baggage. Then we waited, like in the Westerns, till sundown.

Sarah was scared to death and that was the hardest part. She was all for building the Maginot Line at the cottage and waiting for trouble to come. I had an awful time convincing her that you usually lose that way. I reiterated the plan about five times and tried to assure her that if she followed orders everything would be swell (I hoped!).

Dressed in my darkest clothing, I slipped out the back door at dark and worked my way over the rough ground toward the hillside. The thing that really worried me was their moving before I got into position. I allowed two hours and that was ample—but just!

Approaching from the opposite side, I moved carefully to the rear and, as I suspected, a large automobile was parked there out of sight of the cottage. The inside faintly glowed, like someone was using a flashlight.

The luminous dial on my watch showed 10:10. At precisely 10:15, Sarah was to snap on the headlights and start her slow approach. I slipped onto the road and crept to the rear of car. Just one person was sitting in the passenger seat.

"They're coming!" I heard the call from the hillside. I breathed easier; Sarah was following orders. The car window opened in the faint glow and I saw a head protrude. "Get ready!" his voice shattered the silence.

I pushed the muzzle of the Webley against his skull, just behind the left ear and cocked the hammer. I could see the figure start and freeze.

"Hello Sergei," I said as the hammer made a dry click. Kamaroff wasn't urbane like Sparrow. He said a lot of things in Slavic under his breath. I didn't understand them but I was sure they were Russian four-letter words. "Turn on the headlights, very carefully. You wouldn't want brain tissue splattered all over that neat dashboard."

Sergei was a realist; he also had a great affection for his head in its present shape and location, so he did as he was told. The beams flashed catching a ferretty-looking guy standing about 50 feet down the road, jacked like a deer. Another dumpy one stumbled down the hill, carrying a telescope and tripod.

"On the ground, face down and spread-eagled!" I shouted. Mr. Ferret looked confused so I let a round go past his right ear. They both dropped like trees in the lighted roadway. "Join the party, Sergei," I said opening the door. When the old Volks came bouncing over the hill, my new friends were lying there, frisked, relieved of appurtenances, and unhappy—particularly Sergei.

"C'mon over, Sarah," I called. She walked over and stood beside me. "I'd like to introduce you to Sergei Kamaroff. Don't get up Sergei, we know you've had a tough day. The other two are Rosencrantz and Gildernstern."

Some things happen subliminally. Maybe the mind works at some mysterious level below consciousness where thoughts slosh back and forth like water in a tank. I wanted Kamaroff to say something—anything. "I guess you're looking for the casket from Alexander's tomb too, eh, Sergei?" I asked.

As soon as the words were out I felt a flutter. They almost died on my lips. Looking down I saw Kamaroff's face clearly in the glow of the headlights. The little, piggy eyes looked up at me registering both avarice and hatred. I chewed down the excitement and swallowed it. That would be too much, like winning the Irish Sweepstakes!

"It's real nice of you to drop in, Sergei, but as you can see, we were just leaving for the airport. I appreciate the borrow of your neat car though, we weren't sure if the Volks would make it." I threw the distributor cap from the Volks into the darkness. "We have to run, Sergei, so long for now. Arklow is about twenty miles in that direction."

"We'll meet again, Dr. Peete," Kamaroff said through his teeth.

"Don't be a sorehead, Sergei. Hop over to the cottage and wait there. You can soak in the Jacuzzi while Rosencrantz and Gildernstern hunt up some transport." We got into the Jaguar and I flicked on the engine. "If you see Alfie Sparrow give him my love," I called as I turned the car and we headed toward Shannon.

Chapter X

We disembarked through customs at JFK and made the connecting flight to Norfolk. If Sarah Grey was a distinguished visitor (which she wasn't) and I wanted to impress her (which I didn't) our timing could have been a bit better. The small air terminal at Norfolk is set amid the lakes of the area and was, at this time of year, enclosed with a riot of azalea. But we were just ten days or two weeks too late. The dogwood were gone and most of the azalea were past their prime and were fading.

Raphael, the major-domo at Avalon, met us with the big car. No introduction to Avalon could possibly be complete without the inclusion of Raphael and Dixie. Raphael is black, of ancient and indeterminate age, tall as a Masai and about as heavy, and without a hair on his head. Dixie, his wife, is short and spheroid, all bosom and buttocks. Dixie spoke pure Afro-American while Raph had a lilting Jamaican argot.

If you get the image of Stepin Fetchit and Butterfly McQueen, forget it. In the strange hierarchy of Avalon both were powers to be reckoned with. Charlotte's papa was distracted and her mama had "the vapors," so Dixie and Raphael drifted unconsciously into the role of surrogate parents. Dixie told her things a girl should know, and Raphael taught her to sail and fish. While Miz Charlotte is the picture of femininity now, she was apparently a bit of a hoyden in her youth.

Living so long at Avalon, Raphael attained his status as major-domo. The only thing Raph was afraid of was Dixie, and the only thing she was afraid of was God. In addition you could get more good, down to earth, advice from Dixie peeling potatoes in the kitchen than all the Doctors of Philosophy at Harvard put together.

As we wended our way to Avalon, I was interested to watch Sarah's greedy little mind in operation. The Benedict standard contract for researchers was a king's ransom to her and this, plus other hitherto undreamed of aspects of the "Land of the Great Ice Cream Cone," like pizza parlors, Kentucky Fried Chicken and Burger King's on every corner were fast putting her into a state of culinary collapse. She was beside herself and only by her iron discipline did her mind start to move toward things other than consumables.

"An' where is this place yer takin' me?"

"Avalon."

"A town, is it?"

"Actually, it's an independent Duchy. We'll travel north past the Yorktown battlefield, where you'll be elated to learn, we kicked the British out . . ."

"Tis th' only thing you Yanks ever did right."

"You call me 'Yank' once more and I'll pitch you off the Coleman Bridge into the York River. On the other side of the bridge, we'll take Guinea Road and meander into 'Guinea Country.' I'm not sure whether that's part of the United States either."

"So it's a house, is it?"

"Yeah, you'll see a big iron gate with the word 'Avalon' inscribed across the top. That's the beginning of Miz Charlotte's fiefdom. She insists Avalon is an island, but, of course, it isn't. It's really a peninsula with a low area at its base that floods only at the highest of high tides. But don't tell her that, it upsets her."

I was getting a kick out of all this. Little Sarah was getting all her ducks in a row, just like they do at the shooting gallery. Little did she know that Miz Charlotte was really Annie Oakley."

"An' she's rich, of course?"

"She was never poor—there were always investments and annuities from her parents, but she's well-off now; she's done it on her own with fat commissions and finder's fees. She pulled down the old frame house that her father built without batting an eye and built a rambling Tudor barn with genuine leaded diamond paned windows, a forest of chimneys, a swimming pool, and a dock for her nifty 24' sloop on Aquia Creek."

"Aquia Creek?"

"It's one of the navigable waterways that snakes north from the York River into Guinea Country."

We drove in silence for a while, Sarah contemplating her confrontation with Miss Benedict. I could tell she was getting edgy; she knew that a lot was riding on this next few hours. "What's she really like?" she asked in a low voice.

Now there was a question that would tax Charles Dickens. I decided to stay with the obvious. "She's in her fifties, I think—that sort of data is 'Top Secret.' She's smart as a whip and not the type to lie to."

"Why do you say that?" she asked innocently. She patted her make-believe curls and tried to sound casual.

"Just a general observation. You Irish have a tendency toward embellishment; she'll enjoy a little poetic license as long as the truth isn't murdered in the process."

We reached the front gate of Avalon and I opened it for Raphael. The gravel crunched under the wheels as we passed up the drive through the deciduous, pine, holly and dogwood trees on the right and Duck Pond on the left.

"She's a bloody Duchess!" cried our Irish bombshell.

This was going to be great! Being a scholar and a student of human nature, I couldn't wait to see these two together. As I was leading her up the sweeping staircase to the library on the second floor, I said to her: "Be sure to tell her that you contacted her because you thought she was a grand detective."

Charlotte Montaigne Benedict paid a lot of attention to Avalon; it was, after all, her masterpiece, the setting in which she placed the jewel of herself. And the library was her *pièce de résistance*. Taking nearly a third of the upstairs part of the main house, it was a long room broken by dormers with high slim windows. The walls were lined with books from ceiling to floor, some of them quite valuable. At the far end was a huge fireplace and a large pedestaled desk where the lady of the manor sat and worked, sometimes up to fourteen hours a day.

I secretly admit that I am in awe of Charlotte Benedict. I feel like I'm back in the third grade when I'm near her. She has an unstudied ability to keep me on a short leash (a facility that eluded some of the crustiest Admirals in the Navy).

Slim and imperious, she was sitting at her desk as we entered causing us to walk the full length of the room under her riveted stare. I wondered what effect all this was having on little Sarah. She must have felt the aura of meeting Miz Charlotte in her fortress, behind the ramparts of her huge desk.

Charlotte looked as if she had been wrapped in tissue and just taken out of a lavender-scented drawer. Age really had little impact on her. Sometimes she seemed an anachronism, sometimes I thought I detected the effects of incipient old age in her movements and attitudes, and then, almost immediately, she'd flash her vitality and seem like someone more thirtyish than sixtyish. She wasn't pretty, at least not in the conventional sense, but her features were well-molded. She had good brows, high cheek bones, and a firm mouth and chin. Her face had great planes and projected character.

Rising as we neared, her white blouse and jabot crisp and spotless, she extended her slim, long-fingered hand. "You must be Sarah Grey?" she said with a smile and in her soft, Southern accent.

It was interesting to see what armor Miz Charlotte would wear for any encounter in the lists. She could be very tough when she wanted and even Bill Buckley didn't like to bandy words with her. Today, however, she was all sweetness and pleasantry so I figured it was the "spider and fly" routine. Little Sarah was going to get killed with kindness. First the Irish barracuda was ensconced in a comfortable chair by the regal desk under the benevolent eye of her ladyship (I was relegated to my mean, varlet-like stool and churlish roll-top desk to the side and against the wall). Then there were solicitous inquiries—was she comfortable, did she need to use the powder room? Beverages were proffered from tea to beer. True to form, Sarah allowed she could do with a sandwich (she needed something to tide herself over till dinner). I don't know where she put it. I am formulating a new theory that the potato famine is still in full rage and the Irish eat as much as they can as often as they can.

Miss Benedict sat at the desk and then encouraged her to tell the complete tale, from the beginning. Assuming an attitude of rapt attention, Miz Charlotte hung on every word, as if she was interviewing Bill Clinton in the Oval Office. I was sick to my stomach. Scratch an Irishman and you'll find a bard. I guess that's true of Irish girls too. She told it well, in a clear well-modulated Irish brogue, replete with imagery and humor. She lilted on, uninterrupted, for almost three quarters of an hour.

When she was finished, Miss Benedict leaned forward. "That was delightful," she said.

I let out a stream of air, like a balloon going flat.

"Are you in pain, David?" Miz Charlotte asked sweetly.

"Sorry, I find it hard to sit on my old war wounds."

Miss Benedict removed her pinch-nose glasses and judiciously polished the lenses. "Pay no heed to Dr. Peete, my dear, he's an example of our disgraceful institutions of higher learning wherein they educate bumpkins beyond their natural capacities."

Despite my disgust with the interview there were a few items that got Charlotte's attention. She didn't telegraph and you had to know her to detect them. One was the emergence of Kamaroff and his loyal band. Both Kamaroff and Sparrow on the scent even impressed the unimpressionable Miss Benedict.

"Can we talk business now?" I asked. "Did you get anything from the Bahamas on Michael Walsh?" I knew that Miss Benedict wouldn't just sit on her hands while we were getting Sarah's passport and traveling.

"Not much," she replied with a sigh. "Walsh reached Georgetown as you indicated and redeemed his trunk the same day."

"He's there now?"

"No—he's disappeared."

"Oh great! He's been bumped off too?"

Charlotte pursed her lips judiciously. "A possibility perhaps . . . but, if so, it would involve yet another character or characters in the drama."

"What do you mean?"

"Think about it. According to Liam Mullin, Walsh flew to the Bahamas on the 30th of April. Your tête-à-tête with Sparrow was on the 3rd and some time later with Kamaroff. According to my information Michael Walsh disappeared on the 30th. So you see, both Sparrow and Kamaroff were in Ireland when

Walsh vanished. If violence has been done, we must assume some other agency."

I held up my hand. "Wait a minute—that's too fast. Either one of them could have agents in the Bahamas, just like you—you didn't get this stuff from your trusty crystal ball."

"A possibility, but hard to swallow. If Sparrow or Kamaroff knew anything about Walsh then why bother with you two? They, themselves would have gone to Georgetown after Walsh."

"Suppose Sparrow found out about Walsh around the time I saw him . . . if . . ."

"If . . . if . . . 'if pigs had wings they'd fly.' It's possible, I'll grant you, but unlikely."

"So you think someone else might be in the picture?"

Miz Charlotte toyed with a letter opener. "Maybe. There's no way of knowing. There are other unscrupulous dealers that Walsh might have contacted. On the other hand, Walsh may have slipped out of Georgetown."

"Why?"

"Look, David, neither of us knows this Michael Walsh. Oh I know what Mullin found out but it isn't much, is it? He could be a minor felon as we've been led to think, or he could be someone of quite different stripe. Suppose he does know the value of the box—predicated, of course, on the fact that it does have some value."

I had been biding my time, waiting for the propitious time to pitch my hand grenade into the great one's lap. I savored it for a moment. "I think I know what Kamaroff thinks it is."

Miz Charlotte looked toward me sitting at my roll-top desk. "Oh, and what's that?" she asked.

"The Casket of Alexander."

Chapter XI

It was sweet! When you live with Charlotte Benedict day in and day out, you look for small victories; they mean a lot.

There was a dead silence and Miss Benedict wore a particularly pained expression. She was groping and couldn't find the words. I mentally hugged myself; Miz Charlotte at a loss for words was like Hank Aaron forgetting which end of the bat to hold. "That," she said feebly, "is pure twaddle—really, Peete, for one who purports to be of the intelligentsia . . ."

"I never purported anything. We can't fight what we are, you know," I replied, showing her my innocent brown eyes.

"What's th' Casket of Alexander?" Sarah asked, her mouth full of country ham and Swiss cheese sandwich.

Miz Charlotte refused to dignify the question by answering. That would have shown a modicum of interest in the idea that was churning around inside her like butterflies on roller skates. So I turned toward Sarah. "When Alexander, prior to becoming 'The Great,' was a frisky teenager his father, Philip of Macedonia, decided he needed a good tutor and hired Aristotle for the job."

"Och, sure an' everybody knows that Aristotle was Alexander the Great's tutor."

"Good. According to tradition (that's everybody's agreed on lies), young Alexander loved Aristotle almost as much as he loved the Iliad. You know why? Because Alexander wanted to be a god so badly that he thought he became one." I looked heavenward. "It's amazing to think how anyone could have delusions like that."

I said this innocently but Miss Benedict wasn't biting. She had gone off into one of her trances of great wisdom which she often does when gnat-like mortals are bothering her.

"The story persists that Aristotle presented Alexander with a copy of the Iliad *that he had annotated!* Think about that one for a minute, a copy of the Iliad owned by Alexander the Great with marginal notes made by arguably the greatest mind of antiquity.

"Legend has it that Alexander considered this Iliad to be his most treasured possession—that he even slept with it under his pillow. That I find hard to swallow. In any event he started on his business of conquering the world. He crossed the Hellespoint and fought the Battle at Granicus and Issus, cut the Gordian knot, reduced Sidon and Tyre and conquered Egypt. Then he came back to face Darius and the huge Persian army for the second time. Outnumbered five to one, he met Darius near Gaugamela and trounced the Persians for the last time. Darius high-tailed it for the hills.

"After the battle, the story goes, some of Alexander's men were rummaging around in Darius's tent where they found a magnificent casket, covered with gold and encrusted with jewels. It was empty and they brought it to Alexander and asked, 'What is worthy to be put in this?'

"Young Alexander replied, 'There's only one thing good enough for that box!' and he put the annotated Iliad in it. He was supposed to have carried it with him until he died."

Miz Charlotte made a sound like a death rattle.

I knew I had impressed little Sarah because she had stopped eating. "An' what happened to it then?" she asked.

"It's assumed that when the Alexandrian Empire was divided, Ptolemy, who got Egypt, took the casket and put it in the Library at Alexandria. If so, it probably was destroyed in the fire that burned the Library in 47 B.C.

"Of course, there's another fanciful tale. You will recall that when Caesar conquered Egypt, Cleopatra, looking for support in her dynastic struggle with her brother, was supposed to have herself taken to Julius wrapped in a Persian rug. Some think that she was traveling so light that she didn't even bother with clothes. But some think that she took along the famous casket and gave it to Caesar as a present, he being the only mortal worthy to receive it. But this sounds like baloney to me."

"But how would it be gettin' to Constantinople?" Sarah asked, her brows knitted.

"Well, accepting the story of Cleo giving it to Caesar, it would have gone to Rome. After Brutus and his gang did in Caesar at the Forum it's not unreasonable to assume the casket went to Caesar's cousin, Mark Anthony—along with Cleopatra, since she and Anthony were very tight. Anthony got the Eastern Empire which was, of course, centered at Byzantium, so its finding its way there is not completely off the wall."

"An' yer thinkin' this Casket of Alexander is our box?"

"Oh no—I didn't say that. I said that I think that's what Kamaroff thinks it is."

Throughout this masterful expostulation, Miz Charlotte sat exercising her iron will. She hated mindless speculation and by now she was probably registering 9.9 on the internal Richter Scale.

"It all sounds far-fetched to me," Sarah said judiciously, munching on her pickle.

Which says it all. When someone from the land of fairies and leprechauns tells you something is far-fetched, you'd better believe it!

Miss Benedict didn't trust herself to start talking and we broke up. I took Sarah to her room over the garage in the detached wing. We went down the back staircase past the pool and I was pleased to see that Raphael and his minions had removed the canvas cover that shrouded it during the winter. This, and the robins and dogwood were harbingers that Spring had really sprung.

"Och, what a grand swimmin' pool."

"Too bad it's too cold."

"Th' guest bedrooms are in a separate buildin' are they?" she asked as we walked upstairs in the garage building to the two bedrooms on the second floor.

"Yeah, well actually this is the penitential wing of the convent. Inside you'll find sackcloth and ashes. Once in uniform, you can tell your beads and meditate on your sinful ways until you're called to the Mother-Superior."

I left her oohing and aahing at the appointments of the guest room and ambled to my monastic cell at the other end of the house for a quick shower and a change of clothes.

Then something strange occurred. Miss Benedict has two fears that verge on the pathological. One, mentioned earlier, was of litigation and the "willies" of falling into the clutches of "Banzai' Bernbaum and his heartless ilk; the second, physical violence, was born of her dire experiences during the burglary that occasioned my employment. I never exaggerate but the KGB could sneak into the Oval Office and steal Bill's pants easier than getting past the front gate of Avalon. Miz Charlotte had sensors checking on sensors all over the place.

In addition, even though it's downright un-American, all

phone conversations at Avalon are taped (wait until Banzai Bernbaum and the ACLU hear about that one!). The focus of these electronic marvels is Max, the oversized control panel that ogles me from the corner of my room, replete with dials, toggle-switches and little red lights. I have complained sturdily to Miz Charlotte about it but she allows that in the conditions of my employment (a controversial document frequently the subject of long and acrimonious discussions) that in addition to the superior cerebral talents that I bring to bear on sundry problems, I am also security officer of her fiefdom.

One of Max's many blood-shot eyes was blinking relentlessly at me and that was strange since it indicated that a phone call was being made from the guest wing. Sarah Grey must be using the phone! But to whom? I filed the item away; I'd check the tape before I turned in.

Sometimes I wonder who's screwier, Miss Benedict or me? Here are two intelligent people who spend the majority of their waking hours driving each other nuts. And if I thought things were going to change I knew I could forget it as I entered the small dining room that looked out on Aquia Creek.

Anticipating the simple comforts of home, I was dressed in an old shirt, jeans and my favorite soft moccasin slippers. Padding into the dining room, I found Miz Charlotte attired in a long ivory colored dress with cascades of lace like the Grand Duchess of Schleswig-Holstein.

Sarah was already there (she had the scent of a hyena when it came to food) and they were standing by the window. Down the creek about a half a mile was a nest of fishing boats beneath a cloud of wheeling gulls and Miss Benedict was explaining the joys of girlhood and the rich shellfish bounty of the Bay.

This was too much! I preferred to eat in the kitchen with Rafe and Dixie where we could discuss important stuff, like baseball. To have to tolerate Charlotte Montaigne Benedict being charming for another hour or so would drive me bonkers. Raphael, dressed in a white jacket, also couldn't figure out why her Ladyship was putting on the dog for the likes of Sarah Grey.

Miss Benedict turned as I entered, "Ah, David, we were waiting for you. I see you're *en deshabille* this evening."

For the first time I noticed some subtle alterations in Sarah. Her Palestinian Terrorist motif was shed for the "scrubbed schoolgirl" look, i.e., a white middy blouse with a big bow, dark skirt with black stockings and flat shoes. She looked at Miz Charlotte wistfully from behind her large glasses, like a kid sprung from boarding school to visit a rich and fussy aunt. Of course her hair was a problem but it looked as if it had all fallen out with some childhood sickness and was growing back.

The meal was ghastly. Raphael was as griped as I was with the antics of Miz Charlotte and slammed the serving plates down on the table, probably making believe it was her head. Dixie had prepared "Oysters Rockefeller" and Sarah landed on those like an octopus sucking out their innards. During the meal Miz Charlotte rambled on about the American colonies, Irish immigrants, the similarities of country music to Gaelic music, Jamestown, the Middle Plantation (now called Williamsburg) the eating habits of the colonies etc., etc. It was all very civilized and cultured. When coffee was served, Sarah leaned back sleek and benign, like a lioness after gorging herself on a kill.

"Tell me about the Bend Sinister," Miz Charlotte asked politely.

I threw down my napkin in disgust. Holding forth upon weighty subjects at the dinner table was a special privilege of Her Nibs only. Many an hour I sat bored to death by a detailed explanation of how Ubangi women distorted their lips, or the sexual cycle of the Arctic walrus (which was why I usually ate in the kitchen where mundane topics were discussed, like fishing or the lottery). For her to pass the baton to the Irish carnivore was more than human flesh could endure . . .

Sarah explained the "genealogy thing" to Miss Benedict and then took off on the Normans. "Many Normans found their way to Ireland, th' ones that start with 'Fitz'—Fitzgerald, Fitzwilliam, etc., an' also 'De' or 'D'—Delaney, Delacy . . . I became interested in th' amazin' rise of th' Normans at th' end of th' first millennium. Every child in Ireland is well versed in th' Norman Conquest of England, but I became interested in th' Italian branch.

"Thirteen years before th' conquest of England, while Duke William was still starin' moodily across th' Channel to the England of Edward th' Confessor, th' Guiscard brothers of th' Hautville Normans had already defeated th' Papal army at Civitate. Then Robert and Roger Guiscard went on to conquer Sicily in 1072.

"125 years later when Odo turned up in th' south of Italy, th' Normans were spread thin—all over Normandy, England, Ireland an' th' Two Sicilies. Their great political talent was their ability to assimilate themselves into th' local scene. They were fast becomin' French, English, Irish an' Italian.

"King Frederick II of Sicily had founded universities an' was restorin' th' Italian language, so Odo deLacy must have been as much a northern foreigner as a kinsman. He apparently was a fierce fighter an' he took th' cross—probably to everyone's great relief. Everyone wanted to see the back of that boy-o. You've heard about th' Fourth Crusade an' th' box?"

Miss Benedict nodded, a bit painfully, I thought.

"When Odo come back, he must have been at 'sixes an' sevens' to decide what mischief to get into next. In those days issues were decided by th' sword an' the Pope. There was always room fer a good soldier an' the' countryside was alive with free companions sellin' their lances to th' highest bidder. But even th' strongest temporal rulers had to be careful of th' Papacy. A bill of excommunication could end their dreams in a twinklin'.

"So Odo, being a bastard by birth an' not havin' much in th' way of prospects, could be someone's hired mercenary but how far would that get him? Instead, he tied himself to th' Papacy. While Odo deLacy had about as much religion as my uncle Dennis' pig, he applied to Rome to establish an order of knights friars, thirteen in all, who would give their lances to 'good causes.' The idea appealed to Rome. An', of course, th' lads could help themselves to this an' that so they weren't botherin' anybody about their 'upkeep.'

"None of th' friars was ordained, you see. They became th' 'Order of th' Bend Sinister,' each bein' born on th' other side of th' blanket an' in the same boat as Odo. It worked fine fer a while, but apparently deLacy wasn't above a little extortion on his own hook. In any event, there was a fallin' out with his superiors an' th' Knights were disbanded.

"Odo returned to Ireland an' apparently just in time. There were all kinds of discussions regardin' th' Bend Sinister rangin' from outright knavery to devil-worship. . . ."

Listening to all this Irish drivel again was only redeemed by the opportunity of watching Miz Charlotte straining to maintain her equilibrium. It was an uphill fight. "Devil worship?" she asked politely.

"Sure an' you know how it was in those days. Th' surest way to get rid of an organization or a person was an accusation of consortin' with th' Devil—that's th' way they got rid of th' Knights Templar. Count Odo was smart enough to high-tail it back to Ireland but some of his coterie didn't move fast enough an' came to a quick end—at th' stake."

"But Odo got back to Ireland?"

"Oh yes, but not too long after he got in trouble again an' th' Crown confined him th th' Monastery of St. Camillus. He died there around 1220."

"But there is no record of the famous casket?"

"Nothin'. The only mention of it was in th' writings of Geoffrey De Villehardouin on th' Crusade when Odo stole it an' wouldn't give it up."

"It's all very fascinating, my dear," Miz Charlotte lied, "one can't help but speculate on the casket's content but I give no credence to Dr. Peete's flights of fancy."

"Then again—maybe it was the Empress Theodora's chastity belt...." I opined.

Chapter XII

"More coffee, Sarah?" Charlotte asked, ignoring me. "By the way, there is one small office that you could perform for me."

Up till now Sarah had been so busy putting chow to bed that she never had a chance for anything else. "An' what might that be, Miss Benedict?" she asked sweetly.

"Would you call Aloysius Lacy and mention that you are here and the current state of affairs concerning the box. . . ."

So that was it! The lioness of Academia was still a'tremble at the threatened litigation by Lacy and his hired gun, Bernbaum! This was the reason for all the honey-dripping and stuffing Sarah full of oysters and Chateaubriand! It was an acute case of litigataphobia!

"My God, boss," I cried, "you're not still worried about that apple-picker from New York?" I pursued the subject with some of my finest rhetoric but it was no use. All my pure logic and clever syllogism were to no avail. Miz Charlotte was one of the most rational women I've ever met but when she lost it, she lost it. Sarah had been hired by Lacy and Miz Charlotte wanted to see if she could call off the legal dogs.

Sarah, on her part, liked Avalon, sleeping on an inner spring mattress and being filled with enough oysters to satisfy a bull walrus. Her new job paid premium wages and she'd do anything to get Miss Benedict in her debt. So, like kindergarten, when you put three together, it becomes two against one. They tried arguments to shut me up, and that failing they finally ignored me by common covenant.

Sarah and I were both beat after our travels and a buzzing in my ear took the edge off my repartee. Miz Charlotte, having accomplished her mission to get Sarah to act as point man against the nefarious Aloysius, was also ready to call it a night.

Tired as I was, I wandered outside a little before crashing. I went out the door to the screened-in porch and took a little stroll in the full moonlight over the small brick bridge to the front gate and back to what Miz Charlotte grandly calls the circular drive. When it comes to things Benedict, she tends toward hyperbole. I made the usual rounds, checking the sail-locker, a small shed on the east side of Avalon by the "T" dock.

The lights in Sarah's room snapped off. She must have the digestion of a boa constrictor, I thought.

I was yawning when I got back but I had one more thing to do before I hit the sack. Avalon had all the latest amenities and in the butler's pantry near the Kingdom of Dixie (where aliens enter only at their peril) was an intercom and a stereo system (so Miss Benedict could torment everyone with the "Flight of the Valkyrie" in the early morning). I put on the small earphones and snapped on the telephone tape from the penitential wing.

"This is 781-3627," a female voice came on the line.

"Mr. Lacy, please," little Sarah asked.

"Whom shall I say is calling?"

"Sarah Grey."

There was a pause and the typhoon came on the line; that's right, typhoon, not tycoon. "Just what the hell do you think you're pulling on me, Grey? I'm not one of your Irish bumpkins from a peat bog!"

It hit my ears like ice tongs and I fumbled with the volume switch.

"If you'll be calmin' down fer a minute I'll be tellin' you."

"Where's my box?"

Ah ha—so atrocious Aloysius knew about the infamous box.

"I don't know what Fowler was up to—it's missin'."

"Missing? What do you mean, missing! It's my property!"

"Fowler disappeared, then he was found, drowned."

"I don't believe a word you're saying. You've got the box and you've given it to that bitch, Benedict!"

"Och, no—I'm tellin' you, I don't have it but I'm tryin' to get it. Fowler took th' box an' got himself killed. I'm gettin' this Benedict woman to help find it. She sent over her 'smart-ass gofer' to look into it. We're still lookin'. It's gotten very complicated an' I can't be talkin' on th' phone . . ."

"Don't you hang up. girl!"

"Now, now—Mr. Lacy. I'm tellin' you I don't know where th' box is but if it can be found, Benedict'll do it. We've got to sit tight. Have you heard from anyone?"

"What? What are you talking about? You mean Steiner? I can't get in touch with him."

"You can't find Steiner?" she said with a hint of panic.

"I can't locate him in Ireland, I don't know where he is."

"But he left Ireland weeks ago!"

"Well he's not back; he's not at the college. They say that he's still in Ireland."

She was silent for a moment, digesting this. "You've heard from no one else?"

"Damn it! Who else is there?"

"I don't know—sit tight and I'll try to keep in touch."

"I said I want to talk to you."

"Later, not now. This place is a fortress. I can't get out, I've got no transport. I don't even know where I am . . ."

"I'm coming there."

"Damn it, don't be so thick! Don't you understand? This has got to be done carefully. If Benedict finds th' damned thing it goes back to th' Irish Government. We'll get nothin'! There's others involved—real criminal types. You go stampedin' about like a cow in th' parlor an' you'll get us all killed!"

The next two minutes were comprised of hurling recriminations back and forth like a tennis match. I humbly listened as an amateur aficionado. The Irish have a dexterous turn of phrase and Lacy had enough of the Sod left on his boots to hold up his end.

Needless to say I was shocked. Not at the fact that Sarah Grey was a two-timing little liar, I assumed that the first time I saw her punky hairdo. It was her referring to me as the "smart-ass gofer"!

I slipped the tape in my pocket. I don't know if Miz Charlotte ever sleeps; I can never catch her with her eyes closed, so I trudged through the dimly lighted house to her bed chamber. Mortal have bedrooms; varlets (like me) have mean and austere cells, but deities like Charlotte Montaigne Benedict have bed chambers and like royalty, she didn't object to an occasional audience there. I knocked softly and being advised to enter, I found her in her nightie with the lace collar up to her chin. She was ensconced on her elevated four-poster, atop a mountain of lacy-fringed pillows, holding some light reading, like the *Five Great Dialogues of Plato* (in Greek of course) or the *Selected Works of Cicero* (in Latin). She had a small tape player by her bed and I frequently accused her of listening to my phone calls.

"Ye gods! Must I be harried in my very bed!" she croaked.

"I have something you ought to listen to."

"This is ghastly! First you drag me into this thing with that blonde predator, and now I'm denied the sanctity of my own bed!"

"You noticed she has a hearty appetite?"

"I noticed . . ."

"She made a phone call this evening—before dinner."

The banter stopped and she pursed her lips. "To whom?"

"Listen," I replied and snapped on the bedside tape player. She lay back on the pillows, completely still. When it was finished she took off her glasses and looked at me.

"You know, David, there's a lot more to this than meets the eye."

"Who have you got on the Walsh angle?"

"Kepler, out of Miami. I can't imagine Walsh going to the Bahamas with the thing but it's not too difficult for a determined person to get from Georgetown to Florida."

"That's what I thought. Particularly if you don't want a close customs inspection. But the whole thing really doesn't add up. Why the Bahamas? Why not Switzerland? That's a great place to do business and customs are a joke. The banking end is so easy too. Has Kepler got anything?"

"No, and he might never get anything. Checking on midnight runs from the Bahamas to Florida these days can be very dicey."

"What do we do with Little Rosie O'Grady?"

She laced her thin fingers behind her head and looked at the tester above the bed. "We'll keep her for a bit. She knows—but little does she know that I know that she knows."

"Ye gods, I'm going to bed!"

I thought I was going to bed. I shuffled through the halls to my cell but my roommate Max was acting up again. A sensor light indicated that we might have visitors from the sea side, or, of course, it could be an amorous muskrat. I muttered a few expletives to relieve my unhappiness. I can only do that when alone; due to Miz Charlotte's very prissy attitude about profanity, which is hard on an ex-SEAL. With some SEALS four out of every five words are unprintable so I'm stuck with archaic idiom in compensation. I took the .357 Magnum out of my bedside table. I hope her ladyship appreciates all this, I thought as I made my way down the staircase again to the door on the screened-in porch. It was time to earn my "royal stipend."

Chapter XIII

I *hate* "night games"! I hated them in the service. Making my way through the silvery moonlight, I renewed all my incantations calling down beasties and ghosties and things that go bump in the night on the empty head of Sarah Grey. Also, you have to be very careful with prowlers; you can't use "deadly force" except in self-defense.

Whoever it was didn't know our security system. Landing on the "T" dock by the sloop was dumb. And nothing was happening. I mean there weren't a bunch of black-garbed "Ninjas" jumping around and breaking up the furniture. Lastly they had picked a lousy night, with nearly a full moon—very amateurish. It could be some crack-heads trying to steal the Ducal flatware, but I didn't think so. Coming by boat presaged planning, however faulty.

I spotted him in the umbra of the holly and dogwood trees that decorated the loop of Miz Charlotte's circular drive. After watching him for about five minutes I came to the conclusion that he was trying to find out where the hell he was. He didn't seem aggressive and I felt he was alone. I slipped down to the dock. Next to the sloop bobbed a small inflatable rubber boat. If there were more than one, they had to be munchkins.

Taking this guy wasn't a problem; I had him surrounded already.

But if I did grab him we'd have to roust good ole Sheriff Marvin Spooner out of the sack and he'd gallop over. After a lot of jawboning (which was usual with Spooner and Miz Charlotte) he'd be charged with trespass and be out on bail the next day.

Cursing, I slipped into the sail locker. I calculated that this was a reconnaissance and the best course of action was in trying to find out who he was and, more important, who he was working for. My black wet suit was hanging in the sail locker and muttering through clenched teeth, I climbed into it. There's nothing more bracing than a night swim in May!

Moving to a point on the shoreline where I had a good view of the intruder and the dock, I watched as he crept around, checking windows and trying to figure out our security system. I really didn't expect any action from our mysterious visitor, the engineless rubber raft wasn't designed for a fast getaway and anyone really looking for trouble would have planned for that.

A half hour later, he sneaked back to the dock, hunching over a little as he passed the light on the pier head. Great, I thought, this guy is a real apache....

Getting into a rubber boat from a dock is easier said than done and I was afraid he was going to fall in the creek and I'd have to rescue him. Finally, after some sloshing about, he managed to plant his backside in the rubber boat. I slipped quietly into the water—it was lovely.

I knew where he was going. There are a few places on the creek where you can launch a boat but you have to know them. This guy was no native and there was a public boat landing nearby that was clearly marked on any of the county maps.

While he fiddled with lines and got the boat away, I moved across the creek at a good clip but without any wake, staying under the shadows of some overhanging trees. Paddling a blunt-nosed rubber raft isn't very swift and I knew he'd be at it for a while, so I took off again, staying in the shadows, but moving.

When I got to the boat landing there was a Ford Escort with Florida plates parked there. The windows had been left down and I saw a pile of papers and a map on the seat. Using my waterproof penlight, I took a peek. There were written directions for finding Avalon along with a Gloucester County map. The map was "x"ed to show the boat ramp and Avalon. The only other thing on the paper was the name "Aldo Tebaldi." Meanwhile, I kept a weather eye on "Long John Silver" in the rubber raft. A waterman he wasn't; straightening out his meanderings, he could have reached Yorktown across the river.

I slipped into the dense shrubbery by the parking area and waited. The spectacle of his landing the rubber raft, moving and hoisting it onto the roof was painful to watch. It's interesting to observe the differences between conception and execution; I'm sure this all seemed simple when he thought it up. It was cold in the woods, however, and I damn near went out to help him tie the raft on the roof.

Finally, when he sat at the wheel I got a look at him. He was small in stature, about thirty-five with long brown hair and a big moustache. He didn't look very formidable, but you never knew. He closed the door and drove off. I was glad to get back in the water and out of the buggy woods.

I slept for nine hours that night which was unusual. It must have bothered Her Nibs not to have anyone to badger because I know that Raphael checked on me. At noon I stumbled down for a bowl of hot oatmeal that hit my stomach like an anchor. Putting in a call to Sam Kepler in Miami I got his answering service and requested a call back.

Miss Benedict was at her regular stand in the library and in none too chirpy a humor. My day started at eight and by then

Her Highness, a confirmed workaholic, could have already spent a good three hours at it. By now she usually increased the drumbeat to flank speed and us galley slaves would really be sweating at the oars. She smiled brightly as I entered which was always a bad sign. "David! How *charming* of you to come!" she exclaimed exuberantly checking her watch, "and it's *only* 12:30!"

Zooks, I thought, it's going to be one of *those* days!

"I thought maybe you'd be taking the day off. Of course dear Sarah was here bright and eager at 8:30...."

I looked over at the Irish adder slithering among the bookshelves off to the side.

"I suppose you'd consider yourself ill-used if I docked you a morning's pay?" she asked sweetly.

"It's Christmas, Miss Scrooge—tis only once a year...." I have to admit that after the long flight, jet lag and being dopey with sleep, I wasn't up to my usual jousting form. I was going to say something about getting overtime for my nocturnal swim but instead just went to my desk and groused.

The next three hours were a ghastly trip down memory lane. It took me about four minutes to figure out what was going on in Sarah Grey's pointed little head. She was all woolly and tweedy today, hiding behind her big round glasses and oozing: "Yes, Miss Benedict...," "No, Miss Benedict...," "May I do this or that for you, Miss Benedict..." I sat there, mouth agape, as she ran her little back-side off doing errands, fetching books, making tea! So that was it! She was going to replace me, the crude and loud-mouthed Peete.

It was a time-warp—happening before my very eyes! I was transported back to Miss Oxbarge's sixth grade and my most contemptible foe, the unspeakable teacher's pet, Olga Ironmonger! Of course Sarah didn't look like Olga Ironmonger who had been a head taller and a good thirty pounds heavier with plump blonde plaits hanging like ship's ropes from her melon-like head. Olga looked like she belonged on the stage at the Met, holding a spear with one of those hats with horns sticking out. But they both had that same sly, sleek look and tight little smile that let you know they knew exactly what they were about—"May I erase the blackboard, Miss Oxbarge?" "May I have an extra assignment, Miss Oxbarge?" My blood ran cold just thinking about her and her Irish ilk.

Miz Charlotte was lapping it up and this whole business was really depressing. Besides the Irish blather and toadying, we weren't getting anywhere. We still didn't know what the damned box was or where to find it. But if Her Ladyship got her kicks out of playing Sarah against me, God knows how long I'd have to put up with the charade.

I was sitting there, muttering to myself, when the phone rang. Sarah came streaking from the book stacks to get the phone on Miz Charlotte's desk, but I lifted mine first. It was Raphael. "There's a Mr. Kepler on the phone for you, Davie," he said.

"Put him through, Rafe."

A moment later Kepler was on the line. "Hello, Dr. Peete."

"Hi, Sam—I tried to reach you earlier."

"I wuz working for King and Country..."

"I'll bet. Anything new on Walsh?"

Miss Benedict was watching me now from her desk, chewing the loop of her glasses.

"I'm still on it but I don't know, it's a real tough one."

"I might have something for you." I gave him the Florida license number.

"That's Dade County."

"The guy is about five foot six or seven, with long hair to his shoulders and a 'Buffalo Bill' moustache that goes to a receding chin. His name might be 'Aldo Tebaldi,' T-e-b-a-l-d-i. It might be a good idea to check on the name."

"Where did you get this?"

"He was here, last night, on the grounds . . ."

That got Miz Charlotte's riveted attention.

"You got this out of him?"

"Oh, no—he didn't even know I existed. I found his car. I think you should get right on this, Sam; it could be hot."

I cradled the receiver back on its saddle in a room filled with dead silence. One thing that really got Miz Charlotte upset was the thought of prowlers. Little Sarah was completely outflanked and I sat, savoring it all.

"Well, David—do I have to send you a telegram?" Charlotte said testily.

"We had a prowler last night. I picked him up on the boat dock sensor. It was a reconnaissance; he was looking over our security. I swam over to the boat ramp and checked him out."

"You swam?" Sarah asked with big green owl eyes.

"There's nothing like a moonlight swim."

Sarah wasn't buying any of this; she figured it was some ploy to unseat her from her preferred position. She couldn't know that I'd spent most of my adult life under water. But Miz Charlotte knew that sometimes I'd swim to Yorktown and back just for kicks and that I never play games when it came to security.

"But what could he have wanted, David?"

"What indeed—or maybe who," I eyed Sarah. "Someone seems to attract an inordinate amount of attention here." I admit I took sadistic pleasure at her blanched expression. She wasn't so God-awful persnickety now.

"So you passed the information on to Sam Kepler," Miss Benedict said more as a statement than a question.

"Yes . . . our friend was from Florida. You don't have anything 'special' here at the moment, do you?"

"No, nothing other than my things."

I knew that some of those were well worth pilfering. It could be just a gang of run-of-the-mill house burglars, but I didn't think so and neither did she. "Let's let Sam run this guy down," I said.

"His name is Tebaldi?"

"I don't know. That was a name on some of his papers. It shouldn't take Sam too long."

"Maybe I should call Marvin," Miz Charlotte mused.

Sheriff Marvin Spooner was the hombre in charge of the law in Gloucester County and while a great guy, he and his henchmen were the last thing we needed at Avalon right now. "Oh glory—let's not get Wild Bill Hickok and the posse out here now. It would take to next Christmas to explain this thing."

"Well I don't like the idea of just sitting here, waiting."

"Neither do I—I tell you what. Why don't Sarah and I take a quick trip down to Markham College in South Carolina and see Steiner. They'll be watching and that way we can draw them off Avalon."

"But if you're gone?"

"I'll get Tonto to cover . . . and the Lone Ranger. They can sleep on your bedroom doorstep if you like."

Chapter XIV

Of course there was no "Lone Ranger"... That just came out of my fertile brain in a flash of inspiration. I had known Harry Tonto in the SEALS and having used him before, I knew that Miss Benedict had confidence in him. After the Navy, Harry had gone into house repair with a kid named Joel Shapiro who was also quite handy. That's life—if you're a sidekick to a guy named Tonto, you get to be the Lone Ranger no matter what your name is.

Of course little Sarah thought Avalon was a lunatic asylum and I wasn't about to disabuse her of the idea. I was enjoying it all too much. She was now also desolate. All her dreams were going up in smoke—the cushy job, the choice viands... everything. "But we're safe here..." she moaned.

"Not really. The worst thing you can do is stay put. This is a house, not a bunker. Besides, I want to see Steiner."

"But he's not there!"

"Oh, how do you know that, Sarah?"

She maundered about and for an instant I thought she might come clean but her prevaricating nature got the better of her. "He—he told me..."

"Told you what?"

"That—that he wasn't goin' back to the U.S., that he was goin' to Rome—to see what he could do about th' box."

"That's funny, you didn't tell me about that."

She shrugged. "I forgot."

"Really? Well that doesn't make any difference anyway. That was weeks ago, he'll be back by now."

"Why don't you call him on th' telephone?"

I shook my head judiciously. "No, I'd rather flush him out unexpectedly."

Sarah was unhappy but there wasn't much she could do about it since I had cut her phone off. I lined up Tonto and friend and everything fell into place. Tonto Inc. did home improvements and they were glad for the barrel top payments by Miz Charlotte rather than stalking delinquent home-owners. They agreed to be available on the next morning.

That afternoon I suited up in the camp jogging togs that Miz Charlotte had given me for Christmas and trotted down Guinea Road. As I passed the Baptist Church, I spotted the Escort parked off to the side. I grinned to myself; it must be hell to try to surveil someone with all the curious Gloucesterites around.

When I got back, I found the Irish bombshell in bad shape. I could tell because she was off her feed and only the thought of leaving the security of Avalon or a ride on the Titanic would do that.

Of course Miz Charlotte insisted that Sarah call Aloysius Lacy before we left. Our little prevaricator was very nervous since Miss Benedict and I were both on extensions. As soon as Lacy got on the line she blurted: "This is Sarah Grey and I have Miss Benedict on the line with me, Mr. Lacy . . ."

"Miss Benedict! What the hell's going on?" the typhoon blew.

"She asked me to call you," Sarah went on like a machine

gun, "to tell you that I'm here, in Virginia, an' that we're lookin' fer th' relic that I told you about."

It finally penetrated Lacy's thick skull and he retreated to growls, snorts and other animal noises while Miss Fork-Tongue went through all the baloney that she had told him before.

"Hello, Mr. Lacy," Miz Charlotte chimed in like Lady Bountiful about to open her bag of gifts, "we've never met but your Mr. Bernbaum has been in touch with me."

"I want the box; it's my property."

"I don't have your box, Mr. Lacy," Charlotte said. "I've never set eyes on it and I can't assure you it even exists. I don't understand the tenor of your Mr. Bernbaum's correspondence . . ."

"I don't like people horning in on my affairs."

"Horning in? We were contacted by Miss Grey. Our understanding was that she was your agent in this matter. Am I incorrect in this assumption?" I could tell that Miz Charlotte's patience was fraying a bit.

"She was hired by me but I didn't tell her to contact you."

"Well, that seems to be a matter between you and Miss Grey."

"I'm coming down there. I want to talk to you, Benedict. I'll be there tomorrow."

As the specter of litigation faded, Miss Benedict was climbing back into the saddle. "Not tomorrow, Mr. Lacy. I have previous engagements."

"Cancel them!"

"I'm sorry, that's out of the question," then in an aside she said to me, "I want you there, David, when do you think?"

"Monday," I said into the phone.

"Who's that! Who's on this phone?"

I was tempted to say the "smart ass gofer" but we didn't want Sarah to know that we knew about their previous contact.

"He's my associate, Dr. Peete," Miss Benedict answered. "I can see you on Monday."

"I'm coming tomorrow!"

"The gate will be locked, Mr. Lacy, and you'll have nothing to do until Monday." Miz Charlotte was getting riled herself now. After a few more minutes of Lacy's tirades and threats, they signed off.

"What a boorish nincompoop," she said, hanging up the phone.

"I'm beginning to think he must be related to Odo."

Harry Tonto and company showed up at seven the next day and since they were acquainted with the layout at Avalon, I didn't have to spend a lot of time with them. We loaded up the Buick and departed Avalon around 8:30. I headed the car down Guinea Road toward Route 17 at a stately pace. Sarah Grey was quiet and miserable (which was the way I liked her most), her arms folded across her chest. A long road trip with her was going to be no pleasure ride.

Passing Buck Roe's store, I spotted the Ford Escort parked by a few other vehicles. I was sure that our recent intruder saw us. The Ford backed out and he zipped up behind us as I reached for the cellular phone. "He's behind me, Harry," I reported.

"You figure he's alone?' Tonto asked.

"Who knows, it looks like it."

The ten hour drive to Lake Charles, the site of Markham College began quietly. The Escort stayed behind us on Interstate 64 to Richmond. He was still there as we turned south on I-95.

At first Sarah was skittish but finally it penetrated her dense skull that nothing was going down on a crowded interstate. Our tailer also had his problems. I knew that he didn't have a phone in the Escort and I doubted he was carrying one on his scouting mission the other night so I didn't think he was calling his nefarious cohorts (if any). When we turned south on I-95 I'm sure his rotten little heart went thump; he'd know this was a trip, not a jaunt to Kentucky Fried Chicken. Maybe he was crafty enough to have topped off his gas tank that morning as we had. If not, he definitely had problems.

Somewhere halfway through North Carolina, he turned off into a service station and I thought, gotcha! Around five miles down the road I found a good off ramp.

"Stoppin' here, are we?' Sarah hissed.

"This is where we lose our friend," I said.

"Oh—that's grand!" she said, thawing a bit. We pulled up onto the over-pass of the clover leaf with a pretty good view of the roadway and the cars that were coming. After about ten minutes the Ford came barreling down and under the overpass, zipping south.

We took some of the other, less traveled roads to Lake Charles. Settling in a quiet motel about five miles from the Markham campus, we took two rooms for the night. That was for propriety's sake; after all, Sarah Grey and I were now business associates. Her job was lying and my job was catching her at it.

The two rooms were window dressing. As in Whyte's Hotel, I stayed in her room but if you suspect the beginnings of a romantic interlude, forget it. We were like some fractious married couple headed for a divorce court. Everything I did, even the way I brushed my teeth, bothered her and vice-versa. We spent a delightful evening snarling and snapping at each other.

Fortunately there were two double beds in the room so I didn't have to worry about her fanging me during the night. As I lay in the darkness, a couple of things emerged from obscurity. Sarah Grey was up to her trim little behind in this thing. Until now I figured she was at the center of all this because Kamaroff and Sparrow thought she had the box and were angling to pinch it. But this boat was springing leaks at every seam. Why was the intruder interested in our security at Avalon? Kamaroff and Sparrow would know that the casket wasn't there. If Sarah had the damned thing she'd have hidden it somewhere in Ireland. She sure wouldn't bundle it through customs to present it to Miz Charlotte.

Maybe they wanted to snatch Sarah instead—for a little "chat." This made more sense but surely Sergei and Alfie would get someone more professional than the Bozo who was prowling our grounds. Sparrow shouldn't be judged for hiring a dunce like Algie Duncan. If Sarah was a simple grad student, a little muscle via Duncan would have worked fine. Sparrow couldn't know Miss Benedict and the formidable Dr. Peete were on the job. No, our intruder wasn't top quality and neither Sparrow nor Kamaroff would stint on good reconnaissance.

My mind turned to the shadowy Walsh. Our tail was from Florida where we suspected Walsh was headed. If Walsh was after Sarah, he couldn't be as choosy as Kamaroff or Sparrow.

But why? This was an unsettling thought. We assumed that Walsh had the box. If so, why did he care about Sarah Grey? Why send someone all the way from Florida to case Avalon? Unless he wanted her out of the way. Maybe the intruder was casing Avalon not to look for the box but to snuff Sarah Grey!

But again, why? You couldn't believe anything Sarah said. Suppose she knew Walsh and they were in the thing together.... The only person who claimed that Fowler took the casket was Sarah. The only other person who might know (after the deceased Fowler himself) was the equally deceased, Father Hugh!

Suddenly, I began to feel very uncomfortable listening to the soft buzzing coming from the other bed. Have you ever tried to sleep with a rattlesnake?

Chapter XV

Clothing has always fascinated me. My respective professions have taken me to remote regions of the earth and professionally speaking, I think historians should look more closely at society's attitude towards attire. I'm continually amazed at how clean and neat some Third World people are (against overwhelming odds) as opposed to what absolute slatterns and rag-pickers some American kids turn themselves into. In a lot of the Orient, for example, young people might be a bit threadbare, maybe frayed at the collar, but usually starched and scrubbed. Of course during my four year vacation stint at the Virginia Military Institute *I* never had much selection in the attire department.

Expensive and exclusive, Markham struck me as an asylum for "also rans," catering to students with trouble making it in the real world but whose daddies were willing to pony up the cash to get them through college by hook or by crook. The beautiful campus was set on a lakeside with manicured lawns and topiaried hedges, but the vista had one problem; it looked like Custer's Last Stand. The lawns were strewn with what appeared to be slaughtered bodies (it was awful, only grape-shot could have torn the clothing of those poor devils to tatters and rags. A girl under a magnolia tree had the seat of her jeans shot clean out!) As we strolled up the quadrangle walk, I was astounded by this devastation wrought in our institutions of higher learning. Off to the right one of the "walking wounded" tottered to his feet, a pitiful sight, his unwashed and lank brown hair hanging down in sticky twists, one trouser leg lacerated with half a dozen horizontal slashes, the other almost completely severed and hanging by threads. Staggering a few steps, he collapsed amid the other writhing bodies. It's sobering to contemplate what these kids were sacrificing for a college education.

Locating Steiner's office wasn't too difficult; after some trial and error we discovered a more "compos mentis" member of the student body who provided directions, but even with finding the lair of the illustrious Professor Wilfred Steiner, our troubles weren't over. It was empty and we entertained ourselves for half an hour in the small anteroom which was really a shrine to the still-breathing deity. The walls were plastered with photographs of the great man's exploits—Steiner shaking hands with the Governor, Steiner shaking hands with the Senator, Steiner sitting atop a camel with grim fortitude stamped on his noble features etc., etc. Along with these visual offerings were glass cases of artifacts discovered by the great man in remote regions and climes—like Indian digs along the Swanee River. I had never met the guy and already I couldn't stand him!

It was 10:45 and Sarah collapsed into an overstuffed chair, no doubt contemplating lunch. We were wondering what to do next when Miss Byng arrived. Her job was to protect the great one from the incursions of unwashed students and although we were rather old and too well dressed to be mistaken for students, she was still very upset that we were in the anteroom unsupervised. I think she was afraid that we might pick the locks on the glass display cases and steal some of Steiner's priceless shards and bones. She blustered for a bit on general principles.

Ten odd years in the Navy had taught me something about the manipulation of unmitigated asses. The secret is to *out-bombast*, to be the *blusterer*, but never the *blusteree*!

"My dear woman," I said condescendingly, "I am Dr. David Peete and this is my associate, Dr. Sarah Grey, representing Dr. Charlotte Montaigne Benedict. We are here for our appointment with Professor Steiner. Please tell him immediately."

Her face registered a look of coping and groping.

"Professor Steiner is not here . . ."

"Not here! Did you say, not here?" I turned to Sarah, "Heavens, Dr. Grey, this is appalling! I told Dr. Benedict that I had reservations about this Steiner person's ability to handle anything as important as this!" I turned back to Miss Byng. "Do you mean to say that we have motored all the way from Virginia to see this—this Steiner person and he's not even here?"

"The Professor said nothing . . ."

"Well I certainly hope not! Dr. Benedict specifically enjoined him to keep the matter confidential, but if he lacks the common courtesy to keep an appointment, I'm not at all sure we'll need his services. Good day, Miss . . . er, Miss . . ."

"Miss Byng . . . please, just a moment, Dr. Peete. Professor Steiner's not here this semester. He went to Ireland on some very important business and he has no classes at the moment. . . ."

"You mean to say that he's not even here . . . at the school?"

"He's at his summer cottage on Lake Beauregard, working on his latest book. If you just wait, I'll call . . ."

"You most certainly shall *not* call! Look here, Miss . . . er, Miss . . ."

"Byng."

"Miss Byng. Steiner knows the extreme confidentiality of this thing. I told him we would arrive in mid to late May and was given to understand that there would be no difficulties—

absolutely *no difficulties*. Now I find he's not even here and you wish to broadcast our presence...."

The old girl was at her wits end, particularly since she could smell a fat fee somewhere in all this garbage. Being a natural gambler, I decided to raise the stakes a little. "Next I'll find out that he's been in contact with Aloysius Lacy!" I said at my prissiest.

"Oh no, Dr. Peete!" the dragon snapped that up like a trout on a mayfly, "that I can assure you hasn't happened. Professor Steiner has left specific orders to tell Mr. Lacy that he is out of the country."

"And Lacy has called?"

"Oh yes—several times and I've followed Professor Steiner's orders implicitly."

I assumed a face of judicious mollification. "Well, that's something. How long will it take Steiner to get here?"

"It's only an hour's drive . . ."

"An hour's drive! Good heavens, Dr. Grey, I don't know what to do. I can't sit around here for an hour! Maybe we should forget the whole business . . . I suppose we could drive there . . ."

Steiner must have run his shop like an Obergruppenführer because the rest was duck soup. Frau Byng was hopping around clicking her heels—she couldn't give me directions to Steiner's cabin fast enough. I left final orders that she was not, under any circumstances, to phone ahead.

Whizzing down the highway to Lake Beauregard and the elusive Steiner, I was satisfied with myself. I thought that my performance with the Head Matron at the Reform School had gone smashingly well. But as old Admiral Roberts (affectionately known as "Old Stonehead") was fond of saying, "the seeds of disaster are sown at moments of supposed triumph." Looking in my rearview mirror I saw a Ford Escort! It had the same bilious green color and I had that old feeling in my tummy. . . .

Sarah Grey was oblivious to my worries and was in her usual pet. It was noon and she was all for lunch but I nixed that; researchers work first and eat later, I told her.

Any thought that our night intruder at Avalon wasn't tied into Sarah, Michael Walsh, Aloysius Lacy, *et al.*, were gone. We had definitely lost him on I-95 somewhere near Fayetteville North Carolina. For him to rebound at Markham just added up to one thing—that damned box!

There were a number of possibilities. He could be employed by none other than our elusive compatriot, Steiner himself. After all he and the Ford Escort were *here*. After losing him on I-95 maybe he just headed here to check in and stumbled on us. Maybe Steiner had the box . . . but if he did, and the tail behind us was his boy, why bother with us?

I still liked the Walsh angle better since our night intruder was from Florida. If Sarah was double crossed by Walsh then maybe Walsh directed our friend behind us to check out our being with Steiner.

Conversely, if he was employed by Sparrow, Kamaroff or Lacy, a phone call made to any of them could have the same result—check if we were headed for Steiner.

But again, the perennial, why? Why should any of them care if Sarah Grey was riding over the foot hills of South Carolina? Unless . . . Sarah Grey is in the way!

How else could I add it up? If the attempt on her life in Dublin was true (always a dangerous assumption when it came to Sarah) then the intruder could be a Florida hit man. Suppose she and Walsh were conspirators and he absconded with the loot. But maybe Sarah knows something dangerous to Walsh, like his involvement in the thing . . . or even more to the point—why and how Fowler got tanked and decided to swim on a cold Spring night in the Slaney?

Suddenly the windshield of the car was lashed with heavy rain drops. Sarah sat bolt upright. "Is it rainin' now," she muttered.

"Yeah, and we have company in the Ford behind us...."

That got her attention; she spun around and looked through the rear window. "Oh my God!" she whined.

In the directions that Miss Byng had given us there was a small parking area at the foot of the hill below Steiner's cabin with his name on the mailbox. She said that we couldn't see the cabin from the road because of the dense woods. Having never seen the place presented problems. Fortunately, the Ford wasn't following too closely, content to lay back on lonely country roads.

"We should be there soon. When we do, you get out of the car and go up the trail a ways—then hide and stay put."

Sarah Grey might be shifty but there was nothing wrong with her brains. We had been in dicey positions before at Whyte's Hotel and the "Back o' Beyond." Both times things had come out all right so I didn't get any back-talk.

I spotted the old mailbox with the block letters, "Steiner," off to the right and turned into the gravelled parking area at a good clip and with stones flying. Jumping out, Sarah flew up the trail like "Old Horny" was snapping at her bottom and I ran across the road before the Escort came over the hill. The Ford slowed down, looking for a spot to pull in. He drove off on the shoulder a hundred yards past the cut off.

As he trotted to our car, I saw he wasn't carrying a firearm, but a piece of pipe. Stopping for a moment, he listened, but the only sounds were the birds. Then he moved to the back of my Buick and dropping to the ground, he squirmed under. I could see the soles of his protruding feet as I hunched in the wet brush.

Finally, our friend crab-walked himself out and stood—again listening. Then he started up the hill and disappeared into the foliage. Waiting about three minutes I went to the car. It wasn't hard to find—a length of pipe, capped at both ends and duck taped to the exhaust. Attached also by duck tape was a battery and a timer.

Putting stuff in your car or under your bed really galls me. It's so sloppy. He wanted to get Sarah and was willing to throw me in for kicks. It was set for 5 P.M. and God knows maybe we'd be gassing up at a service station and we'd take out a dozen people with us.

Sometimes I have a devil in me. I should have done something proper and legal at this point but I guess I was tired and frustrated. I took the pipe, reset the timer for ten minutes and hoofed it to the Ford Escort, slipping it into the glove compartment.

I hoped he wasn't the belt and suspenders type. I suppose he could take a potshot at Sarah but I didn't think it was his style. He might miss and somebody might shoot back. I was worried that he might come back and drive off so I waited. The gadget blew on schedule, removing the doors, hood and setting the tank off. He came a-running out of the woods, figuring the timer misfired and he'd better get lost. His expression when he saw which car had popped was lovely. He didn't see me as I came up from behind.

"Hi, neighbor," I said, standing behind him. "You're having a little car trouble, eh?"

He jumped and spun around with a stupid expression on his face. We looked for a minute at the burning wreck.

"I'm no expert on cars, but gosh, I'm afraid you're in for a big bill," I said, shaking my head sadly.

I left him there and went up the hill to find the cabin empty.

So much for my handling of Frau Byng. She obviously had called and the bird had flown. Then Sarah appeared.

"What was the explosion?" she asked white-faced.

"Our friend has some car trouble . . . and Steiner's gone."

"Where is he?" she whispered hoarsely.

"Steiner? Oh, you mean our pal. He's down below tinkering with his engine but don't get excited, he's not going to try anything."

"An' how would you be knowin' that?"

"I'm omniscient, it's part of my charm."

"When we got back down the hill, he was still by the Ford trying to figure what the hell was going on. I knew we'd have company soon in the person of the Highway Patrol so I got Sarah into the Buick.

"Now where are we goin'?"

"Home. If Miz Charlotte wants Steiner, she can get somebody else to track him down."

Chapter XVI

"So you blew up his automobile?" Miz Charlotte asked, testily.

"That's not quite accurate," I replied, "he blew it up himself."

"But you put the bomb in his car!"

"Yeah, but I didn't know *a priori* that it was a bomb, did I?"

"If it walks like a bomb and quacks like a bomb, it *is* a bomb!"

"Oh, I don't know. I couldn't see inside the pipe. It could have been filled with popcorn—besides, it was *his* property. He took it out of *his* car. I just returned it."

"And then you left the scene?"

"Sure, I didn't want to explain that to the State Police, besides, he was there—it was his bomb, not mine."

"It seems a rather heroic way of doing things."

"I have a flair for this stuff."

It was Sunday morning and I was debriefing the Lady of the Manor on our fallow expedition to the wilds of South Carolina before she left for services at Abingdon Episcopal Church. Tonto and sidekick were paid off and were heading back to their secret hideout. Sarah Grey had been sent to her cell to meditate on her many sins.

"They're after her, you know," I said.

"It would seem so. I wonder why?"

"Because she's in on it, Milady. It's the only explanation that holds water." I expounded my Walsh theory.

"He has the box but Sarah is a threat. . . ." she mused.

"Yeah, the Irish reptile is trouble. I think you should buy her a one-way ticket to the 'Auld Sod' and call her a taxi."

"That would be like signing her death warrant."

"That's easy for you to say but I'm getting tired of putting my tender bod on the line to protect the Irish Medusa. You can do it; just make believe you're 'Goode Queen Bess.'"

The phone rang. I picked it up and Raphael said that Mr. Hammerschmidt was on the line from Zurich for Miss Benedict. "It's Oskar the Great."

Charlotte picked up the receiver. "Oskar, what a pleasant surprise—how are things in Switzerland?"

"The snows have melted and the land abounds with flowers, my dear, it only lacks your presence to make it perfect."

Hammerschmidt spoke with a British accent. You might have thought him to be English except for some faint guttural nuances.

"That's very sweet, Oskar—is there anything I can do for you?" Miz Charlotte chirped.

"I continue to press my suit. I again ask for you to make me the happiest of men—to grant me your hand in connubial bliss."

This had been a running joke for longer than I've been around. Each time they met the gallant Oskar would offer his tricky self on the altar of married bliss and Miz Charlotte would daintily refuse. Well, not exactly refuse but dance all around the thing. Actually, I hoped that one day it would happen—then they could go off to Valhalla and have a Götterdämmerung together.

"I'm not sure it would work, Oskar," Charlotte said coyly. "There are all those 'French pastries' you like to keep about."

"But this would be a union of dynasties, my dear—one mustn't be bourgeois. A little browsing in other pastures is to be expected. After all, you can keep your Dr. Peete."

Ye Gods! He thinks that I'm a consort to a battleship! But this was the wrong tack with Miz Charlotte; I could see her gorge rising. I don't know why she never married but suspected there was a tale to be told. But when it came to things like God, country and marriage, Charlotte Montaigne Benedict was very conservative.

"I don't know, Oskar. If such a union is merely to join our collections, we might better endow a museum. Besides," she added chillingly, "Sergei is also pressing and he has a Title."

I could almost hear the Swiss barrage balloon deflating.

"I should warn you about Kamaroff, my dear," Hammerschmidt replied crisply, "the man is, I'm afraid, violent—but I'm sure that you are aware of that. I understand that Dr. Peete has returned from Ireland with Miss Grey?"

"Yes—and he had a charming luncheon with your Mr. Sparrow."

"I take it that you don't have the casket?"

"Casket? What casket, Oskar?"

It went on like that for another five minutes but he couldn't even get Miz Charlotte to admit the existence of the box.

"A fishing expedition," Miss Benedict said as she hung up.

"What about Sarah Grey, do we send her packing?"

"Not yet," Charlotte replied, lost in thought. She was hooked. The fundamental impetus to all scholarship is curiosity. She suspected that this was something big and wanted to know all about it—a big find, or a big fraud.

"Fowler thought he had something valuable in that relic,"

she said. "He was well informed enough to go to Kamaroff and Hammerschmidt to get their tenders—to bid them one against the other."

"That's tricky. Maybe one of them tried to take it?"

"He wouldn't have it with him."

"Then why kill him—at least before they had it?"

"More likely it was this Walsh person. He's the key right now. We've got to try to locate him."

We forced ourselves into our patterned routine until three the next day and the appointment with the now steaming Lacy. I wasn't looking forward to the meeting; judging from his antics on the phone, Lacy was a real pain in the fundament. Looking on the bright side, however, maybe Miz Charlotte would let me throw him out the window.

He arrived in a big rented limo about 15 minutes early with horn honking and arm waving. I waited on the front steps as the car made its way up the loop drive and was slightly taken aback when three people got out. It was easy to pick Aloysius out; he was of medium build with big ears and a bossy manner. He was joined by an attractive woman carrying a laptop computer who looked all business and a big gorilla who had been driving. Lacy reminded me of a rooster, the lady of the "Ice Queen" and the gorilla of "King Kong" with bulges where even King Kong didn't have them.

Miss Benedict has all kinds of rules concerning the operation of Avalon, but I have a few of my own. One of them is that no one goes to see Miz Charlotte armed except good old Sheriff Marvin Spooner.

Lacy started up the front steps like T. R. up San Juan Hill but I held up a restraining hand. With the other I pushed the alarm button in Raphael's hangout. We don't use this often but it's proven mighty handy at times.

"Mr. Lacy?" I asked, standing in the doorway. "How do you do? I'm Dr. Peete."

"We're here to see Benedict."

"You're a bit early," I said. King Kong moved up beside him.

"I've got no time for this nonsense. Who the hell does she think she is, the Queen of England?"

"She does here, Mr. Lacy. She sees people at appointed times—and unarmed. That's a rule."

The gorilla smiled (I think) and putting his big paw on my chest, pushed. I backed away as he stepped through the entry. Off to the side was the doorway to the serving areas. It had a Dutch door that was closed at the bottom. In the doorway was Rafe with a double-barreled shotgun. King Kong looked from Rafe to me.

"Don't even think about it, pal; you're in the South now. Folks hereabouts take a dim view of other folks bustin' through their front doors. But if you insist, would you mind standing off to the side a little that way? The painting behind you is a genuine Corot and we'd hate splattering you all over it."

I relieved him of his weapon and he was very unhappy. I told him I'd return it on leaving but I threw the bullets into the shrubbery. "Now can I offer you some refreshments while you wait?" I looked at "Beautiful over Forty" "You're not Bernbaum, are you?" I asked. She told me to chill out.

At precisely 3 P.M. I led them up the curved staircase to the library. Miss Benedict sat behind the battlements of her big desk with Atrocious Aloysius directly across from her. Miss Withers (so called for the way she looked at everyone, especially me) sat next to him, laptop at hair-trigger, a model of bristling efficiency. The gorilla sat looking upward (contemplating how swell it would be to swing on the overhead beams). Sarah, a mere shell of her former conniving self, sat nervously off to Miz

Charlotte's right, looking like a school-girl about to get chewed out by the Headmistress. I sat at my desk.

"Well now, Mr. Lacy . . ." Miz Charlotte started tentatively.

Lacy was the soul of tact and diplomacy. "I'll brook no nonsense in this matter. Your services are not, I repeat, not, required. Simply stated, Miss Grey exceeded her authority in contacting you. I understand that there have been some expenses? I'm a reasonable man and willing to pay what is justified. You can submit a documented bill directly to Miss Withers or forward it by mail."

"Excellent," Miss Benedict replied, "that will be most satisfactory—David?"

Walking over to the library table, I punched some commands into the computer. The expense sheet appeared on the screen and I printed it. Tearing it off I handed it to Miss Prissy. "When we get to know each better my computer would love to go out with your computer," I whispered.

She snarled and ran her eye down the sheet. All her wheels and gears were humming at full tilt. "There's an item here for weapons?"

"Yeah, a .38 Webley and a .22 Remington."

She looked over her glasses at Lacy. "I hardly think . . ."

"Not now, for God's sake, Gladys! Discount whatever you think is padding." Lacy turned to Miz Charlotte. "I take it from this that I can expect you out of this business?"

"You can expect that any employment arrangements instituted by your agent, Miss Grey, are terminated."

"That's not what I asked."

"I know, and contractually we are kaput. Any arrangements that we had only go that far."

An angry expression covered his face. "What are you trying to pull here? I said I want you out!"

"My dear Mr. Lacy, I'm a free agent. My business is antiquities. I search for them where and when I wish. I've made it abundantly clear that you have no financial responsibility for my efforts. I think that terminates our business."

"But you wouldn't even know about this if it wasn't for me—and that fool of a schoolgirl over there!"

"That's true," Miss Benedict said sweetly. "But this is an expression of the vagaries of fate. Miss Grey, with appropriate intent, did contact me. We were party to subsequent events. Whether we continue to have an interest in the matter is solely at my discretion, not yours."

Lacy jumped to his feet. "You're making a big mistake taking me on, Benedict! You've got my box from that Irish bitch and you're going to try to keep it . . ."

I had risen also. "Sit down, Lacy."

"Who the hell do you . . ."

"I said, *sit down*!"

Lacy planted his keister back in the chair.

"Now let's not get excited," I said, turning to Her Ladyship, "do I throw them out now?"

"You have no right to take my property," Lacy muttered.

"Don't be Neanderthal, David. That's sinking to their level and I won't have it. As for you, Mr. Lacy, my patience is worn ragged. I've told you at least three times that I don't have the box. Whether it is your property is a matter of profound conjecture that could only be established in a court of law. In that environment I suspect that your claimancy to be rather thin."

"It was placed there by one of my forefathers!"

"That argument is specious. You have no proof that Odo deLacy was even related to you. If we take the number of generations at 16 from the time of Odo's living he would be one of 131,000 direct lineage. If your forbears were sexually active and had say 18 generations, the figure would be over a half million. Anyone in this room might be related to him. Then there's the Irish Government laws concerning National Treasures and, Rome, since it was discovered on Church Lands. . . ."

Aloysius almost had a stroke. His face got whiter and his big ears got redder. He kept looking at Miz Charlotte with beady eyes. I was afraid that he'd turn the gorilla loose to break up the furniture. Then I got a flash of inspiration. "We don't have the damned thing. We've been trying for weeks now to get Kamaroff to give it up . . . Uh oh . . ."

Lacy was on it like a hound dog on a June bug! "Kamaroff? Who's this Kamaroff?"

"David!"

"Sorry Miss Benedict—I . . ."

Lacy signaled King Kong who came over to my desk, looming over me. "Now wait a minute, Lacy—call off your goon!" I said.

"Who's Kamaroff?" Lacy growled.

I shrugged my shoulders. "Sorry, Miss Benedict," I said again. "Sergei Kamaroff is a collector. He's from Zurich but I have a feeling he's headed here. We think he has the box . . ."

"No, David—really Mr. Lacy, that's not the thing to do. My advice to you is to stay away from Sergei Kamaroff . . ."

A look of profound craftiness crossed Lacy's face. "That's your advice, eh? Well I'm a free agent too, Benedict. C'mon, let's get out of here!"

After performing my surrogate host duties at the front door seeing Lacy & Co. off, I came whistling up the staircase to the library.

Miss Benedict was standing at her desk when I entered. "You, David, are a middle-aged juvenile delinquent."

That really hurt—I never considered myself middle-aged.

Chapter XVII

Life in Avalon settled down into the hum-drum routine of a Borgia castle. All of sly Sarah's grandiose schemes for supplanting me in the heart and mind of Miss Benedict had fizzled. Why Miz Charlotte didn't pitch her out I didn't know.

But Sarah didn't get off the hook. Each day she slithered in to the stacks of stuff that Charlotte had waiting for her to do. Occasionally I'd catch her looking at me with enough electricity to light up Newport News so I always sat with my back against the wall.

In spite of the excitement in the Carolinas, we were still nowhere. A package of papers came from Liam Mullin containing some sketchy information on Walsh and a copy of the proceedings of Fowler's inquest. It contained a transcript including Sarah's identification of the remains, the post-mortem report on Fowler and what little the Irish police had on Walsh. The stuff on Walsh did contain a police mug shot plus information that Walsh had been discharged for cause by a Caribbean ship line, but didn't say what the cause was.

Everything was riding on Kepler in Miami. Miz Charlotte had given up on Steiner for the moment. He seemed to be just a windbag caught up in something he couldn't handle. Unless we had some leverage on him like collusion or theft, tracking him down would be futile.

Finally the call from Kepler came through. We were in the library and Charlotte nodded to me to take it. That way she could listen and make acerbic comments.

"This is Sam," Kepler said. "I got a few things. The Escort belongs to a guy named Joab—a real sleaze ball. He has a record but it's all petty stuff. The local police and the DEA are interested in him. I can't find him so he might still be up your way."

"Do you have any background?"

Sam described our intruder to a "T." "He was born in Tennessee, aged 32. Did a stint in the army where he got some training in explosives."

"That sounds like our boy . . ."

"The Law thinks he was doing 'odd jobs' because of his explosives background. As I said, it's not much . . ."

"Anything else," I asked hopefully.

"Maybe. The name Tebaldi doesn't mean a thing down here. I was about to scratch it when I decided to take a long shot. I checked Vital Stats. An Aldo Tebaldi, born August 22, 1959, died about six years ago in a boating accident. A buddy in motor vehicles checked and guess what? Dead people in Florida now drive cars. A driver's license was issued to an Aldo Tebaldi on May 4th. The address is a phony unless he lives in a pizza parlor."

It was an old dodge. You find someone who's about your age and dead and get a copy of the birth certificate. With that you get a driver's license and a new identity. It couldn't stand much scrutiny but it would do for a character like Walsh who probably didn't plan to stay long in the USA.

"Do you have any dope on this Tebaldi character?"

"Only that he was a ghost before May 4th. Do I go on?"

"Yes, Mr. Kepler," Miz Charlotte interjected, "it's very important that we find him. I doubt if he'd stay in a hotel or motel—probably he has a room somewhere. See if he has a phone."

Sam was hurt. He was a pro and didn't like advice from amateurs any more than Miss Benedict did. "Hell, Sam—you know what to do better than we do. Just give it a real push, will you?" I added diplomatically.

With nothing better to do, I called a contact in Zurich. It's always a neat idea to know where all the men are on the chess board. It took under twenty-four hours to find out that both Sparrow and Kamaroff were in the USA and that Kamaroff had a connecting flight to Richmond. I called Harry Tonto to check and see where Sergei came to earth.

So the middle game ran as follows: Tricky Oskar and Kamaroff knew, or thought they knew, what the box was but had no idea where it was. They hadn't yet tumbled to the Walsh angle. Their only lead was Sarah and both were probably headed here where they knew she was. Walsh seemed to be in Florida, probably Miami, with the box but he was worried and hired Joab to relieve little Sarah of "the thousand natural shocks that flesh is heir to."

I reminded Miss Benedict that this was getting expensive. Between transatlantic flights, forays into the Carolinas, hiring people in Virginia, Ireland, Miami and Zurich, *and* feeding the bottomless pit in the guest wing, the bills were adding up. I was carrying coals to Newcastle. Miz Charlotte had her own internal computer and used the desk top in the library for error checks.

Sergei Kamaroff coming through the air terminal at Richmond would be as inconspicuous as Jumbo the Elephant. Both Sergei and Alfie Sparrow had standards that were never compromised. They traveled first class, used big expensive cars and stayed in the best hotels. It was the only civilized thing to do.

Arriving unexpectedly in the end of May, Kamaroff couldn't get into the Williamsburg Inn so he settled for the Lafayette House. He probably already had us under observation from the holly and dogwood. Tonto had dug this up in a few hours.

Kamaroff was an odd duck. He liked to gamble, particularly at bridge and since there were no racetracks within striking distance, I expected him to stick pretty much to his suite. I thought it might be a good idea to let Sergei know he was playing on our turf.

One person always welcome at Avalon was good old Sheriff Marvin Thomas Jonathan Jackson Spooner. Marv's from one of those old Gloucester families; you can find Spooners everywhere and they take up half of the Confederate War Memorial up by the Courthouse. Sheriff Marvin and Miz Charlotte had known each other for years (although he was a good dozen years younger, Miss Benedict knew his sisters and had dandled little Marvin on her knee). He had gone off to Vietnam, won medals, came back and ran for Sheriff. Since half the county was kin it wasn't much of a contest. Marv had a soft southern accent and those "country boy" airs but was sharp as a tack as many an evildoer found to his dismay. I dialed his number and waited for Doris, his secretary to put him on the line.

"Hello, Davy, how were things in Europe?"

"Everything's fine—the 'Spice Girls' want to know when you're going to visit them again. Are you free this evening?"

"Sure."

"I'd like to take you to dinner."

"At Avalon?"

"No, over in Williamsburg."

Marvin agreed. He knew something was up but he was too polite to ask directly. Arriving around 7 P.M., we had drinks while the Sheriff and Milady reminisced about the old days.

About 40, Marv was exceptionally good looking with finely chiseled features. He coiled his long lank form into one of the chairs and softly racketed the sparrow of conversation back and forth with Miz Charlotte. Sarah Grey was very silent, raking the Sheriff with calculating green eyes. I couldn't tell whether she wanted to stab him with a hat pin or carnally assault him.

After the chitchat we ambled to the Buick and sat for a moment before leaving. "As you no doubt have gathered, I need a little help," I said.

"Figures."

"We're working on something—a relic that lots of people are interested in. Some of them are very nasty."

Marv didn't say anything. He was a great listener.

"One of these characters, a real bad-ass named Kamaroff is presently over in Williamsburg. An ounce of prevention could save a lot of grief."

"I always like preventive stuff."

"I think Kamaroff would like to talk to our Miss Grey."

"I wouldn't mind talking to her either."

"Don't kid yourself, she's bad news."

We drove over the Coleman Bridge and up Colonial Parkway through the pleasant May evening.

"Tell me about this Kamaroff character."

I gave him a rundown on Sergei. "I'm hoping to catch him in the dining room. I suspect he's been in his suite all day—playing cards. Leg work's beneath Sergei's dignity. He probably had lunch in his rooms and I'm hoping he'll come up for air."

The Lafayette Inn, just south of Williamsburg, caters to business conferences, weddings and such besides normal tourists. When we arrived in the dining room the evening rush was tapering off and I figured a Continental character like Kamaroff would dine late. Sitting off to the side we ordered the roast duck. I had the house wine (with my palate I can't tell a good vintage from ginger ale) and Marv, being a good Baptist, continued with his tonic water and lemon.

Time passed and I was afraid that we'd have to seek Sergei in his lair (which would be like swimming in a creek full of water moccasins) but at 9:15 he bounded in with two muscle-bound Neanderthals in suits. He was led to a table where he could look out on the swimming pool, now empty of frolicking naiads.

"That's him?"

"Yeah, ugly, isn't he?"

Chapter XVIII

Kamaroff wasn't much to behold. Short and squat, he sat hunched over his menu. We waited and after coffee I led Spooner to the small porch where Sergei and his hearty crew had just gotten their soup. I moved to a place directly behind Sergei's chair. I leaned over with my mouth next to his ear.

"Howdy, Sergei," I whispered. "I heard you were in our neck of the woods and I just couldn't wait to pop in and say hello." I had the warmhearted pleasure of watching him drop his spoon and splatter the front of his $600 silk jacket. He swung his large, dark-maned, grey-streaked head around, his glance boring into my eyes with a look of pure venom.

"You picked a swell time to visit, Sergei. Have you seen Colonial Williamsburg with all the restored buildings? You ought to go and take a look at the jail, Kamaroff. It's awful to see how they used to lock people up in those days."

"Is Mr. Kamaroff interested in jails," Marv asked softly.

"I bet he is! And are you lucky, Sergei. This is Sheriff Marvin Spooner in charge of all law enforcement in Gloucester County where Miss Benedict lives. If you're really interested Marv would be glad to show you the state electric chair . . ."

Marv leaned over and faced Kamaroff with a smile. "Are you staying in these parts for long, Mr. Kamaroff?"

Sergei wasn't his usual jovial self.

"You ought to drop over to Avalon and see Miz Charlotte, Sergei. She'd be hurt if she knew you were in town and you didn't call," I said gallantly filling in the awkward pauses in the conversation. I nodded to his companions. "And do bring along Bonzo and J. Fred Muggs."

Kamaroff slowly regained his composure. "We always meet by chance, Dr. Peete. One of these days we'll have a real assignation—and a little tête-à-tête."

I gave him my brightest smile. "I'll look forward to that Sergei, more than you could imagine."

"Will you and Sheriff . . . er . . ."

"Spooner."

". . . Sheriff Spooner share some wine with us?"

"I'm afraid not, Sergei. We have to get home. You know how Miss Benedict is when she's hot on the trail of something—just work, work, work, day and night."

Kamaroff dabbed his mouth daintily with his napkin. "Perhaps I shall drop in on Miss Benedict," he said softly.

"You do that, Sergei, but call ahead. Miss Benedict is fussy about appointments and I wouldn't want you to fall afoul of the roving mastiffs on the grounds. Well, ciao for now . . ."

Back at Avalon I dropped Marv off at his car. I found Miz Charlotte at her desk in the darkened library, in a pool of light from the green, hooded desk lamp.

"David?' she asked, her eyes straining into the darkness.

"None other."

"Did you see Mr. Kamaroff?"

"I did. I introduced him to Sheriff Spooner and we had a swell conversation on jails and the electric chair." I gave her a rundown of our meeting.

"He might come here?' Charlotte asked, a little taken aback.

"That's what he said."

"But why would he want to see me, I wonder?"

"Well, he knows Oskar is after you and maybe he wants to press his suit in person. After all, you said he has a Title . . ."

"For heaven's sake, David, do be serious . . ."

"I'd love to. Look Your Ladyship, this is getting out of hand. We've had a probable hit-man on the grounds, an attempt on Sarah's life (not to mention, yours truly), and both Sparrow and Kamaroff and their assorted ruffians hiding in the highways and hedges . . . It's time to lean on the 'Rose of Tralee.' "

"I doubt if she'd tell you a thing."

"Oh, I don't know—I can be very persuasive."

"You wouldn't touch her. You're a big fraud, David."

"I wouldn't have to. If she won't talk, we're going nowhere and she's a liability to us—she's dangerous. Then it's simple, I march her to the front gate and kiss her good-bye."

"And leave her to Kamaroff's tender mercies?"

"Sure, that's how you live in shark-infested waters. You chum a little. You've told me in the past that our business is pure Darwinism. Sarah Grey's skin is Sarah Grey's lookout, not ours. She's perfectly happy to bed down here and let you protect her (and *feed* her, Lord help us) while she's not telling us a damned thing. And I can vouch that she doesn't talk in her sleep . . ."

We beat this around until after midnight. I was hopeful Miz Charlotte was coming around. It was obvious Sarah knew something and leaning on her might bring us closer to the box. Finally, we called it a night and went our respective ways.

I guess age is beginning to ambush me. Roast duck is great going down but you might have to sit up holding its hand later on (or webbed foot as the case may be). I took an antacid and got out the "Decline and Fall of the Roman Empire" to put me in a state of stupor. The churning and burning had subsided and I was settling my limbs for Morpheus when Max grunted.

He was like a roommate who never slept. Most of the sensors that Max plays with are located on the grounds or at entries like doors and windows, but some are set inside the house where valuables reside. A soft hum accompanied the blinking light indicating that someone was in the library!

It could be Miz Charlotte. She tended to wander the night like Marley's ghost but she was usually careful about tripping the switch on her bedside table that deactivated the library system. I threw on a robe. No other sensors were blinking indicating this was an anomaly. I slipped down the hall to the library door. It was locked! Damn. I didn't have the key! I sprinted back to my room and got it—and my .357 Magnum. Miz Charlotte's bedroom was on the other side of the library and that's what worried me most.

I doused the lights on the landing and slipped through the library door. Total darkness enveloped me and it was comforting. I padded to the side door leading to the back hall and Miz Charlotte's room. I listened again—nothing. As I snapped on the lights, Her Ladyship appeared, covered with lacy stuff.

"What in the world . . ." she said.

"We've got company—go to your room!"

Those rare opportunities when I could order Her Ladyship about, and she had to obey, did my soul good. I was ready to accuse Max of having a stroke and needing brain surgery except for the locked library door. Then I spotted the typewriter on the library table. Typewriters haven't been used at Avalon since the last millennium. Why Charlotte hung on to that old Underwood was a mystery; it usually sat on a shelf in the corner collecting dust. I touched the green hood of the table lamp next to it. It was warm.

A few minutes later I tapped softly on Miz Charlotte's door. On entering, I found her sitting in a chair by the window in the soft glow of her night table lamps.

"Did you find anyone, David?"

"No, the library alarm went off. Maybe we have rats in the wainscoting."

Sheer terror covered her face; she'd rather face Viking raiders storming ashore from Aquia Creek than vermin near her precious books. I took pity and told her about the typewriter. "As my mentor, Sherlock Holmes used to say, 'eliminate the impossible and the remaining, however improbable, must be the solution.' Since neither of us used the typewriter, and Rafe and Dixie haven't, and since no one has skulked in from the outside according to Marvelous Max, then the rat in the wainscoting must be none other than—Sarah Grey!"

Miss Benedict was silent; the lines around her mouth were hard.

"Do I go and get her?"

"No—we'll have it out in the morning."

For the first time in weeks I had the feeling we were going to get this thing off the dime and moving. My indigestion was gone, Max's indigestion was gone; it was lovely.

The next morning I was ready to eat Sarah Grey alive. I bounded up the stairs whistling to find Miss Benedict already in the library. "Do you wish to be present at the foot of the scaffold? If so I'll fetch your knitting."

"Great Scott, David, let's keep a little decorum, shall we? Yes, I wish to be present while you talk to her."

Since her fall from grace, Sarah didn't work any overtime. At 8 A.M. I waited, humming and cheery, when the phone rang. Raphael was probably out doing something because it came straight through to the library. I picked up the receiver. "Avalon," I said.

"Mr. David Peete, please," a strange voice replied.

"Speaking."

"This is Sergeant Gomez of the Miami Police Department, Mr. Peete. I'd like to talk to you please, it's important."

I had that sinking feeling in my stomach. I put my hand over the mouthpiece. "It's the Miami Police—I don't like the sounds of it." Miz Charlotte picked up the phone.

"Go ahead, Sergeant Gomez. I've asked my employer, Dr. Benedict, to get on the line."

"Do you know a Samuel Kepler?"

"Yes."

"Have you employed him?"

"That's a confidential matter, Sergeant—what's this all about?"

"Have you employed him?" We bounced that back and forth for a while. Finally, Gomez realized he wasn't getting anything for free.

"He was killed last night . . ."

"Killed! How?"

"Hit and run."

"An accident?"

"Apparently."

Apparently, my foot. The Miami Police don't make long distance telephone calls to Virginia to ask about the employment of traffic statistics. "Yes, he was employed by us. My employer is a collector with some valuable objects d'art in her home. We had a prowler on the grounds but managed to get his license number. Mr. Kepler was a private detective and was checking. The alleged prowler's name was, Joab."

"Roscoe Joab?"

"I don't know his first name, Sergeant. Why all the interest? Is there something wrong?"

"How did you get Joab's name?"

"Kepler called the other night. He said he had checked out the license plate and the car was registered to Joab."

"How did he do that?"

"I have no idea. I didn't ask."

"Why did you go to all this trouble?" Gomez was a real terrier.

"Aw, c'mon, Sergeant, someone was trespassing on our property; we wanted to know who he was."

"Why didn't you call the local police? They'd have followed it up and it's a lot cheaper than hiring your own investigator."

"Are you complaining about citizens actively engaged in 'Crime Watch'? Check with Sheriff Spooner of Gloucester County and you'll find that a report was made. It seems to me how we spend our money is our business—unless it's illegal."

"Don't get huffy, Mr. Peete—I'm just following things up."

"But why?"

"Let's say that I don't like the smell of this one or I don't like loose ends hanging around. Are you folks located near water?"

I could tell exactly how his mind was working. "We're on the water and we have our own dock. Look Sergeant, I'll save you some time and money. There are no drugs involved. Put a call through to Sheriff Spooner or call the Governor's office. You'll find plenty of people who'll vouch for Dr. Charlotte Montaigne Benedict.

"We had a sneak thief and from time to time we handle some very valuable objects on a referral basis. If we find someone on the grounds, we like to know who they are and, hopefully, who they're working for. For us, that's good business."

"Did you find out who Joab is working for?"

Gomez was good. He was asking all the right questions and if I wasn't careful I could be flirting with an obstruction of justice charge. I looked inquiringly at Miz Charlotte; she nodded.

"No—Kepler didn't have that yet. There was another name we came across in the car—Aldo Tebaldi. It might mean nothing but he was checking it out." I spelled it for him.

"How did you get this again?"

I went through it again. There was a long pause.

"What's going down there, Mr. Peete?"

"Look, Sergeant, you have everything that we have. We assumed intended robbery at this end, don't you?"

The phone call lasted another five minutes but went nowhere. He wouldn't say what it was about Sam's death that stirred him up, and we wouldn't say anything more.

Putting out respective receivers down, both Charlotte and I were upset. Sam Kepler was no close friend. He wasn't an old Navy buddy, but our employment apparently led to his death. Of course he was in a risky business but that didn't really help to make it easier.

I thought about Joab. Maybe, after our little ructions in South Carolina, he found out that Kepler was checking on him. It made me uncomfortable. I didn't tell Sam what happened in Carolina and I could have neutralized Joab a half dozen times. So we weren't in our best humor when Sarah Grey walked into the library and announced, "Good Mornin', all."

Chapter XIX

I knew that Charlotte Benedict was capable of sharp business practices. Never one to outright lie, she wasn't above a little "half-truthing" now and again. But I was also aware that she carried a lot of moral baggage. In issues of right and wrong Miz Charlotte had a finely tuned sense of proportion. No coup was worth the price of personal integrity.

Unfortunately, neither of us was above a little self-deception on occasion. Did Fowler get drunk and fall in the Slaney? Did Father Hugh shrive a sinner and then die of a heart attack? In the official papers Liam Mullin had forwarded, Fowler died of "misadventure whilst intoxicated" and Father Hugh of heart failure. Of course the officials didn't know all the stuff that we did. We could speculate all we liked but the fact always remained that it *could* have happened as the officials indicated.

It had been like a finely poised balance scale but Sam Kepler's death tipped the balance scale and sent it spinning. Knowledge is generally derived in two ways: one through the accumulation of single facts; the other in detecting relationships between these individual facts and then the whole is not necessarily the sum of its parts. The trail of bodies strewn from the tomb of Odo deLacy was too long, Fowler, Father Hugh, maybe—Sam Kepler, no way! Somebody was out there who wanted the box and was willing to kill for it. That somebody also wanted Sarah Grey dead.

Sarah looked at our faces. She didn't need to be a genius to know that something was wrong. "What is it now?" she asked.

I had developed a full head of steam. Primed before for a showdown with little Molly Malone the news from Miami pushed all my dials into that red zone that indicated imminent eruption. "Sit down!" I growled, pointing toward a chair. She walked across and sat and even through the mists of anger and frustration I was surprised at her composure.

"The fun and games are over girl," I said as quietly as I could. "Sam Kepler bought the farm last night."

"Bought the. . . ?"

"He was the victim of a hit and run in Miami."

I figured she'd start to unravel a little, particularly with the hit and run business, but she just swallowed a few times and blinked at me with those green eyes behind the big glasses. "We figure it was your Mr. Walsh," I added.

"What do you mean, 'my' Mr. Walsh?" she asked in a low voice.

"What do you think we are, a pair of idiots? You think that we believed your cockamamie story with the drivel about the Bend Sinister and women with broken necks? I say *women* because there's a good possibility that there'll be another one shortly.

"It doesn't wash, Sarah. Starting back in Ireland someone was out to kill you. Why? Because they don't like your punk haircut? Not bloody likely! You're up to your lying Irish mouth in this thing. Walsh is after you. Oh sure, Sparrow and Kamaroff would love to talk to you, but they don't want you dead—maybe just hurting a little. So now you're going to tell us the whole story."

I had that sinking feeling. I had it all figured out, you see, because I was so devilishly clever and worldly wise. By now Sarah was supposed to be all a-quiver. Instead she lit a cigarette and looked at me with a faint smile. Sitting by Miz Charlotte's desk she reached out, picked up the phone and dialed a number and waited for a moment. "Hogan's Taxis? This is Sarah Grey at Avalon off Guinea Road. Can you have a cab here in half an hour? . . . Good . . . No, I'll tell the driver th' destination . . . Thank you." She replaced the receiver and smiled.

"You two are so bloody clever it makes me fair weak in th' knees. This's th' big threat, eh, Peete? Tell all or out you go an' never darken th' door again. Th' two of you make me sick at me stomach with your fine clothes an' grand houses an' your all-knowin' ways. What's th' matter, Peete? No smart-ass comments? What are you goin' to do now—if you lay a finger on me I'll have you up fer assault!"

She turned to Miss Benedict. "An' th' great lady of th' manor has naught to say either? I'll tell you a little secret Miss 'Know-it-all' Benedict. I needed a safe house an' you gave it to me. An' I needed someone strong enough and stupid enough fer me bodily protection an' your 'monkey on a string' over there did just grand. His muscles bulge right up between his ears."

I sat there and gripped the arms of my chair—hard! Here was this lying Irish bitch, who I'd put my butt on the line for three times, who I'd shoveled food into like a stoker into the firebox of a locomotive, carving me up and preening herself!

Charlotte Benedict calmly appraised Sarah. She was cold as ice. Maybe that's the litmus test of quality. I was ready to blow up but she functioned with her usual incisiveness. "I would be careful about baiting Dr. Peete too far, my dear," she said softly. "He has a primitive element in his nature that he keeps in check only by the strongest chains of willpower."

She leaned back in her large chair, still very much the lady of the manor. That's quality, I thought admiringly. "The gambit might work, Sarah—you might pull it off, and then again, you might not. If the ploy fails, I suspect that you'll be dead within a week. I presume that you've calculated all that? You are, after all, a very calculating girl . . ."

Sarah's laugh wasn't pretty. "So now we're playin' that we know exactly what's afoot?"

"Oh, it doesn't take any genius, my dear. You wrote a document last night on that typewriter. It's probably a detailed account of Walsh's and your activities dealing with the demise of George Fowler and possibly even Father Courtney. Now you'll put one copy of the document in the hands of a lawyer or possibly in a safe deposit box and you'll keep the other to wave in Mr. Walsh's face when he appears.

"Candidly, there are a number of weaknesses in your plan. For one thing, you're seriously underestimating both Kamaroff and Hammerschmidt. They're professional blackguards, you see—and you still have your amateur status. They've been around the course many times and while we've moved a bit faster so far, on your own you'll be crossing steel with people quite out of your league."

Sarah just looked at her with narrowed eyes, but she was nervous, viciously stabbing out her cigarette.

"Then there's the question of Mr. Walsh himself," Miz Charlotte continued. "I don't know the gentleman but he strikes me as most unreliable. He befriended your Mr. Fowler, obviously with his hand in Fowler's pocket as far as it would reach, and then, when Fowler discovered something of real value—did away with him. And you're linked to Mr. Walsh. What that relationship is, is purely conjectural. If he was responsible for Fowler's death, then Father Hugh's death was also by his hand, as was the attempt on your life in Dublin. He's hardly a stable character.

"And look at the hand that you're dealing him. 'Touch not a hair of me head,' as you would so eloquently put it, 'or I'll expose th' whole perfidious plot!' So you've chained yourself to this violent and dangerous man for a slice of the profits.

"Finally, it's instructive to think about Mr. Walsh. Have you spent sufficient time on that? I think not. Mr. Walsh is no longer Mr. Walsh—he's Mr. Tebaldi. Do you really think if he successfully peddles the box he'll go back and drink ale in 'Maggie's Bloomers'? Hardly. He's dreaming of a non-extraditable country in South America. He took great care in dealing with Fowler and Father Courtney in Ireland; he was in jeopardy then, but that jeopardy diminishes dramatically with each passing hour. Even if your deposition was aired now it could take months, or even years, for the authorities to act. And where would they find Walsh? He might not even be 'Mr. Tebaldi' any longer. He might need your cooperation in the consummation of the deal, then he will change identities like a suit of clothing. And your status will change very rapidly from a needed asset to a dangerous liability. If I were you I would be very careful about how and where you receive your cut. As I say—it might work, for a time, but I wouldn't put any hard cash on it."

Sarah wilted under all this. It's hard when you're being very clever to have all the leaking seams in your little boat pointed out with relish. Her face set in a mask of enmity, she walked silently toward the back door and the stairway to the guest wing.

"When you see Mr. Joad, give him my best," I said. She slammed the door on the way out.

I reached for the phone, punching out Harry Tonto's number. I got a recording and slammed down the receiver in disgust. "Nuts!" I said, "Tonto's not in."

"Don't be upset, David, it's childish."

"Don't be upset? Are you kidding? Three times I put it on the line for that Irish . . . that Irish . . . that—three times! And she says my muscles run up into my head!"

"And you want Harry Tonto to follow her? In that abominable pickup truck with all the paint cans and pipes rattling? Why not dress him up as Bungles the Clown so he'd really be conspicuous?"

"So what's your idea?"

She didn't say anything but picked up the phone and dialed. "May I speak to Marvin? This is Charlotte Benedict." I picked up my phone.

"Marvin, this is Charlotte."

"Trouble with Kamaroff?' Marv asked laconically.

"No, but the root cause of any misunderstanding with Sergei Kamaroff is in the process of leaving Avalon. I mean, of course, Miss Sarah Grey."

"Oh, what's she up to?'

"No good, I'm afraid. As a concerned citizen always dedicated to the tranquillity of Gloucester County, I felt obliged to call you."

"She's goin' to tear th' county up?'

"Perhaps not that but I suspect that she might become the set piece for some difficulties. It appears that someone might wish her grievous bodily harm—of the worst kind." ("Yeah, me," I muttered.)

"This is a bit late, isn't it, Miz Charlotte?'

"Perhaps, but I'm not clairvoyant, you know. May a private citizen make a suggestion?"

"Sure."

"I think it would be in the interests of the county to know where she goes. If she leaves the county, which I suspect, you might even wish to take broader action."

"I think we'd better talk."

"My suggestion would be to act now and talk later. If you like I'll send Dr. Peete over."

"I think you'd better do that."

"We'll just delay until she leaves, all right?"

I had to hand it to Miz Charlotte. I had been trained since I was a little tyke to do all my own up and down lifting but she was a real executive. She knew how to push buttons.

"We're still in the thing?' I asked.

"Possibly, I don't know. It depends on what happens. Right now I have responsibilities as a citizen."

"Do you want me to open up to Marv."

"Of course—tell him everything."

Chapter XX

Charlotte Benedict went back to work, but that was all play-acting to demonstrate to us insignificant mortals how Zeus's daughters acted all the time up on Mount Olympus. At the window, I watched Sarah climb into Hogan's taxi and then take off.

"She's gone. I guess I'd better run up and talk to Marvin."

You could get the mistaken idea that Marvin "Stonewall" Spooner was in our vest pocket and nothing could be further from the truth. Adept at playing the political game, he knew how to treat important residents like Miz Charlotte, but he was no patsy. Knowing that Avalon, and all the valuable stuff that found their way there might be interesting to unsavory characters, he cooperated at being responsive to our needs. But he still viewed himself as the Wyatt Earp of this particular Tombstone and he didn't like things going down that he didn't know about. It was an unhappy Marvin Spooner that I met in his office up by the courthouse. I felt a distinct coldness in his gray eyes.

"Tell me about it," he said quietly.

So I told him, starting at the sidewalk table in Wexford when I first ran afoul of Sarah Grey, down to the time of her stepping into Hogan's taxi. He said nothing during the recital, just leaned his long body back in his chair.

"For God's sake, Davy—you mean to sit there and tell me you thought those folks in Ireland had been snuffed," he said quietly after I'd finished—but with an edge in his voice.

"I said I had 'suspicions,' Marv. Those weren't the official verdicts at the inquests."

"Yeah but hell, they didn't know all this other stuff—the casket and so on . . . You had an obligation to come forward."

"That's 20-20 hindsight, Marv, and you know it. All I had at that time was this cock and bull story from the Irish colleen who wouldn't know the truth if she was tipped head first into it. Until I left the sacred soil of Ireland I thought it was all an elaborate scam. It still might be—probably is."

Despite his calm exterior I could tell that Marv was steamed. "Well you and Miz Charlotte sure didn't let me know that this Joab character was a soldier from Miami."

"Damn it, Marv—I didn't know that. You got a report of the trespass and the license number and you didn't do much about it. I'm not griping, you understand—he could have been from the National Inquirer trying to get a picture of Miz Charlotte in her teddy."

"So you blew up the poor bastard's car and left him?"

"It's better to give than to receive. Sure I did. Why not? It was *his* bomb."

"What about the South Carolina Highway Patrol? They would have liked to know what was going down."

"Aw, c'mon, Marv. What good would that have done? Can you imagine what some smart lawyer would have done to the switching of the damned thing back and forth between cars? I probably would have been arrested for attempted murder. And even if we got Joab, so what? We would have put one, not very intelligent, Rover Boy in the slammer and the guy who's really behind it all would just dig in a little deeper with another identity."

Spooner was silent for a moment. "Yeah, maybe he would—or maybe Sam Kepler would still be alive."

That really hurt. "Yeah, maybe he would, or maybe he wouldn't. Neither one of us knows that."

Marv was getting past the stage of being incensed which I was happy to see. He began turning it over in his mind again. "Going back to the Irish end, I can see getting someone blind drunk and tipping him into the freezing river at a selected spot—but what about the priest?"

"He had a bad heart to begin with. There's lots of things can make a bad heart worse—much worse—like atropine, nicotine or digitalis."

"But where would this Walsh get atropine or digitalis?"

"We don't know much about Walsh, do we? Look, I could isolate enough nicotine from a box of cigars to give half the county heart trouble. Maybe Walsh isn't just a common thug. Look at Sarah—I thought she was just a greedy Irish kid on the make for 'grand' things and she turns out to be Lucrezia Borgia with a lot more grit and staying power than I ever expected."

Marv stood up and walked to the window, looking out sightlessly. "And now you think she's put herself in real peril."

"Hell, she's been in real peril since this thing started."

"Maybe she never had any choice."

Good old chivalrous Spooner, I thought. "Don't get romantic, Marv, there's lots of things she could have done."

"Like what?"

"She could have gone into a convent and taken the veil. She could have gone to relatives. Where did she go, by the way?"

I wouldn't have blamed him if he told me to get lost but Marv, despite his country-boy ways, was shrewd. He knew his limits, areas of his own expertise and those regions where he hadn't the knowledge to operate efficiently. This game was being played in

Miz Charlotte's specialized court. I might be a real pain in the sitter but he recognized that he needed our input.

"She went to the First Virginia Bank on Route 17 and rented a safe deposit box . . ."

"Bingo!" I said and then explained about Charlotte's speculations during our last conversation with Sarah.

". . . then she went from the bank to the Post Office. Then to Butterfield's motel and took a room. She's there now."

"She's still in Gloucester? That's a surprise. I expected her to go someplace else, but it makes sense. She doesn't know the States and she's more familiar with our stomping ground than anywhere. Butterfield's is cheap; if she went over the bridge, she'd pay more. It suits her purposes."

Marv turned and looked at me. "What purposes?" he asked.

"To get in touch with Walsh. She knows where he is. She's telling him that she's wired the thing, that she's left papers in a safe deposit box that will blow it wide open if she has an 'accident'—and that she's in for her share of the loot. Whatever that damned box is, she and Walsh think it's worth a bundle. Kamaroff and Sparrow are buyers. Sooner or later Walsh will try and peddle it."

Back at his desk Marv toyed with his pencil and then threw it down in disgust. "Sometimes I wish you and Miz Charlotte would move out of my county."

"*Your* county? That sounds pretty feudal, pal. Who the hell do you think you are—the Sheriff of Nottingham?"

"If I am, you're no Robin Hood. Look, Davy, I'm just a country copper. I can't peddle this to the State Police—they'd think I had a screw loose. I don't have people to watch this gal even if I wanted to. I have trouble enough keeping up with run of the mill crime . . . and Kamaroff and Sparrow aren't even in the county. Until something happens, there isn't much I can do . . ."

In a way I was glad. I knew Miz Charlotte was ambivalent but the virus of curiosity had infected her. In spite of this siren's song we could be weeks half in and half out of this cockamamie thing and that would be very hard to live with. The bullet-headed military mind likes to know what the objective is and how to get there. Marv's inability to do much made it fish or cut bait time. I phoned Miss Benedict and she was snappish; she didn't like being jostled. She also didn't like to spend money so I sat doodling, while Miz Charlotte's curiosity fought it out with her penuriousness. Finally she spoke and I hung up the phone. "Guess what?" I said to Marv. "The Lone Ranger, Tonto and Robin Hood are all coming to the rescue of the Sheriff of Nottingham."

I asked Marv to deputize us so we'd be a posse but he wasn't in the mood for shenanigans. I haven't gotten so many instructions on what I could or couldn't do with my trumpet since I was the Angel Gabriel in Miss Oxbarge's sixth grade Christmas Pageant and the unspeakable Olga was the Virgin Mary.

So there we were on the outside looking in, along with Kamaroff and Sparrow. They say one of the secrets of chess is to seize the initiative in the center of the board. That's where we were as long as we had Sarah Grey. Suddenly we were pushed to the periphery with Sergei and Alfie. All we could do was wait.

Waiting didn't help the atmosphere at Avalon. The days dragged into a week with Harry watching Butterfield's motel and we were all getting stretched in the nerve department. But if it was tough on us at Avalon, one ray of sun-shine was that it was sheer hell on Sarah Grey at the motel. At least we had some semblance of work to occupy us; she was just sitting and waiting.

Harry Tonto and Shapiro were also getting antsy. Nothing was happening. Sarah Grey stayed in her room for hours at a clip watching all that intellectual stuff on the tube. Despite

Marv's injunctions, Tonto got friendly with Gus Butterfield and managed to get into Sarah's room while she was shopping. There was nothing to report except that poor Sarah had really come down in the world. No more oysters Rockefeller or "T" bones for our Irish Carnivore; it was now canned stew heated on an electric ring. But Sarah must have been fairly well set for cash; she had banked all of her salary while she was with us and eating Miz Charlotte right into the poor house.

I threw down my pencil and faced Miss Benedict. "I have a great idea—why don't we dump it?"

Did you ever notice how when you recommend doing something unpleasant that others are already thinking about, they get mad? Miz Charlotte looked testily over her glasses. I could see one of our classic confrontations looming on the horizon.

"I beg your pardon—'dump'?"

"Dump, drop, abandon, forsake, desert, jilt, ignore...."

"If I need a Thesaurus, David, I have one on my shelf."

" 'The Queen was in the counting-house, counting out her money, the maid was in the garden eating bread and honey' ... and oysters and caviar and joints of beef and anything else she could lay her hands on ... It's over, Miz Charlotte. We're out of the game—lurking in the rhododendrons along with Alfie and Sergei. I hate losing too, it's so undignified, but Sarah Grey has played us for patsies. It's time we retire with what shreds of dignity we have left."

"David you couldn't recognize dignity if it fell out of the sky and landed on you."

"What do you mean? I'm an officer and a gentleman."

"If only you weren't so abrasive with her."

"Abrasive! What about her apple-polishing all over the place with you lapping it up? I thought you were going to adopt her—like 'Mommy' Warbucks and Orphan Annie!"

"That's what I should have done . . . Oh, that would have put you in your place, Peete! Why didn't I think of it? I could have had the delicious pleasure of watching her order you to jump!"

"You're forgetting Yin and Yang, Miz Charlotte. In that case I wouldn't have any choice but to marry the girl. It would have been great—you, me and little Molly Malone, all one big happy family. And I could call you . . . Mom!"

I am well aware of my shortcomings, the worst of which is running my mouth while my brain is in neutral. I always had to be careful about sailing too close to Miz Charlottes bows, and now I really rammed her! I was afraid that she'd hit me over the head with her expensive French telephone when it rang. She picked it up with all kinds of lightning discharging around her head. "Yes?" she said, eyes flashing.

There were some phone noises.

"It's for you," she said. She held out the phone but I was afraid to touch it, I might get electrocuted. I slumped at my desk and got mine—still contemplating my imminent unemployment. It was Harry Tonto.

"The bird is ready to fly," he said.

"Who the hell is this, the Audubon Society?"

"What's eating you? Sarah Grey is moving. She's rented a car from Hogan."

"You mean a taxi?"

"No—a car. It's parked in front of her room at Butterfield's now."

Chapter XXI

Saved by the bell! The best treatment for "hoof in mouth" disease is to remove the hoof, the mouth and all other tender anatomical parts from harm's way as quickly as possible. In the SEALS my sense of self-preservation was whetted to a razors edge so, more by reflex than cognition, I shouted: "Ye gads—I'd better check this out right away!" . . . jumped up and booked, man, as fast as my legs could carry me!

Sarah might be renting wheels because it's cheaper than paying as you go, or maybe she was planning to visit the Washington Monument while she was waiting for Walsh to contact her, but I didn't think so. Of course running off to look at a beat up rental car in Butterfield's parking lot was pretty silly, except that by staying in the library at Avalon I could be incinerated at any moment by a lightning bolt.

Butterfield's Motel, set back from Route 17, was just a row of dismal looking units with the office set close to the road and under the perpetual "vacancy" sign. There were two vehicles in Butterfield's lot, a black van and a bit further up, a Chevy that had seen much better days. The place was deserted except for Gus Butterfield in the glassed-in office area. I memorized the plate number of the Chevy and the van on general principles.

On the opposite side of Route 17, a few hundred yards to

the north was a small shopping mall with the majority of units empty. Edging the Buick amid the cluster of parked cars, I waited. I knew that Sarah shopped in the small supermarket and I didn't want to bump into her. I finally slipped out and went into a vacant store where Joel Shapiro was sitting at an old desk. He was a funny guy who looked like a fugitive from a rock group. He wore his brown hair long with a sort of Fu Manchu beard and clothing that would usually be rejected by the "King's Daughter's Thrift Shop."

"Is she around?" I asked.

"Nah, she's in her unit. She shopped this morning so she won't be out this afternoon."

"Hers is the Chevy?"

"Yeah, but there's something going down, Davy. I was just fixin' to call you."

"She's packing?"

"No, it's the black van. It pulled up around 10:30 this morning with three guys in it— real sleaze balls."

Looking at the Lone Ranger's sartorial magnificence I thought: Zounds! But "beauty is in the eye," etc. "Sleaze balls" to Joel might be guys with buttoned down collars and wing-tip shoes.

"What about them?"

"Well, there were three of them. Most people don't look for a motel unit until later. Then they stayed inside. I don't know— maybe they drove all night and were tapped out."

"They've got Jersey plates—to drive all night they'd have to come at five miles an hour . . . That's it?"

"No. I had convinced myself that it was nothing until they came out at noon."

"To eat?"

"That's what I thought but instead they drove over here and parked right out in front. They *stayed* in the car and that was weird because the sun is hot and in a closed black van it must have been hell, man."

"No one got out?"

"No, they just waited about 15 or 20 minutes. Then this big black job with tinted windows rolled in."

"What make?"

"Lincoln—here's the plate number." He passed me a slip of dog-eared paper.

"Who was in the Lincoln?"

"I don't know, but our three pals got in the limo and stayed for 10 or 15 minutes, then they went back to their room. You think they're goin' to snatch her?"

"It looks like it." I was ambivalent. After days of frustrating inactivity it was great to have something to react to. The trouble was that we were reacting, not acting. I felt like the little-leaguer who can't get the other side out and never leaves the outfield. On top of that, it had all the earmarks of Alfie Sparrow or Sergei Kamaroff. Which meant it was all a sideshow. The main event was Walsh, who little Sarah was obviously waiting for. Whoever these three were working for, their timing couldn't have been lousier.

"Where's Tonto?"

"He's getting some shut-eye. He was up all night. Cheeze, this is a crummy job."

"Roust him out, will you. He can sleep later if he wants to."

I was betting that the guys in the van would wait for the cover of darkness to go into action. From a professional point of view, I thought this was a mistake. Sarah would be much more wary after night had fallen. A half hour later Tonto arrived, awake and bitching (which was always a good sign).

"I had just fallen asleep," he muttered.

"Tell me about it. You're the only person I know who can

sleep with his eyes open." I went over the plan. Tonto and I would take care of the three guys in the van while Joel would hang back and keep his eye on Sarah. I told him not to blink because she was very fast.

"You're goin' to take on the three of them?' Shapiro asked.

"Sure—they can't be that good if it takes three of them to handle one, 115 pound, girl."

We settled down to one of those long and very boring afternoons. Shapiro was mad because I wouldn't let him play his boom-box but I didn't want to attract any attention from the hairdresser's next door. Rousting *that* bunch would be worse than shooting off flares. We played cards for a couple of hours and I lost consistently—I always do.

"Do you think we ought to call the sheriff?" Tonto asked.

"What for? Nothing's happening."

"Yeah but kidnapping's against the law."

"It is when it happens, but we don't know what they're up to. Besides, this is snake-napping—I'm not sure there's a law against that."

We had a delicious meal of pizza washed down with beer. It was awful; I realized that all that good living at Avalon was making me soft. Finally, around 9:30, Tonto and I got in the Buick and drove over. Gus Butterfield was less than enchanted to see us.

"What's goin' on, Tonto?" he asked pushing his paunch against the counter top.

"Nothing, Gus—we just want a room, that's all."

"Now wait a minute, you guys . . . I got patrons to think about. I'm callin' th' cops!"

"You don't want to do that, Gus. It would make your hourly clientele very nervous. Just relax."

After paying for the room we parked the Buick down at the

end and waited in the car. About 11 P.M. Tonto turned to me. "It's a good time now," he said and slipped out of the car. He was gone about twenty minutes and then he returned, sliding into the passenger seat. "I sure hope these guys aren't just traveling salesmen from Hoboken," he muttered.

At 2 A.M. Tonto was getting very testy and I thought that maybe nothing was going down when the door opened to the unit where our Jersey friends were staying. Two of them marched to Sarah's door while the third hopped behind the wheel of the van. Not bad, I thought professionally as the door was opened and the restraining chain cut with bolt cutters in under ten seconds. The Irish cobra never had time to hood up and show her fangs.

In a minute or so they frog-marched her out and I could see that all the fight had gone out of her. The sliding door was opened and Sarah was pitched in like a sack of old potatoes. The other two followed her in. When the door closed, the lights popped on and the van backed out. As it surged forward, the front wheels fell off. Then the left rear dropped. The right rear stayed in place and spun a bit.

"You didn't take the lug nuts off the right rear?" I asked.

Tonto scratched his stubbly chin. "It must have hung up."

Walking quickly to the van, Tonto took the driver's side and I took the other. When I reached the sliding door it ran open and the two came out, muttering to each other, their heads bent over. The next thing they saw were heavenly constellations. Moving fast, we hauled the trio into their motel unit, trussing and gagging them with duck tape.

In the crippled van, who should I find huddled in the corner but the Rose of Tralee. " 'Pon my soul—it's Miz Scarlett. Them Yankees dint bother you none, did they Miz Scarlett?" She didn't say a word, just ducked through the door and ran to her room in her skimpy nightie.

I really wanted to make sure she was still breathing but I had other fish to fry with the Three Musketeers who were beginning to come around in the other motel room. I left Sarah and went back to Tonto and our new friends. Tonto had set them sitting on the floor against the wall and under a lamp with duck tape across their mouths.

I always loved amateur theatrics and working at Avalon with Sarah Bernhardt allowed me to keep my hand in. Our three pals on the floor were naturally very unhappy and uncomfortable. They were also very confused. It seemed like such a simple job; just snatch a slip of a girl and after delivery head back to the wilds of New Jersey. I'm sure that the wheels falling off their van and being set upon by ruffians like Tonto and me were not anticipated.

I made my grand entrance back to their motel room eyeing the trio like one of Al Pacino's boys in the *Godfather*. "We'll have to get rid of them, Rocco!" I said out of the side of my mouth.

"I can dump their bodies out in the western part of the state, Boss," Tonto said following the lead.

"No—get Rudy's oyster boat . . . and three 55 gallon oil drums and three bags of sackcrete . . . And hurry—I want it over by morning."

By now our three friends, whoever they were, had enough. They were hired help, after all. They weren't buying our little drama but they couldn't be sure they hadn't fallen into the clutches of a pair of homicidal loonies. I looked appraisingly. The one on the end looked the worst for wear and I roughly tore the duck tape from his mouth. Putting my face up to his, I asked: "Where were you taking her?"

He couldn't blurt out directions fast enough.

"That better be right, Bubba." I went to the phone and called Marvin who was very unhappy. While I was explaining to him how, by fortunate happenstance, Tonto and I blundered by during the commission of a felony, a door slammed, an engine revved and a car zoomed out of the lot.

"That's our little bird; she's headed north on 17," Tonto said. I heard a motorcycle kick on.

"There goes Shapiro," he added.

About 25 minutes later Spooner arrived, blue lights and eyeballs flashing.

Chapter XXII

"Why don't you turn off those pulsing blue lights, Marv? All Gus's 'hourly' guests are climbing out the back windows."

"I'm beginning to think I can't trust you, Peete!"

"Trust me? C'mon, Marv—Tonto and I observed a felony in progress and after adroitly reconnoitering the situation, made a citizen's arrest..."

Marvin took a few minutes to look over the scene. "You just happened to be passing by? What happened to the lug nuts on the van?"

I shrugged.

"I suppose that you and Tonto just happened to have rolls of duck tape with you?"

"We did happen to have a roll in the glove compartment..."

"Damn it, why didn't you call me before?" When good Baptists start swearing you know they're really mad.

"Look, Marv—if we had called you what would have happened? You'd take them in, wait for their smart Yankee lawyer and then ask questions to the smart Yankee lawyer, who would (after a lot of jaw-boning) relay same to the Three Musketeers. Before we found out anything we'd be old men with long white beards. This likely lad at the end, who we'll call 'Porthos' for the purposes of our discussion, has seen the error of his ways and voluntarily turned state's evidence."

"Yeah—and what part of his anatomy were you 'turning' to convince him to perform this noble act?"

"Nothing, I swear . . . after the initial contact, which was in the heat of the moment, I never touched him. Look, let's continue this discussion later over a beer and tonic water. We know where they were taking her—I suggest we get there ASAP."

"Sarah Grey has run off?"

"Shapiro's on her trail. What is this, the United Nations? We've got to move—now . . . and without blue flashing lights."

Another cruiser showed up and Marv turned our three new pals over to a Deputy. I got into the Buick with Tonto and Marv followed in the cruiser. "He seems pretty mad," Tonto said soberly.

"This has been a lousy day—everybody is misinterpreting my good intentions."

About five miles north of Gloucester Court House we headed east on a secondary road for three or four miles. "Porthos" had identified the dirt road that led off into the dense woods. In the clearing was a single-wide mobile home with a big Lincoln parked off to the side, about as inconspicuous as a dinosaur. I trotted up the steps and knocked while Tonto ducked around to the back.

"Open the door in the name of the Law!" I shouted. Ever since I was a kid I wanted to do that. Who should open the door but a very distressed Alfie Sparrow.

"Alfie, old bean! Fancy meeting you out here in the bush." By this time Marvin was reading him his rights.

It was 7 A.M. before I finally got out of Marvin's office. Everybody was still mad at me. Of course even though Spooner had the four of them I recognized that the wheels of our legal system grind ponderously. It was all too tenuous. Sarah would have to sign the complaint against the three guys at the motel but some more stuff than Joel's seeing the Lincoln in the parking lot would have to be dug up to tie Sparrow with them. Marv was very unhappy.

Alfie was also pissed at me which was very unchivalrous. Even Tonto was sore because he didn't mind a little high jinks now and again but hated getting crosswise with the law. Contractors have to be careful of this sort of thing. Finally, last night's pizza was complaining. I asked Marv for an antacid and he said something very ungentlemanly.

Driving back to Avalon, unwashed, unshaven and with my clothing reflecting my arduous activities, I wasn't my usual example of sartorial splendor. I opined that by this time Miz Charlotte would be in the library, nose to grind-stone, for at least an hour. I figured it would be good for her soul to observe 'yours truly' in my current red-eyed state, dramatically attesting to my exhausting labors during the night whilst she tranquilly reposed abed.

Dimly I recalled that we had parted under less than ideal circumstances but that was yesterday. The balm of time should have narded up all tender areas and I was confident that the very sight of my pitiful form would melt her heart . . . wrong again! A withering look blasted me as I entered the library.

One of the greatest pundits of our age, Yogi Berra, said it all: "It ain't over till it's over!" To the masculine gender herein lies the definitive difference in all the realm of Yin and Yang. When two men carve each other up they either descend to the level of fisticuffs, or, more likely, break the engagement in smoldering resentment. When next they meet (provided fisticuffs haven't been resorted to) they feel a bit sheepish and try to ignore things. If this is unendurable, one might mutter: "I say, old chap—sorry about yesterday . . ." We are, as Professor Higgins rightly observed, "a truly marvelous sex."

I don't mean that God goofed when he made women out of an extra rib but it seems like he got distracted. Maybe the serpent was hissing in the weeds. Anyway he endowed all women whomsoever with a 10 jillion megabyte computer that gives them total recall and the masculine approach of "soonest forgotten, quickest mended" will never do. An autopsy is required with endless iterations of: ". . . and you said and I replied . . . ," or, what I hate the most, the quiz game: "Do you know what you said?" How the hell do I know, that was yesterday! How can they remember all those words?

I won't relate the carving of the corpse—or the exquisite details that were uncovered, recognized, considered, evaluated etc. When the dust settled I was exhausted. Miz Charlotte was considering going through it all again and I had to head that off at all costs. As she raised an accusing finger, I mumbled in desperation, "Alfie Sparrow's in the clink . . ."

Her finger was arrested in mid-flight.

"I beg your pardon?"

I had broken her serve! Like any good player I moved to exploit the advantage with everything I had. I related the night's activities in copious detail.

"Sarah Grey was getting ready to move . . . I figured you wouldn't want her whisked away before the game got started."

"Poor Alfred," she mused, "I'm sure that all this has done irreparable damage to our professional relationship."

The uneasy truce that followed was a real drag. For weeks I had anticipated how great it would be when Sarah got pitched out on her ear. Gad, what an imperfect world!

Precisely at noon, Sergei called. He disdained to bandy words with underlings and asked for Miz Charlotte. Sergei was looking for a little free information and I listened in awe to the conversation which was like hearing Cardinal Richelieu and Otto von Bismarck trying to steal each others pants. In the end Sergei asked for, and the chaste Charlotte granted, a 3 P.M. audience.

The big car arrived promptly on time and disgorged Sergei and party. I didn't want his simian friends in the library so I dispatched J. Fred and Bonzo to the kitchen where Dixie could feed them bananas or flatten them with a frying pan if they got rambunctious.

Sergei was a model of continental gallantry. His hair was plastered flat on his large head and his chin was shaved to a tone of blue steel. As he sat at the desk in his vanilla suit, hands folded over the head of his stick, the ferrule placed precisely between his out-pointed shoes; he reminded me of a shifty Roman art dealer. "Time prezzes, my dear lady, we can no longer stand the luxury of these games with your Dr. Peete."

"Games?' Miz Charlotte asked.

He shrugged. "Must I apologize for my taste for the rare and exotic? I covet the casket, as you do, but at cross-purposes we but add to our confusion and frustration. With our separate pieces of the puzzle we can see no pattern, but together. . . ."

"You're proposing a partnership?"

A look of primitive craftiness crossed Sergei's features. "But of course! It makes sense . . . I admit that I would take the prize if I could, but alas, that is impossible . . ."

I could tell that Miz Charlotte was intrigued, not with the idea but rather how Sergei's tortuous mind worked. "And how would we establish protocols, Sergei?"

"To start with facts; I know what the box is . . . your Miss Grey knows where it is. She obviously hasn't told you and intends not to. She wants it for herself."

"And, of course, you do not?"

He shrugged again. "Naturally I do, dear lady. We have one basic difference, however—you think that treasures belong to the masses, to be gazed at in public places by ignorant louts with no idea of their significance. What a travesty! They should be possessed by ones capable of savoring their true meaning and value."

"And who might be rich enough to pay for it?"

"Of course! You will forgive my bluntness but you have no qualms about enjoying the fruits of your success. The Corot hanging in the entry to this building is not being enjoyed by the common cattle."

Miz Charlotte's back stiffened a bit at this. "It was legitimately purchased," she said.

Sergei smiled unctuously. "Was it? I find questions of ownership abstract. The Mona Lisa was painted by an Italian and stolen by the French who legitimized the theft by declaring it a 'National Treasure.' Why relegate such rights only to governments? Look at my country. From bitter personal experience the rights of governments, rather than individuals, to appropriate things is not a persuasive argument."

"Then I fail to see how we can reach any accommodation."

Sergei again leaned forward with his slippery smile. "Of course it involves risk. I propose merely an exchange of information without further obligations. I reveal to you what I know, and you allow me to talk to Miss Grey."

"You realize, Sergei, that the girl doesn't have the box?"

"Of course."

So that was it! Kamaroff was dangling information in front of us solely to see and suborn Sarah (a laughable idea). How he proposed to seduce our Wild Irish Rose, I couldn't imagine but it might be instructive on the limits of human cupidity to watch those two together. Miss Benedict was basically after the same item—only she wanted to turn all this deception and greed to the advantage of "Truth, Justice and the American Way."

"You realize that Sarah Grey is a free agent, Sergei. I can't force her to talk to you."

"I ask for nuzzing more than your tacit cooperation."

"Very well—but now comes the question of sequence . . ."

Sergei waved his hand as if whisking away a fly. "To demonstrate my trust in your impeccable sense of fair play, dear lady, the box is, of course, the Casket of Alexander."

"Which, I believe, Dr. Peete has already pointed out to you." Miz Charlotte was really good. She said this with all the conviction of Carrie Nation at a Drys' Convention.

"And which neither you nor the good Dr. Peete really believe—but I do."

Reaching into his briefcase, Sergei extracted a fragment of parchment pressed between glass and passed it to Miss Benedict. Dying with curiosity, I looked over her shoulder. It was papyrus, and while I'm not as fast as Her Nibs at Greek, from the Iliad. "In early April, Mr. Fowler contacted me in Zurich concerning the casket. He said that he found three scrolls within: a copy of an ancient Iliad—a fragment of which you now see; Aristotle's commentary on the Iliad, and a *third* scroll that he said would stun the academic world."

"Fowler proposed to sell you the relic?"

Kamaroff scowled. "He sought an expression of interest. He also contacted Hammerschmidt as the subsequent activities of Herr Hammerschmidt's minions show . . ."

Charlotte slowly shook her head. "I still find it hard to believe."

"Many strange finds have occurred in our business. Now—may I please speak to Miss Grey?"

"I'm afraid that she's not here."

Sergei really lost his cool! "What do you mean? You said she was here!"

"No, Mr. Kamaroff—you inferred she was here. I said nothing whatsoever. I am not responsible for your assumptions. And I have no objection to your conversing with her when you find her."

The major explosion that was brewing was interrupted by the phone ringing. I picked up my receiver.

"Davy? This is Joel. Sorry I couldn't call before this . . ."

"Have you got that crab meat Miz Charlotte wanted?"

"Yeah, I sure do."

Chapter XXIII

Sergei went ballistic. Jumping up with a wild look in his eye, he was shouting in Russian and I hoped that Miz Charlotte didn't understand it because it sounded very ungentlemanly.

"Can you hold on?" I asked Joel.

Miz Charlotte's square chin was defiantly up but I could tell by her eyes that he was scaring the hell out of her. Moving quietly beside Kamaroff, I slipped a restraining arm-lock on him; the kind that doesn't hurt if you don't move but feels like you're going to break in four places if you do.

"Now, now—Sergei, let's not get excited."

Kamaroff went limp. With his two trained chimps in the kitchen getting a lesson in table manners from Dixie and with me calculating just how and where to break his arm, he reluctantly abandoned violence as a viable strategy. But there was still plenty of fire in his eyes. "You dried-up old bitch!" he said through his teeth. "Kamaroff has a long memory and a longer arm!"

I gave him a little jerk that brought him up on his toes. "You keep talking like that, friend, and I'll shorten your long arm by about twelve inches."

As we marched down the staircase, Sergei kept muttering things under his breath. After depositing him in the back seat of the limo, I invited his honor guard to leave and was pleased that they marched off like third-graders. There was a lot of shouting and arm waving but finally they took off down the drive. I made sure the gate was locked and went back to the library and the phone.

"Where did you go, out for a beer?" Joel was cranky.

"Where'd she go?"

"She went up to the supermarket and parked in the lot—she stayed until morning. It was the pits, man—have you ever sat on a motorbike in the dark for three hours? The mosquitoes . . ."

"Yeah, yeah, is she still there?"

"No, she drove north to Urbanna, to a motel."

So little Sarah was still in the game despite her harrowing experiences. "Suppose she takes off again, can you see the unit now?"

"Look, man—she's in bed. Can Tonto relieve me?"

"He was up all night too."

"Suppose I get Ernie?" Joel was getting desperate.

"You mean your ding-a-ling brother in law?"

"He's okay, boss—he follows orders pretty good."

Zooks, I thought, the 'Baker Street Irregulars'! "All right," I said reluctantly. "But tell him to call here, I want to talk to him."

The library was empty. Miz Charlotte was in her boudoir which was off the back hall on the way to the guest wing, probably for a stiff brandy (which she considered medicinal). Fortified but pale, she returned.

"Have they gone?" she asked, making a real stab at dignity and falling a bit short.

After clearly demonstrating that she still needed my services as "Official Greeter and Disposer" at Avalon, I was feeling more relaxed. "Yeah—you shouldn't take these lover's spats too seriously. I understand they're quite common . . . 'boy meets girl' . . . 'boy proposes to girl' . . . 'boy fights with girl,'"

"David shut up!"

"Look at the bright side, you've still got Oskar . . ."

"David!"

Fortunately the phone rang curbing my suicidal tendencies. It was Marvin. He wanted to know Sarah's whereabouts. I knew that if I told him, he'd have her brought in to straighten out last night's mess and heaven's knows when we'd get the ball rolling again. I crossed my fingers and said we were still looking.

"Now look, Davy," Spooner said, "don't play games with me on this one. I want that girl!" He rang off.

I napped at 6 P.M.—something I almost never do but who knows what games little Sarah might be playing that night? I wasn't completely there when the phone rang at 7 P.M. It was Spooner again and he sounded happy, which made me nervous. "Is this Dr. David Lee Peete?"

"No, this is Arnold Schwarzenegger."

"You know a New York lawyer named, Bernbaum, David?"

"Great Caesar's ghost!—not 'Banzai' Bernbaum!"

Marv was obviously savoring this moment. "He's in my office right now, jumping up and down and waving his arms. There's a little guy with big ears with him, a Mr. Aloysius Lacy, also from New York. Do you know him?"

"What is this, a quiz program?"

"Lacy has signed a complaint against you."

"What for?"

"Felonious assault."

That really hurt . . . to be charged when you haven't even enjoyed doing it! "You're kidding! I haven't touched him, besides he couldn't be assaulted, he travels with a gorilla about eight feet tall."

"If the gorilla's name is Dunlevy he's in Mary Immaculate Hospital . . . being reassembled. Lacy looks like he spent the night in a bowling alley—in the company of the pins. He signed a complaint against your pal Kamaroff *et al.*, for attempted murder, felonious assault and indecent language."

This really sounded like Kamaroff and his crew. "Gosh, they didn't hurt Miss Winters, did they?"

"Who's Miss Winters?"

"The Snow Queen . . . Anyway, I don't see what all this has to do with me?" I added innocently.

"She's okay, I think. And you're part of the 'et al.,' buddy. Bernbaum said that you knowingly and wittingly and with malice aforethought sent Lacy and company to accost Kamaroff while fully aware that said Kamaroff was a homicidal maniac and would 'accost' back."

"Oh for Pete's sake! I merely suggested that Mr. Kamaroff, as a connoisseur of antiquities, might be of some assistance to Mr. Lacy in his quest for knowledge and wisdom."

"I think I'm goin' to have to pick you up, Davy."

"Oh yeah? On what charge?'

"I'm thinking of putting you in protective custody. You'd be in and that would protect the community at large." He cradled his phone.

I had hit my nadir! Suddenly all the world was conspiring against me. Miz Charlotte's attitude toward me had all the warmth of an Arctic white-out; Marv Spooner was sore about Sarah's disappearance and planned to run me out of the county as a public nuisance; Tonto and Shapiro were ready to quit in disgust; even Dixie was mad at me for sending those two baboons to the sacred precincts of her holy kitchen during Kamaroff's visit, and now, out of pure spite, Awful Aloysius was passing up Miss Benedict's deep pockets to sic me with that fiend right out of hell, "Banzai" Bernbaum!

Fortunately for our side, Sarah Grey stayed put during the

bucolic Ernie's watch. I guess that she was as tired as I was. I got back to bed around midnight and was really tapped out. Max and I had a wonderful night.

I had Tonto relieve Ernie with my Buick since it had a phone. Meanwhile I plowed into the latest excavations of Professor Dorphmann at Troy. I was gripping my chair with excitement when the phone rang. It was Tonto.

"She's on the move—heading south on 17."

"Be careful, she'll be skittish about being followed."

"Don't worry, I'm giving her plenty of space. When we get past Gloucester I'll close up a little."

"Keep in touch." There was nothing to do but wait. If she went over the Coleman Bridge and out of the county, Tonto would call again.

"The bird is flushed," I said to Miz Charlotte.

She came out of deep submergence and blinked a few times. "Sarah Grey?"

"Yes ma'am."

After that even Dorphmann's scarlet prose couldn't hold my attention. I wanted to ask Charlotte what she thought of Sergei's claim about the box but that was taboo; Miss Benedict never made bricks without straw. The phone rang again.

"I thought she was headed over the Coleman Bridge but she hooked left just past the shopping mall and went to the beach."

"The beach!" This was too much!

"Yeah—there are people around and she just parked."

"Where are you?"

"I'm in the VIMS parking lot."

I scratched my chin and pondered. "I'll be there in a few minutes." I gave him the phone number in the Cadillac and took off.

The Coleman Bridge from Yorktown came right over

Gloucester Point and the beach. There was a single entry road that led down to the beach just past the Virginia Institute for Marine Science. Extending from the Point to the VIMS installation, the small beach on the York River was favored by the locals. At this time of year, day and night, there were plenty of people around. Past the bridge abutment and around the point was a public boat ramp and the large VIMS boat basin. Fifteen minutes later I slipped into the Buick beside Tonto in the VIMS parking lot.

If Sarah was finally going to make contact with Michael Walsh the beach wasn't a bad spot. Even at night there were fishermen using the pier with cars coming and going. They wouldn't be noticed. I was excited at the thought that Walsh might be in one of those parked vehicles.

"She's still there?"

"Yeah, she got out and walked around a little but she's not going for a swim this early in the year."

I kept trying to see into the other parked cars with my folding binoculars when Sarah started her engine.

"What the hell," I said.

She backed out and drove past us at a stately pace.

"You'd better follow her, Harry," I said, getting out of the Buick. "And for God's sake, don't lose her."

So she wasn't meeting with Michael Walsh—now. But if I were going to hold a conversation with that gent, I'd be very choosy about where. That was it, she was checking out the location. About twenty minutes later my car phone rang.

"Yes?"

"I think she's heading back to the motel. We've passed Gloucester on our way to Urbanna."

"Call me at Avalon when she gets there." Back at Avalon I sat at my roll-top desk and thought hard. Sometimes, even in my case, dim flickerings of intelligence may be observed. I had played this as far as I could. As it was, good old Marv was ready to have me tarred and feathered and ridden out of Gloucester on a rail. If things worked out, it probably would be okay (although scratch one sheriff and bass fishing buddy as a "friend"); If it went wrong I'd be in real trouble. I leaned forward and dialed Marv's number.

Chapter XXIV

"You'd better not be calling to tell me you know where Sarah Grey is, Peete!" greeted me. No salutation, no "how's things goin'" or anything like that . . .

"I know . . ." I said, holding the receiver at arm's length with my eyes scrunched shut until the metallic squawking began to subside. I thought I detected an interrogatory squawk. "Marvin?" I asked.

"Damn you, Peete! I had to let Sparrow and his bunch go!"

"Look Marv—Joel had a hard time following her and couldn't get to a phone. He . . ."

"Oh yeah? Where was she? In the Congo?"

"Worse—she's in a motel up in Urbanna . . ."

"I'm getting her to sign a complaint against Sparrow."

"I wouldn't do that, Marv. If you bring her in, you'll never see her again." I explained about her trip to Gloucester Point Beach. He was still breathing hard but at least he was listening.

"You think this is the meeting?"

"Yeah, I do. I think Grey has contacted Walsh and she picked the beach for the rendezvous because it's safer with all the people around."

"Once you get past the dead-end side roads, there's only one way in," Marv mused.

"Right, we'll have them in a sack. I think we ought to be patient, Marv. Sparrow isn't going anywhere—he'll be hanging around for the box. You might bag the Irish reptile and Walsh. If Walsh doesn't show you can run Grey in after she makes her play—Sparrow will still be there."

My impeccable logic won out and I settled down for another wait. Walsh must know that his departure from Ireland had been discovered along with his connection to Fowler and the box. Sam Kepler's murder, and I was sure it was murder, did that. His two main buyers, Sparrow and Kamaroff were here as was his main threat, Sarah Grey. The clock ticked on and Miz Charlotte was still testy.

We went down to supper at 7:30 P.M. The meal was grim, emphasized by the deafening click of silverware against the china. I poured myself a glass of port after supper; that always made me sleepy and it was a silent signal to Miz Charlotte that I didn't expect any action that night. As usual, I was wrong. The phone in the dining room buzzed.

"She's moving," Tonto said.

"Where are you?"

"We're turning south on 17."

"Keep in touch."

It would be close to 35 minutes before she reached the south end of the county. I dialed Marv's number. "She's heading south."

"That's a surprise, it's only 9:45."

"I'll meet you at the VIMS parking lot."

The beach was still alive with people. Of course the early Spring sun worshipers had long gone except for a cluster of frisky teenagers playing about in the dark. But the fishing pier was dotted with anglers with probably two dozen cars in the narrow lot. Marvin arrived in his personal wheels. He got out and sat in the back of the Cadillac with me.

"She's not here yet?"

No . . . You know, Marv, being as we're so helpful to you in all this, Miz Charlotte and I hope you'll be considerate . . ."

"Helpful!"

"Sure—look what we've set up. If things go down right old 'Stonewall' Spooner will have cuffed an international crook and probable murderer before sun-up. That's big time, pal . . . it'll look great on your résumé."

"The only consideration you deserve is about 6 months on the county road gang. What does Miz Charlotte want?"

"To look at the box. It's going back to Ireland but she wants to examine it first. You'll need an expert to look at it anyway and it won't cost the county a cent . . ."

"Here she comes!" Marv said. "What time do you have?"

"10:26."

She parked the old Chevy down in the lot in front of the fishing pier and Marv stepped over to his car and the police radio. When Tonto showed up we were all set.

Nothing happened. Now and then a car would come and we'd tense up, but it was always just a fisherman. An hour went by. Sarah got out of the car, walked around for a bit and stood under the lamp light at the foot of the pier. Then she returned to the car.

"What the hell's goin' on?" Marv said.

"He's not showing, damn it!"

The time crept toward midnight. Sarah did her little act under the light pole a number of times but it illicited no response. At midnight she switched on her engine and popped her lights. Marv got out and returned to his car. "I'm taking her, Davy," he said over his shoulder.

Sarah's car started on the upgrade and he pulled out in front of her, blocking the road. I walked down to the entry of the parking area where both vehicles were stopped. Marv got out and walked over, opening Sarah's door. "Step out please, Miss Grey."

"What's th' trouble—I've done naught," she lilted. Then she spied me. "You bastard, Peete!" she muttered.

"I'm taking you in for questioning, Miss Grey. You'll have an opportunity to call your Embassy and a lawyer if you wish," Marv said officially. Then he barked a few orders into his radio. A short while later two county cruisers came down the road. Marv leaned on the door of the first cruiser. "I want the area searched. Nobody leaves without giving proper ID. We're looking for a guy about 40, Irish, probably speaks with a brogue."

"Can Tonto and I help?" I asked. It was a good-sized area running around to the VIMS boat basin on the other side. There was no way of cordoning it off, except to vehicular traffic. Somebody on foot would be gone already.

One cruiser went around to the boat basin to check vehicles there while the other stopped in the beach parking area. The deputy went out on the pier to talk to the fishermen. Tonto and I started to check parked vehicles. The fifth one down was a Toyota sports van with tinted windows. A guy was sleeping in it and as I rapped on the window I got that old sinking feeling in my stomach.

He didn't move so I gave a whistle to the deputy. Moving cautiously around to the front, I shined my pencil flashlight through the windshield. The deputy sauntered over.

"What's up?' he asked.

"There's somebody in the van . . . dead, I think."

Everybody got excited after that. Tonto (being a man of parts) opened the locked van. He was a guy around forty, with light brown hair and a full beard. A round black hole decorated his right temple and in his right hand was a small, cheap, .22 pistol.

"He did it himself," one of the deputies commented.

"Don't bet on it," I said. "You'll lift his prints off the gun but I bet you twenty bucks you won't find power burns."

"I can't make head or tails of this," Marv said. "We were watching the girl the whole time—she didn't do it."

"Yeah, it looks like she didn't know he was in the car."

"So it must have happened before she got here."

"Unless it happened right under our noses," I said unhappily.

As we were talking, a police cruiser came slowly around the curve from the boat basin hidden behind the bridge abutments, its blue lights flashing.

"Now what the hell . . ." Marv said.

Behind the cruiser was a stretch black limo. Both cars parked near us and Marv walked over. The window of the limo slipped down and I saw the very unhappy face of Sergei Kamaroff.

"I found these guys parked over by the boat basin," the deputy said, "it didn't look right to me so I brung them over."

Kamaroff got out. He didn't see me, being fully absorbed by the uniformed deputies. He drew himself up to his full height, effecting the visage of an outraged diplomat. "Who's in charge here?" he demanded in his heavy Slavic accent. "What is the meaning of this—this travesty!"

"Howdy Sergei!" I called. "What are you guys doing, a little night crabbing? I bet your pals eat them alive, eh?"

Poor Sergei—I've become his nemesis, his evil genius. Every time he hears my voice something unpleasant happens. He probably figures if he ever does get the casket, when he opens it I'll jump out like a jack in the box!

"Guess what, Sergei? There's a dead body over there. You want to know who's in charge? You remember good old Sheriff Marvin Spooner? He's in charge. . . ."

None of this was making any sense. The corpse must be

Walsh. Sergei might think snuffing Walsh and taking his money back would be a peachy idea except a search came up empty of either the box or the bushel of money needed to purchase same. If Sergei didn't get it, why kill Walsh unless it was in a fit of pique because Walsh was selling it to Sparrow. Suddenly Marv's radio started squawking and he had a protracted conversation. Marv leaned against the side of the car and looked at me. "This is the damnedest mess I've ever seen. Who do you think they just picked up on Route 17?"

I took a wild guess. "Alfie Sparrow."

"Nuts! I told Joe Hogg in the other cruiser to hang around by the turn off to 17 and he saw a big Lincoln barreling out. Sparrow claims he wanted to look at the beach on a pleasant evening but saw all the police cars and decided to leave."

"I'll bet he did."

"He could have parked on one of those dead-end side roads and walked down to the beach to do his dirty work."

"My God, Marv, you're going to need a Greyhound bus to take all these suspects back to the courthouse!"

It was also obvious that Marv couldn't handle all this alone and he put in a call back at the ranch for assistance. Sparrow and company were escorted down to the beach and watching Sergei and Alfie sitting side by side in their separate limos trying to ignore each other was hilarious. I climbed into the back of the Caddy for a snooze—it was going to be another long night.

But I didn't sleep—for the first time parts of the thing began to come together.

Marv's detective contingent arrived and the whole business began all over. Spooner wrangled some space in the VIMS building and everyone was herded inside. I just had to peek at this bunch all together in one room. There they were in the reception area; an unhappy Sarah Grey with her arms folded defensively across her breast; Sergei planted in another chair like a stuffed wart-hog; Alfie still protesting the Gestapo-like tactics of the American police; plus assorted riffraff. It would make a great TV sitcom; they were all making believe they didn't know each other.

There were deputies with flashlights searching the point, collecting all kinds of tidbits while looking for the box and money that would have cooked Sergei's goose. They never found it.

One by one the suspects were paraded down from the lab to view the remains for identification. Nobody was dumb enough to own up on this point, but it was an interesting spectacle and I roused myself from a prone position to enjoy it. Kamaroff, Bonzo and J. Fred Muggs all looked at the body without the flicker of an eyelid. Sergei shrugged and muttered; "How would I know some person here? I'm Swiss." Alfie was filled with righteous indignation in his denial.

Then one of the deputies interrupted the proceedings with an elderly fisherman in tow. "A boat came into the ramp at around 9:30 last night. This guy was fishing nearby."

"What kind of boat?"

"I dint look close," the old bird replied, "I think it was a metal 'V' boat—it had an outboard . . ."

"What happened?"

"A guy came ashore and left."

"What did he look like?"

"I dunno. He come back about a half hour later an' took off."

Great! So somebody could have come from the water side . . .

Sarah Grey was finally hauled down and looked a little queasy in the bright lights as she stared at the husk huddled in the corner of the van.

"Do you know this man, Miss Grey?" Marv asked solemnly

"It must be Michael Walsh," she said hoarsely.

I couldn't take this any more. "Come on, Sarah. You know that's not Michael Walsh—that's *George Fowler*. . . ."

Chapter XXV

Sarah Grey was tough. After the initial jolt of my identifying the corpse as Fowler, she denied everything. But in the instant that I said it her mask slipped and I knew I was right.

But that wasn't what worried me. It was Marv. He was sore as hell. The banter about my assisting the county on a few public works projects at the end of a shovel wasn't so funny now. "Now, Dr. Peete, just how long did you know the deceased was Fowler and why did you feel the sheriff's office wouldn't be interested in this little item?" (The address, "Dr. Peete," chilled my spleen.)

"Look Marv, I know you feel I've been holding out . . ."

"That's a fair characterization, Dr. Peete. You've continually withheld vital information and this irresponsible action may have contributed to a homicide."

I could see the massive doors of "durance vile" swinging open. "How long did I suspect that Walsh might be Fowler? I'd figure about 120 seconds before I said so to Sarah Grey."

"That's convenient."

"It's true! What reason would I have for holding that out? I was in the Caddy thinking over all the screwy things about the whole business and then I walked down to watch you parade all of them out to look at the corpse. As Sarah approached it began to add up differently. Who knows how the mind works?"

I felt like I was swimming up a waterfall.

"Go on."

"Okay—I couldn't figure Walsh out. Here's this sneak thief who is clever enough to bump people off 'by accident.' Let's grant that Fowler tells him about the casket. Let's grant that Walsh is smart enough to know how to peddle it. Let's even assume that Fowler is stupid enough to tell him about Kamaroff and Hammerschmidt. What does Walsh do? He comes to America!

"That's crazy! His two potential buyers are in Switzerland so he comes here, to a country he doesn't even know? Why not go to Zurich, a town designed for shady deals with Swiss banks available—where he could throw a stone and hit either of his potential buyers? It was incredible.

"So Walsh heads for the Bahamas, but he knows his way around, doesn't he? In Miami he's clever enough to phony up a new identity. Pretty good for an Irish bozo who's spent his life holding up his end of the bar at 'Maggie's Bloomers'!

"It didn't compute. I thought he had an American partner, like Steiner, to help him over the rough spots. But that wouldn't explain why he didn't take the easier route straight to Zurich.

"Then we come to Sarah Grey. She's been in mortal danger from the beginning, yet she's hung in there. She's had an attempt on her life, not to mention the threats to her comfort represented by Sparrow and Kamaroff but she's still here. Why?

"And lastly—why do in Father Courtney? Maybe it's because he'd know the corpse in the Slaney wasn't Fowler . . .

"This stuff was bubbling around in my head with a few obscure facts I had lost track of with all the other garbage—like the infamous Bend Sinister and skeleton's with broken necks.

"I'm convinced that Sarah Grey and Fowler had a thing going. When I asked her about Fowler, she told me he made advances and she virtuously re-buffed him. I don't think so. I think they were playing 'patty-cake' to pass the time. If she's so virtuous why was she typing and editing for this randy American who was trying to get her to bed?"

Marv started to say something but I held up my hand.

"Hear me out, Marv. The next fact that I lost was that when Fowler went missing, Sarah and Father Hugh went to the Garda. She said Father Hugh identified the corpse but the document on Fowler's inquest said that *Sarah Grey* identified the corpse! When I got the papers from Ireland that didn't sink in—but in the back of the Caddy I remembered it . . ."

"So you think it was Michael Walsh in the Slaney?"

"Sure I do. Look at the setup. Sarah goes to the police to declare an American visitor named Fowler to be missing. A body is found in the Slaney with Fowler's ID. Sarah identifies the corpse as Fowler. Michael Walsh, the drifter, wanders off . . . who cares?"

Spooner scratched his jaw in thought. Maybe I wouldn't be getting one of those suits with the horizontal black and white stripes after all. . . . "So they were in it together," he mused.

"I think so. They find the reliquary and Steiner and Father Hugh won't let them open it. Steiner wants to hog the glory and Father Hugh wants to see the Bishop. Fowler and Grey see it slipping away. So they steal it and open it—it looks like big time! Fowler knows about Kamaroff and Hammerschmidt. Anyone in our business hears about them. He flies to Zurich to peddle it, contacting both Hammerschmidt and Kamaroff with samples. But there are real problems. He doesn't know Zurich, it's not his home turf. Also, Father Hugh and Steiner know about the relic; the priest will go to the Bishop, Steiner to the Garda. I think he told Hammerschmidt about this little problem so Oskar sends Sparrow to make sure that Steiner gets lost and keeps his mouth shut."

Spooner shook his head. "But neither Sparrow nor Kamaroff identified the corpse as Fowler . . ."

"This is a murder investigation—they're not stupid."

"But why didn't Steiner go to the Garda at once?"

"Because he's as greedy as the others and thought he could get it back. He's after the glory, not the money, but he sees it slipping away just as they did. So he waits a bit to see what's happening. Then Sparrow sends Algie Duncan to scare the hell out of him. He's been in hiding ever since.

"But Fowler still had Father Hugh to worry about. Steiner might be scared off but priests are different. There's a whole different chemistry there, isn't there? The Bishop could cause an uproar with the police looking a lot closer into the body in the Slaney. At all costs, Fowler had to silence Father Hugh."

"And you think he did?"

"I do."

"And he tried to finish Sarah Grey also—why?"

"C'mon Marv—you can think of as many reasons as I can . . . greed, fear of exposure, misogyny . . ."

Marv was silent for a few moments. "So Fowler decided to keep it all for himself . . ."

"I think so. I don't think that Sarah was in on the Walsh business but he talked her into identifying the body even though it was all a bit too convenient. Then they cooked up the 'disappearance of Walsh.' But in the end, she was a threat—just like Father Hugh and Steiner."

"And he tried to get her by running her down with a truck?"

"Right. He must have figured it was all over when he muffed that, but she didn't go to the Garda. He completely misjudged the avarice of Little Molly Malone there! She came to us instead . . ."

While Marv still wasn't happy, he bought it. I exaggerated

when I said that I cottoned to the idea only two minutes before Sarah made her bogus identification of the corpse; it was really closer to twenty minutes before that, but the fact remained that I passed it to Spooner in a reasonable time.

By 7 A.M. the sun was warming the York River and the morning rush-hour traffic was rumbling over the Coleman Bridge. The box was still missing so Marv and I drove to Avalon to see if Miz Charlotte had any ideas from her vast experience at finding stuff. We staggered into the library looking like Butch Cassidy and the Sundance Kid on the run.

"Great Scott!" she said from behind her pedestal desk. "Is this going to be a nightly occurrence?"

"Walsh, who is really Fowler, is dead," I said.

She looked quietly from one stubbly chin to the other. "Tell me."

So we told her the whole bloody business. Miss Benedict was in top form and it was like feeding data into a computer. There was no: "Gosh!" or "Oh, I say!" or "Well I'll be dashed!" —all the gears just clicked and hummed.

"We've got to find that casket, Miz Charlotte," Spooner said quietly. "It doesn't solve what happened, but it's central to any legal steps to be taken—like indicting anyone."

"Have you let them all go?"

Marv wilted a little. "Yes ma'am—I've nothing to hold them on. I've told them not to leave town. You know what I'm worried about? That it's not here—that it's in Ireland."

Miss Benedict shook her head. "I think it's here, Marvin, and probably close by. Don't all these people at our modest beach facility suggest anything?"

"You mean they were all here by appointment?"

"Yes. Fowler had reached the point where he had to move with some dispatch. It was all coming apart, wasn't it? He had pulled it off rather well but that sort of thing wouldn't last forever. He never knew what dear Sarah might do. Sam Kepler somehow tipped him off that his identity as Tebaldi was unraveling. He had to get in touch with Sparrow and Kamaroff quickly."

"But how would he know they were here—in Tidewater?"

"With a few phone calls to Zurich. After all, they wanted to contact him too. But their interest in Sarah Grey must have been unnerving to Fowler. If Sparrow or Kamaroff ever found out about Walsh from dear Sarah, it could really complicate things."

"So he arranged to see them all last night?"

"Why not? 'If it be done, it best be done quickly.' He probably staggered the timing; he'd see Sarah at, say, 10 P.M.; Kamaroff at 12 P.M. and Sparrow at 2 A.M. . . . something like that. But he'd never have the box with him. Once the bargain had been struck there would be further, more complicated, exchanges of commodity and fee. Tell me, Marvin, did you find out where he lived?"

"We got a latch key. It fits a lock—somewhere, in what—a fifty-mile radius?"

"That's what you'd best concentrate on, Marvin, the key. And one other thing—I would hold all detailed information on the happenings at the beach close. I would release no details to the press."

That wasn't much help but it was all that poor old "Stonewall" Spooner was going to get.

We settled down again to waiting. Sooner or later something should turn up. Fowler bedded down somewhere and eventually a motel owner would wonder where he'd gone off to—unless Fowler checked out incident to making the deal and immediately moving on. Then we might never know. The police were far better equipped for this sort of thing than we.

Chapter XXVI

Marv circulated the details through the local "Crime Watch" network and I admit that I was dumbfounded when it hit pay dirt in less than 36 hours. He called me on the phone: "I think maybe we've found Fowler's hole," he said.

"Where?"

"In Virginia Beach, near Pungo on the Carolina border."

"How did you come up with it?"

"Through the Virginia Beach Police. A guy named George Smith, known around there as 'Grumpy,' rented a room to him."

"'Grumpy'?"

"Do you want to come—I got clearance to see him."

"Yeah, I sure do . . ."

Marv and I found Grumpy's place without difficulty since he was advertised with signs up and down the route. His far-flung financial empire reached out like the tentacles of an octopus into almost every area of commerce. There was "Grumpy's Bait & Fishing Boats"; "Grumpy's Outboard and Lawnmower Repair"; "Grumpy's Fresh Vegetables"; "Grumpy's Chimney Cleaning Service," etc., etc. Reaching the hub of all this activity I expected a grim, soot-covered mill with a forest of stacks belching black smoke. Instead we meandered off onto a dirt track and picked our way through the hulks of old automobiles and clucking chickens to a tin-roofed cottage. The door was answered by a behemoth gal, weighing as much as Marv and I together and who could pitch us both and the car back out on the state road.

We were directed to a detached garage cum workshop out back where, at last we met the enterprising Mr. "G." Smith, Esq. He was short and wiry, bald, with a big nose, a receding chin and a moustache comprised of only individual hairs that grew any way they wanted. Little beady eyes swept us from head to foot with probably a better appraisal of our combined net worth than Dun and Bradstreet.

"I'm Sheriff Spooner from Gloucester County."

Grumpy was disappointed. He was hoping we were two dumb city slickers with a dirty chimney. All his dreams of selling us stainless steel flues at $70 a foot went out the window. He spat tobacco juice at our feet.

Taking this as a gesture of friendly greeting, Marv continued. "I understand you rented a room to a Mr. Tebaldi?"

"'T were mother's room . . . she passed on." Old Grump didn't let any grass grow under his feet; he probably rented it before the old girl's bed was cold.

"We'd like to look at the room, please."

"Understand he were done in? You kin look at th' room but don't take nothin'. He owed me fer two weeks."

I'll bet he did, I thought. Grumpy had all the predatory instincts of an African vulture. He took us to an add-on wing with a separate entry. A grim room with an old bed, a curtained recess for a closet, a battered ancient dresser with a portable black and white TV standing on a tiled floor, was Fowler's cell. He would have been better off in jail. Looking through the windows with their broken venetian blinds, I could see the workshop.

"How long was he here?" Marv asked and Grumpy began frantically to calculate his two weeks back rent.

"He come three weeks ago yesterday . . ."

"What did he tell you about himself?"

"He dint say nothin' much. Said he were lookin' fer work—sellin' stuff. Had Florida plates on th' van. Said he weren't sure he were stayin' here abouts."

"Did he go out every day, looking for work?"

"He did some. Went out at night o'course."

"Say where he went?"

"Nope. His business, not mine. I'm worryin' over my rights, Mister, he owed me fer two weeks. I got a right to keep his things." Grumpy was about a subtle as a bull peeing on a flat rock.

"You can take that up with the proper authorities, Mr. Smith. As for now, nothing belonging to Mr. Tebaldi is to be touched—absolutely nothing. I should remind you that this is a murder investigation and any tampering with evidence carries stiff penalties." Grumpy was *very* unhappy with that.

There was nothing in the bedroom. He had some old clothes but no papers, no box, nothing that would distinguish him from the 280 million or so other Americans wandering about.

"We'll look around a bit, Mr. Smith," Spooner said.

Grumpy was addled at this. He figured Fowler had stashed a bank heist somewhere but he had to be careful since he was a bottom brick of the commercial world hereabouts. While Marv poked around the outside of the house, I wandered back to the workshop. Neatness didn't count with the Grump and parts of internal combustion engines were strewn everywhere with tools and other paraphernalia. It looked like the Battle of El Alamain. One wall had bins filled with odd-sized junk protruding in random fashion.

"Them's my parts bins," Grumpy muttered.

"Yeah, I can see all the stock numbers." I got a beat-up ladder and set it on the dirt floor behind the cluttered counter to have a look.

"Don't take none of that stuff—it's valuable."

"You ought to take some of this old junk and bronze it, Grumpy—to make lamps and sell to the tourists."

"You think so?" he asked. Gad, I had hit upon an avenue of commerce that the Grump hadn't thought of yet! I could tell by the light in his beady little eyes that I had achieved new heights in his estimation.

I spotted it on the top shelf, pushed toward the back of a deep bin behind some mechanical junk. It was a metal box of the size we wanted, painted with a thick black enamel with chips and scratches showing a greenish substance underneath.

"What's this?" I asked.

"It's my . . . my . . ." Grumpy stammered.

I carried it down and put it on the counter. "Look, Grump," I said, "I'll give you a little free advice—this here is a murder investigation, you get side-ways in this thing and you might find yourself in charge of all the lawnmowers up at the State Farm. Hey Marv!" I called.

Spooner came into the workshop a few minutes later. "Is that it?" he asked quietly.

"I think so—I haven't opened it."

"Take a look."

It was strapped shut with two heavy luggage belts and the seam between the lids was sealed with a heavy commercial tape. Slitting this I gingerly lifted the lid. It was packed with envelopes of chemical drying material and beneath that, in plastic bags, were the scrolls.

"Bingo!" I said.

THE BEND SINISTER

* * *

As I held the casket in my hands a mighty strange feeling came over me. If it was what Kamaroff and Sparrow thought, other hands had been placed on it in the past—some over 2300 years ago ... Darius, Alexander, the people in Byzantium and even nasty Count Odo himself. More sobering and closer to home, the blood of four people that I knew of stained its existence.

I sat in the back of Marv's cruiser, behind the steel cage with the thing on my lap. I bet it gave my fellow Gloucesterites a thrill; they probably figured that at last Marv was hauling me off to toss me in the county oubliette.

Before we left Pungo, I couldn't resist one parting shot at poor old Grumpy. He had looked at the old enameled box and scratched his head. "Is that worth sumpin', Mister?"

"I don't know ... 10 million, maybe ..."

I had ruined his entire life forever. Poor old Grump had been cleaning carburetors in Fort Knox all this time and didn't know it. He wanted to do away with himself but couldn't decide amid the gas stove, shooting himself, self immolation or a swim with concrete boots. I left him pondering.

Miz Charlotte frequently worked on old manuscripts and the "clean room" she had constructed in a small storeroom off the library was her pride and joy. It had sensitive humidity and temperature control and the air conditioning was designed to maintain a slight overpressure keeping out any dust laden air.

I silently placed the box into her quivering hands. There was no smart-aleck dialogue—she just went to the section of the bookcase that concealed the door to the clean room and popped it open. Since then I haven't seen her for days. Every once and a while I rap on the molding and shout: "If you're still there, rap back ... once, if your still alive ... twice if you're dead!"

Time passed microscopically. Being alone in the library was like sitting in an empty cathedral. Fortunately, Marvin came at least once a day. Needing answers, he couldn't understand the ponderous wheels of Academia.

Miz Charlotte was Olympian, but she's not that Olympian. Even she visited the little girl's room now and then. So biding my time, I ambushed her for a limited conversation. The next time Spooner showed up I was waiting.

"The authenticity of the scrolls is yet to be established."

"What the hell, David, how long does it take?'

I shrugged. "How should I know, I'm just mortal, you know. I don't go into sealed rooms and commune with Zeus."

"Well, I don't have forever."

"I know, I know," I held up my hands, "and I pointed this out to the Great One."

"And?"

"And she said, quote: 'Illusion is Reality,' unquote."

"Oh great! Chinese Philosophy! What the heck is that supposed to mean?"

"It means that whether the relic is authentic or not is not so important as whether folks *think* it's authentic. If it is a forgery, the quality is such that you have a case."

"So she thinks we could proceed?"

"Right! She's not ready to commit herself yet. What's she's saying is regardless of the outcome of her investigations, you've got a motive."

Marvin slumped back in his chair. "That's great—and that's all we've got . . ."

"No glimmers, eh?"

"Not a danged thing. Any of them could have done it. I was wondering—do you think Grey could have hoodwinked us?"

"Hoodwinked? How do you mean?"

"At the beach, in the beginning I was really watching her every move, but as time passed, I'm not so sure. She did get out of the car. How much time does it take to blow some guy away?"

"Aw, c'mon, Marv—under our noses?"

"If you had to swear in a court of law with maybe a life hanging in the balance, could you say it was impossible?"

"Well I . . ."

"The van was parked on the other side of that guys camper. We were a little higher up but it was still almost completely shielded."

"But why would she hang around, she'd be off like a shot?"

"Maybe—maybe she *knew* we were there."

I was getting more and more confused.

"Any one of them could have done it, Davy. Kamaroff was there. Sparrow could have sneaked down in the shadows. Somebody could have come by boat. Sarah Grey could have blown him away while we sat there. I've got bad vibes about this whole thing!"

After Marv left I felt lousy. I had really screwed him up. Guilt is an awful thing cause there's no place to hide—it's chained to your being. Had I caused this? Should I have just left the whole thing to Marv?

Of course we were successful. We followed the trail of the box from the crypt through the deaths of Father Hugh, Kepler, Walsh and Fowler; from Ireland to the Bahamas to Florida and finally here. We had beaten everyone to it and now it reposed under Miz Charlotte's penetrating view.

If we were so successful, why did I feel so guilty? Because maybe our mixing in the thing had also drawn all these characters to the Gloucester Point Beach—and murder?

When in doubt—eat. I went to the kitchen and sat a while Dixie, the Oracle of Avalon, made me a ham sandwich.

"What are you moonin' about, Davy?" she asked bluntly.

"Oh, nothing. It's this business at the beach. I feel sort of responsible."

"What do you mean, *sort of*? Either you is or you ain't."

"I guess I is."

"Did you cause it?"

"Well—cause sounds pretty strong. Contributed would be better. I sure made a mess for Marv."

"An' you're feelin' guilty?"

"Yeah, I guess so . . ."

"That's the way you're *supposed* to be feelin', young man. That's th' way th' Good Lord made you. All these psychologist folks keep sayin', 'We gotta eliminate guilt,' so they works overtime tryin' to 'splain to folks why they ain't responsible fer nothin'. They drink an' shoot drugs cause their mamas dint love em. They tear up the schoolhouse cause they got 'glands'! That's nonsense, Davy. You feels bad cause the Good Lord 'spects you to feel bad when you done wrong. Sounds to me like you was so busy gettin' what you wants, you dint care what happens to other folks."

"That's great! I come down here for a little solace because I feel rotten and you tell me I'm supposed to."

"In this life you gets 'sactly what you deserves—you sows an' you reaps."

"So what am I supposed to do?"

"What do you mean . . . do? Don't just sit there on your behind, man—go fix it!"

Chapter XXVII

Sitting in the library watching the clean room entry for hour after hour was maddening. I felt like Ahab waiting for the White Whale. I had to get Miz Charlotte off the academics and on the case so I prepared an impassioned speech that would move her. It was a bit maudlin but reeking with all the old-fashioned virtues that she held dear. I kept polishing it and telling myself, no smart-mouthed commentary, no matter what the provocation.

I decided that even my eloquence might be improved if I spiced it up with a good quote or two from Robert E. Lee (whom Miss Benedict greatly admired). I was atop a library ladder, reviewing a quarto tome, with another firmly between my knees when the bookcase opened and the Lady of the Manor sailed out.

Carpe diem! Striking a heroic pose and in my best stentorian delivery I started with a quote from Marse Robert: "And I say to you: 'Duty is the sublimest word in our language. Do your duty in all things. You cannot do more. You should never wish to do less'!"

She stopped and blinked up at me. "Be careful, David, you'll break your neck up there. See if you can get Marvin Spooner."

I was stopped just as I was raising my finger to add emphasis to my deathless eloquence . . . "What do you want him for?"

"To see if we can unravel this mess. The trouble with you, David, is that you have no civic responsibility."

Marv didn't need much persuading. He arrived, if possible, more unhappy than he was before. "What about the box?" he asked.

"That can wait," Miz Charlotte said briskly. "Where do you stand on the beach investigation?"

"Nowhere—I can't make a case against any of them. They all decided it was a lovely night to visit the beach."

"What about physical evidence?"

"Fowler was murdered. There were no powder burns on his hand. The pistol's a 'Saturday night special' a .22 cal. derringer type with four barrels and a rotating firing pin. It sells for about $95 and I'd be afraid to shoot the danged thing."

"Any possibility of tracing the sale?'

Marv rubbed the bridge of his nose. "We're looking . . ."

"Are Sparrow and the rest still here?'

"Yeah, but not for long. If I had something, I might be able to hold them as material witnesses. I'm afraid it's all over."

"Oh, it's not as bad as all that."

"Really, why not? In a day or so they'll all be going."

Miz Charlotte shook her head. "We'll keep them here."

"And how are y'all goin' to do that, may I ask?" he jerked his thumb at me. "Have 'Rambo' over there kidnap them?"

"A good general," Charlotte said pedantically, "always seeks out the weaknesses in his enemies' dispositions. If there is one weakness in this affair, it's greed. The chains of greed, Marvin, are stronger than any legal chains you might forge."

Then she laid out the screwiest idea she had ever come up with, and that took some doing. We figured she'd finally flipped, so she patiently explained and reexplained without getting excited. Of course the charade might turn into a fiasco, but she was willing to try. Marvin assented mainly because it was either this or maybe a witch doctor.

When it started to move, like most things when Miz Charlotte set her hand to the plow, it moved with dispatch. Doc Ravensford, the Benedict family physician, was called and after a protracted conversation was in the boat. Miss Benedict then called Mr. Mumpers of the Dickensean firm of Mumpers, Mumpers and Thornwhistle who handled her legal affairs. After being resuscitated poor old Mumpers also agreed.

We had more trouble with Dixie than anyone. Dixie is one of those straightforward types who doesn't get confused by modern thinking. Either something is right or wrong and she didn't need anyone to figure it out for her. In the end, after judiciously reviewing the plan, she made the call to WAVY TV.

Televisions were verboten in the library (Miz Charlotte maintained that its cultural potential was forever destroyed when the sitcom was inflicted on us) but that night a special dispensation was given. It happened about a third of the way through, before the break between the top of the news and the weather. Alveta Ewell intoned: "On a somber note, WAVY TV learned today of the death of Dr. Charlotte Montaigne Benedict, the noted antiquarian and art expert. Miss Benedict, a native Virginian, unexpectedly passed away at her home on the Middle Peninsula."

At 10 A.M. the next day, Oskar called from Zurich. "Iss it true, Dr. Peete—this terrible report that I have heard?"

"Yeah, it was pretty numbing, but in a way she's better off. It was a massive stroke."

"Terrible."

"Yeah, it was—she was working on the casket, you see . . ."

"The casket!"

"Didn't Alfie tell you? We found it . . ."

"I see . . ." Oskar sounded like his world had ended.

"Life goes on, Oskar. You don't mind my calling you Oskar, do you? I have to see to all the business details and such. It's such a responsi . . ."

"Business details?"

"Look Oskar—there's a downside and an upside to everything. Now you take the casket. What in the world should I do with a thing like that?"

"You know what Miz Charlotte would wish."

"Sure, but it really didn't belong to her, did it? I mean, ownership seems to rest with the guy who has it last. I was talking to Kamaroff the other day about the concept of ownership . . ."

"Why not come to Switzerland and we could discuss the question?"

"Oh, I'd love to but I can't get away right now, Oskar."

"Then I'll send my Mr. Sparrow . . ." Oskar was getting eager.

"Can I be completely honest, Oskar? I haven't been overly impressed with your Mr. Sparrow. I was thinking perhaps of a discussion here at Avalon. I'd love your input. That way I'd be sure that a neophyte like me was doing the right thing."

He belly laughed. "You're a scoundrel, Dr. Peete. I see the possibilities of a long and prosperous relationship."

Miz Charlotte and I replaced our phones simultaneously.

"Oskar took your demise very well considering his deep amorous feelings. But then he always had a stiff upper lip."

"Stop being ghoulish, David."

"Like I said to Oskar, life goes on."

I figure there are two kinds of crooks, the honest ones and the dishonest ones. The best example of this is Oskar Hammerschmidt and Sergei Kamaroff. Now Sergei is a good honest crook. He has no phony delusions about his crookedness; he lies, cheats and steals to make more doubloons than the next guy. Not being fettered by useless baggage like a conscience, he just slithers along. Oskar, on the other hand, is as big a crook, but he makes believe that he's not, or what he does (no matter how dirty) he really should be doing cause he deserves it. Which meant my approach to Sergei Kamaroff, the most honest of all the honest crooks I ever met, was more to the point. He was still at the Lafayette when I put the call through.

"Sergei, I'm glad I caught you before you left. This is Peete."

Sergei said something in Russian.

"Don't be grumpy, Sergei. Have you heard the terrible news? Miss Benedict is dead . . ."

"Dead!"

"Dead, kaput . . . finished. She dropped dead yesterday while working on the casket."

Dead silence. . . .

"I really appreciated your help the other day . . . working together, uncovering the great mysteries and truths of history."

"You have the casket?"

"Yeah—I was telling Oskar about it a little while ago. I've got the casket, Sergei, and you know what? Nobody knows about it but Miz Charlotte and me . . . and now Miz Charlotte knows about it in heaven. Are you interested in a little dealing?"

Sergei got oily. "Suppose I come over?"

"Don't bother, Sergei, my mind is running more along the lines of an auction. I'll let you know and be sure to bring plenty of kopecks." I rang off.

Miss Benedict hadn't been on the line. "Sergei was really choked up and could hardly talk. He wants the casket as a reminder of you. Do you want Lacy?"

"Oh yes, and Steiner too. We need to have them all present."

"Gosh—just like in the mystery stories, trite but exciting. Can I play the part of the master detective, Dr. Falstaff Merridue, and say . . . 'Someone in this room is a murderer' . . . ? And then watch all the shifting eyes."

"I don't think so, David, as I recall Dr. Merridue is usually about 20 stone. It's a question of type-casting."

"We can get Lacy but I don't know about Steiner."

She was silent for a moment. "Let's let Marvin handle him," she said at last. "He can exert pressures that we can't."

I had a score to settle with Lacy. I was still sore about him siccing that hellhound Bernbaum on me. I put the call through and got warm-hearted Miss Withers. "Is he there? This is Dr. Peete," I asked.

"With respect to what, Dr. Peete?"

"Suppose you put him on and I'll tell him."

"I'm Mr. Lacy's confidential assistant. If you tell me I'll pass it to him—if appropriate."

"Oh well, it's not important. It's about the casket that he wanted and I now possess. Just forget the whole thing." I hung up.

Miz Charlotte looked up. "He wouldn't talk to you?"

I held up a finger and in about 30 seconds the phone rang. I picked up the receiver. "Dr. Peete," I said.

"Dr. Peete? This is Miss Withers, I . . ."

"One moment, Miss Withers, I'll put on my confidential assistant." I clicked her on hold and than switched her back, pitching my voice to a falsetto. "This is Myrtle . . ."

"Will you please get Dr. Peete back on the line . . ."

"I'm sorry," I cooed sweetly, "Dr. Peete never confers with underlings—Is Mr. Lacy there?"

"If he'll just . . ."

"I'm sorry," Myrtle chirped, "have a nice day." I hung up again.

It took a little longer for the phone to ring again. I picked it up. "Peete here."

"What the hell is going on, Peete . . ."

"Is this Lacy?"

"Yes, I . . ."

"Then shut up and listen. Benedict's dead and I have the box. It's available for auction here at Avalon on Wednesday night. Call when you get in for further instructions and bring plenty of dough!" I slammed down the receiver.

Miz Charlotte was watching with rapt attention. "You know, David, you really ought to bequeath your brain to science. The abnormal psychologists could have a field day. . . ."

The other cats and dogs were swept up. Sarah was very snappish until I mentioned that the tables would be groaning. It was interesting to watch fear battling it out with gluttony. Gluttony won. Marv tracked Steiner and the good professor had other pressing engagements until Marv started talking about subpoenas. So we pushed toward a dramatic climax or a big fizzle. Marv was nervous as a cat but once committed, he stuck to it.

When the big evening arrived, he camped in my room with Max and put one of his deputies by the back door to the library, out of sight. Miz Charlotte planted herself in the clean room where she could play with her scrolls during the times when things got boring.

Marv had me wired for sound. He wasn't going to miss anything if he could help it and, in addition, he had the library bugged so that you couldn't burp in it. He was recording but he had headsets for himself and Miz Charlotte.

The party was by invitation only—no goons or baboons allowed. Hammerschmidt, who had flown over from Zurich, brought Sparrow, of course, and we made an exception permitting Lacy to bring Miss Withers because Lacy never appeared in public without Miss Withers or his pants. Out of sheer meanness I told Lacy she could come but without her lap-top computer. Miss Withers without her lap-top would be as nervous as Lady Godiva with a hair cut.

As a final obeisance to convention, we put suits on Tonto and Shapiro. Tonto passed muster but the L. R. was something else. "You can dress 'em up" . . . etc.

Chapter XXVIII

Kamaroff arrived first. Sergei had a very straightforward nature and when he wanted something, he made a beeline. Bonzo and J. Fred were with him and I held up my hand. "No way, Sergei—only you or beat it."

Sergei was unhappy but then Sergei was always unhappy. After our last session in the library he didn't want to go up there without his blocking backs, but he acquiesced. I saw his pals off the grounds and led him to the front door which was festooned with an old-fashioned black wreath. I thought it added a touch of class. Kamaroff looked at it and stopped momentarily, an inquisitive look on his face. "Is she . . . ?"

It was delightful, Miz Charlotte was listening to every word. "She was cremated yesterday—a very private service. I don't like bodies around, they can get dug up."

Sergei looked at me, his eyes filled with unfeigned admiration . . . he figured I had poisoned the old girl to get the box.

Tonto did the honors. We don't believe in electronic sensors and the searching was done by hand. Sergei was then invited to the dining room where a buffet and bar had been set up.

Sarah Grey came next and primly objected to being searched which didn't impress us very much. Dixie, who was mad as hell, did the frisking. I wasn't taking any chances; Sarah might have a hand grenade in her bloomers. She passed in and I saw our first mistake in not wiring the dining room. The conversation between our Irish adder and Sergei was lost to posterity.

Steiner pulled up and I was interested in this bird since I had never met him. He was medium build with pop eyes, dark brown hair suspiciously without a strand of gray, and a very huff and puff air. He squeaked at the search and I pulled him gently aside to a corner of the entry hall. "We're so glad you came, Professor Steiner, but one word about your being invited by the police and we'll make more trouble for you than you ever dreamed of."

He sputtered and I could tell he was good at it—that and taking umbrage; he was obviously a master umbrage-taker. I'm sure it struck terror in the hearts of all undergraduates but I was unimpressed. Like a puffing lizard, after inflating and turning purple, the show was over . . . no fangs.

Hammerschmidt came fashionably late. Probably six feet, three inches in height, he was a picture of sartorial perfection in an expensive black suit with a white carnation, which was a nice touch for the solemn occasion. I judged him to be about sixty, elegantly handsome with a small goatee beard hiding any sag around the jowls. His perfectly cut suit also masked any signs of dissipation caused by his Epicurean life style. Alfie danced around him and seeing them together set me chuckling; Alf reminded me of Oskar's man, "Crumpet."

Of course packing hardware was beneath contempt with Oskar but he amiably submitted to a search. What should we find on dear old Alfie, however, but an ankle holster with a small Beretta.

"Oh, I say, bad form, Alfie," I muttered. Oskar thought it was all very amusing. Then he got a bit maudlin.

"I can't believe she's really gone, Peete," he said with a hint of the sibilant. "The world has lost a great mind and a fine lady."

"Buck up, Oskar, we're both going to our rewards."

Oskar started chuckling but held it in out of propriety. I was afraid he might fracture a blood vessel. "You're a rascal, sir . . . a true rascal!" he said.

Lacy and Miss Withers showed up last. I enjoyed the liver-colored patches on his face even though they were starting to fade. Without her lap-top, Miss Withers didn't know what to do with her hands. Unarmed and defenseless in a cruel world she looked warily about, expecting to be attacked at any moment by CPA's in war paint. During the search she reacted with all the sensitivity of a manikin; I had forgotten her nerve endings were disconnected.

The dining room had taken on the appearance of a cocktail party. Sarah Grey hit the table and ate her way about a third of the way down. Steiner was explaining to Hammerschmidt how he was an expert on nearly everything and Miss Withers had just tossed down her third club soda in wild abandon. I watched admiringly as Oskar, like an old bull walrus, elbowed Sarah aside and landed on the oysters, tusking up a half bushel or so. When everyone reached the proper level of conviviality, I went to the door.

"Ladies and Gentlemen, I hate to be a wet blanket but it's time to move to a more profitable time of the evening. Y'all are invited to follow me to the library. Please bring your drinks or build a fresh one if you wish."

Up the stairs I went, through the double doors to the big room like the Pied Piper leading the rats. The library was dark and theatrically staged. I sat in Miz Charlotte's big chair behind the flat expanse of her desk, swept clean save for Miss Benedict's work diary and my .357 Magnum. On the small, high table at my side, artfully lighted, was the old enameled casket.

Maybe there *is* something to the atavistic idea that some objects are intrinsically evil. Maybe the old relic still worked its emanations. In its presence the boisterous group changed abruptly. All eyes were on the box. This part of the program was going to be a great strain on me, but Miz Charlotte threatened me with bodily harm if I cut up.

"Ladies and Gentlemen . . . *The Casket of Alexander* . . ."

A silence followed and I let that sink in. Then I continued:

"This Casket is, beyond question, the most important find since the Dead Sea Scrolls. It is truly priceless, but unfortunately we must attempt to assign worth to it.

"Before continuing any mundane discussion of intrinsic value, however, I'll give you some idea of what it contains. We know the trail of violence in its wake and of the deaths of at least four people that can be attributed to the box . . . God knows how many more there might be.

"The Casket claimed its last victim four days ago. I mean, of course, Dr. Benedict herself . . . her stroke was truly the result of the remarkable contents of the box. It's only fitting to review excerpts from her working diary as she carefully investigated the scrolls.

"I refer now to her notes of 9 June: 'The first scroll is of papyrus and has been damaged. The initial 90 cm of the document, the outermost part of the scroll and most unprotected portion, is aged and unreadable save for isolated sections. It is obvious from cursory examination that some of the more legible parts near the 90 cm point are missing. (I might add parenthetically that we know Fowler removed some fragments as samples for Messieurs Hammerschmidt and Kamaroff—but to continue from the notes.) The balance of the scroll is, in my judgment, a copy of the Iliad by Homer on an excellent quality of papyrus of very ancient age.'

"There is, of course, considerably more commentary concerning this copy of the Iliad, which is priceless in itself, but for our purposes we need go no further. If you have additional questions I will provide information from these records after my remarks.

"The second scroll purports to be the commentary by Aristotle on the Iliad. Rather than read directly from Miss Benedict's lengthy notes, I think it better if I preface her findings, which I will support by excerpted material.

"Unquestionably, the commentary of Aristotle is the most important document unearthed thus far relating to the Hellenistic Era. For the first time the personalities of both Aristotle and Alexander are starkly revealed rather than a mere revelation of their activities. This document is not so much a commentary on the Iliad but rather on the personality of Alexander, as perceived by one of the greatest thinkers of antiquity.

"By inference, we find Aristotle a deeply concerned tutor, not by those unusual talents that Alexander possessed, but rather by the dangerous flaws he finds in his personality. Alexander loves the Iliad, and Aristotle, his patient and determined mentor, uses this love to expose Alexander's venality, arrogance, and manic aspiration to become a deity. This is no literary appraisal but rather a terse, but gentle, denunciation of the flaws the mentor finds in his charge. Here, Alexander is not the Achilles-like blond semi-god presented in history, but an arrogant, fractious teen-ager, who never really grows up and who is narcissistic and cruel.

"Into the hands of this youthful megalomaniac was placed the most formidable military machine existing at the time. Is it any wonder that Aristotle would be aghast at such a turn of events.... So the wise man, with admirable dexterity and courage, uses the Iliad, which Alexander held most sacred, as a means to correct his pupil.

"But the chemistry of human relationships is complex. Against all odds, Alexander fell under the thrall of Aristotle who constantly defied him. It seems that Alexander needed the respect of this man. He found in him, perhaps, the father figure that Philip of Macedon never provided.

"Alexander eventually departs on his great venture and is separated from the gentle persuasion of his mentor. Crowned with success, Alexander is christened 'The Great' and retreats further into his narcissism. He is no longer Macedonian or Greek—he deifies himself.

"Yet it's interesting to remember that despite all his astounding successes he cannot forget that one small corner of the world that he can never conquer, the mind of Aristotle. In the midst of all his pressing military, life and death, decisions he finds time to send back samples of natural life to his old tutor in Macedonia—like a schoolboy showing his butterfly collection to his teacher."

It's a great strain on my psyche to talk that long without a few pregnant asides, but Miz Charlotte had coached me for hours and if I didn't do it right, she'd come out of the clean room and break the Casket of Alexander over my head. My audience sat there in stunned silence. Oskar opened his mouth to talk but I knew if he started, we'd be there till Christmas. I held up my hand. "Later, please" I said.

I gave a long and involved reading of excerpted material from Miss Benedict's working diary. It was difficult deciphering her spidery copperplate and I kept it as short as possible—just enough to substantiate my eloquent précis. After that there was no holding Oskar.

"What about authenticity?"

"Unfortunately, Miss Benedict passed on before she had completed her research. They are on papyrus consistent with that period and the ink was sepia, squid secretion, which is also consistent. I haven't the expertise to make a formal judgment. The documents are for sale, by auction, as is, where is."

"That affects the price!" Kamaroff shouted.

"We shall see. The management reserves the right to reject all bids if the bidding doesn't meet expectations."

"This is not fair!" Kamaroff exploded. "We were led to believe it would be auctioned to the highest bidder! What right have you to make such conditions?"

I leaned over and patted the .357. "This is my right . . . here," I replied.

There was a lot of huffing, puffing and cross-talk.

"If these are forgeries you shall hear from me!" Sergei said through his teeth.

"You gotta find me first, Sergei," I smiled. "Do I continue now with the third scroll?"

In all the excitement I think they had forgotten about the third scroll.

"What in heaven's name iss it?" Oskar asked.

"The Pact between Alexander and Baalzibul—The Lord of the Flies."

Chapter XXIX

"Great Heavens, Peete," Sparrow moaned. "I hope you're not leading us into the wasteland of Satanism!"

"I'm not leading you anywhere, Alfie—I'm just telling you what's in the Casket."

"Mr. Sparrow iss correct, Dr. Peete," Hammerschmidt interjected, "this raises questions of authenticity. I think we should view the scrolls."

"You can inspect them later, Oskar. Shall I continue?"

The group settled back into a grumpy silence.

"Miss Benedict knew that anything smacking of Satanism raises questions and was as skeptical as any of you. But she was, first and last, a scholar. She withheld judgment. The view of the godhead was different in the millennium before Christ. A whole pantheon of gods, acknowledged by Alexander, were mischievously intruding into men's affairs. Before great ventures, soothsayers and oracles were commonly consulted; people we'd call warlocks and witches.

"The Bible has injunctions against congress with other gods. Not so with the Greeks and other peoples. The Iliad is replete with attempts by mortals to propitiate fickle gods.

"Baalzebul, or Beelzebub, is the Lord of the Flies. There are others; gods of serpents, frogs, rats and who knows what else that we read about with mild interest. Benedict rightly points out that Baalzebul is special because he is mentioned in the Bible. Had Alexander visited the Temple of Apollo at Didyma it would be an historical footnote. No one would say: 'Lordy, he has congress with Apollo!' Our Judeo-Christian heritage gives his visiting the Temple of Baalzebul a sinister connotation.

"Benedict also points out that gods had geographical precincts. When crossing the Hellespoint, Alexander made offerings to Poseidon. In the kingdom of the flies, why shouldn't the prudent commander try to propitiate the Lord of the Flies?

"Nothing profound happened in the hills around Gordium at the Temple of Baalzebul. There were no terrible rites or human sacrifices. Just a simple contract was drawn; a statement that Alexander recognized the satrapy of Baalzebul while in Asia Minor. For this he was promised the favor of the god for *ten* years."

"This occurred when?" Kamaroff asked.

"Around 333 BC, after the battle of Granicus."

"Which was the only battle that Alexander almost lost, along with his life! Was this before or after the Gordian knot?" Hammerschmidt mused.

I shrugged.

"And ten years later he had conquered the known world . . . and then— he dies. . . ." Sparrow said.

"That, Ladies and Gentlemen, concludes my presentation."

"The scrolls, I would like to inspect the scrolls . . ." Hammerschmidt said.

In the next few minutes we'd know whether Miz Charlotte's loony scheme would work or not. Oskar placed his pince-nez on the bridge of his nose with an air of expectancy. Kamaroff's black eyed gaze bore into me, his face in natural repose—that is, scowling like a gargoyle. Sarah Grey was out of it and she knew it. Lacy was beside himself, his mouth opening and closing, like a goldfish. Miss Withers was calm, watching with a kind of detached interest. Steiner just sat with his bug eyes trying to look in all directions at once.

"There's just one further precondition for bidders, Ladies and Gents," I said, "he, or she, can't be a murderer."

They all started babbling at once.

"What iss this imposture?" Oskar rumbled.

"He is an agent of the police!" Kamaroff screamed. "He has been from the start. He is always in the company of the tall one . . . the sheriff!"

Poor Sergei, I had hit an ancient resonating chord; the deep-seated hatred for the police agent and informer that had been woven into his very soul. His usual saturnine face seemed pasty and saliva bubbled at the corners of his mouth. Lacy was on his feet, shouting and pointing. Sarah looked at her male counterparts with contempt and Miss Withers with the detached interest of a prissy undergraduate biology student observing the scurrying of rats under stimuli. I held up my hands for silence.

"Look at my side for a minute," I said over the babble. "Somebody in this room plugged George Fowler and that muddies the waters." I turned toward Oskar who I felt to have a leadership of the group in matters cerebral. "Let's take a hypothetical case: let's say, Oskar, that good old Alfie parked above the VIMS installation and strolled down to Fowler's van and did the job . . ."

"Why on earth would he do that?" Oskar asked.

"Let's not get into the whys, we're just hypothesizing, right? Now suppose you outbid Sergei for the box but also suppose that old Alf made a mistake—say he left a clue."

"This iss ridiculous!"

" . . . and then say Stonewall Spooner nabs both of you for

conspiracy and murder? Then the business of the box comes out and what am I—an accessory after the fact? Or maybe they stop payment some way, or grab me as I'm leaving with the loot 'cause it's State's Evidence. It's not a question of ethics but good business practice.

"Now look at the bright side for a minute—from your perspective, not mine—it might narrow the bidding field. If it's either you or Sergei, Oskar, that's a big saving for those who are left."

Hammerschmidt threw up his hands in disgust. "But the local police could never unravel this thing . . ."

"Don't underestimate the local police, Oskar. There are good, smart people here. And they aren't alone—Spooner can go to the State Police for all kinds of scientific help and we're involved in a conspiracy crossing state lines. That could enter the jurisdiction of the FBI. None of you would like to talk to the police or the Feds. I'm making it in your self-interest to talk to me. If you do—we'll reduce the bidding field by one."

Hammerschmidt narrowed his eyes. "You would turn the killer over to the police?"

"C'mon, Oskar—there's some honor among us crooks. After a 24-hour head start, I'd pass what I know to the cops."

Oskar shook his head. "But there's still the question of the Casket . . ."

"By the time the local posse sorts that out I'll be long gone someplace where they don't extradite folks. You might like to take a little time to think this over. The bar's open and anyone who wants to leave, can—for keeps."

They sat there thinking. Hammerschmidt and Alf held a quiet communion, as did Lacy and Miss Withers, although theirs was more one-sided. The typhoon howled and Withers, without her data base, didn't know what to do.

"This is insufferable!" Steiner bellowed. "Why should I be exposed to this charade? You'll hear from my lawyers, Peete, and I'll personally see that you're stripped of all your credentials . . ."

Everyone turned and looked at him—appraisingly.

"Well you certainly can't think that I . . . this is ridiculous!" Steiner swallowed a few times. "I don't trust you, Peete! You'd better not try to gin anything up with these . . . these . . ."

"Scoundrels? Blackguards? Cads? I'm surprised at you, Steiner, they're your professional colleagues . . ." I was really enjoying this.

"You'll hear from my lawyers!" he shouted but he sat down again.

"Have them send their stuff to my beach house in Rio."

An uneasy truce settled over the group.

"For openers, let's talk about Fowler's schedule. The police figure that his van arrived before 10:30. We know that Sarah had an appointment at 11 P.M. and that she stood under the street light pole, making sure she could be seen—Miss Grey?"

"Your daft," she lilted. "I had no idea Fowler was there. How would I know?"

"Because you contacted him. You had arranged that back in Ireland before he tried to terminate your partnership with a truck. He was to disappear and head for Miami while you sat on Father Hugh. When things quieted down you were to contact him through a Miami convenience address.

"He pulled a few surprises, like the corpse of Walsh but we'll assume he told you that Walsh drowned accidentally and all you had to do was identify the body. When he tried to run you down, you couldn't believe it, but finding Father Hugh dead, you knew. You contacted us to help find Fowler; if anything went wrong, you were just a poor Irish lass looking for the relic.

"But you still wanted your cut and you covered yourself with a document outlining everything and stashed in a safe-deposit box . . . with a copy to the convenience address in Florida. He contacted you for a meeting at 11 P.M. to discuss things."

"Yer so damned smart, Peete—then why would I kill him?"

"Maybe he told you to pound sand. Maybe you were afraid he'd try to finish the job and hide your body and he'd be long gone before your letter was found."

"Well, he never showed up," she said, sulking.

"But you did go to see him?"

She shrugged. "He phoned th' motel. He said we should meet at th' beach an' make arrangements."

"At eleven?"

"Aye, I got there early."

Meanwhile Kamaroff was his usual grumpy self but seemed to reach the conclusion he had nothing to lose by playing the game. "Tebaldi called that day. I didn't know he was Fowler. He proposed a meeting at midnight to discuss the relic."

"But you also came early?"

"Of course, around 10:15. I wanted to see the place. When he told me it was a beach, I thought it would be deserted."

"But it was almost two hours to midnight—why didn't you leave after you looked it over and come back later?"

Sergei looked at Hammerschmidt. "I wished to see if anyone else was coming. I couldn't park in the lot; the car would attract attention. So we drove around the point and parked there. My assistants watched the parking area but saw nothing."

"How were you to make contact with Tebaldi?"

"He would flick his headlamps on and off. Then I was to go to his car."

"With the money?"

Sergei looked at me as if I was crazy. "Of course not, we would negotiate."

"So you knew that he didn't have the relic with him?"

Sergei wore a greasy smile. "I assumed that he wasn't a fool. The first meeting would be to agree on terms and the method of transfer."

"And you never approached the van?"

"No, it was not time. I didn't know it was his car."

I turned to Sparrow who was sitting next to Hammerschmidt and looking for all the world like a nervous headwaiter. "Well, Alfie, how about you," I asked.

Sparrow was sitting with his head high (so he could look down his nose at me) and his frog-like mouth had a definite downward turn. This was to let me know that I was beneath contempt in his gentlemanly eyes. He shot a quick peek at Oskar, sitting in an overstuffed chair and lighting a long, overstuffed cigar. Oscar's gaze flicked toward Alfie transmitting permission. Gad! I hoped I never looked like that around Miz Charlotte . . . it was positively humiliating! Sparrow turned back toward me.

"Yes?' he said as if I was asking him the way to Piccadilly Circus.

"Aw, c'mon, Alf—we don't have all night to play tea and crumpets (Oskar sort of gurgled at this which I interpreted as a guffaw). What was your deal at the beach?"

"Mr. Tebaldi had contacted me also," Sparrow said with a real stab at dignity, "he referred to the relic and proposed a meeting at 12:30 A.M. with a view toward effecting a transaction. The instructions given were similar to those propounded by Count Kamaroff. At the appointed time, Mr. Tebaldi would flick his lamps on and off."

"But you also arrived early?"

"That seemed prudent under the circumstances. I had never met the gentleman and a reconnaissance seemed wise."

"But you didn't drive down to the beach?"

"Of course not. I had rented a Lincoln saloon for my use. To drive such a vehicle to the beach amid the American pickup trucks (there was a distinct curl of the lip) would have been like arriving with a Fire Brigade. No, I parked on one of the side lanes and sauntered down."

"At what time did you arrive?"

"At approximately midnight."

"So you must have been acquainted with the general layout of the beach—the single access road and so forth?"

"Oh yes. I drove through the area around 4 P.M. I knew it was a cul-de-sac."

"What happened when you sauntered down at midnight?"

"I never got there. Nearing the place I saw it was alive with blue flashing lights and police cars. I felt I could serve no useful purpose by remaining."

"So you decided to do a 'bunk'?"

Patches of color rose in Alfie's cheeks. "Really, sir, I would hardly call it a bunk. Mr. Tebaldi would not wish to transact business amid the flashing lights of police cruisers and I was confident that he would call again with alternate arrangements, so I withdrew."

"Until the cops nailed you?"

Again Sparrow bridled. "That carries an unwarranted connotation, Dr. Peete! I was not 'nailed' as you so crudely put it. I was flagged down and I saw no earthly reason not to assist, where possible, with subsequent investigations. After all, I was merely meeting a business compatriot to discuss the sale of an artifact. The arcane circumstances were solely the invention of Mr. Tebaldi. I would have preferred the more congenial atmosphere of a good restaurant."

"But you can't prove you didn't arrive earlier than midnight and take your saunter before 10:30—say at 9 P.M.?"

"No. But I claim the same logic as Miss Grey. I came to negotiate the sale of a valuable relic. What possible reason could I have to do such an odious thing? Even if it could be demonstrated that Mr. Tebaldi intended to sell to another, the idea of killing him is quite inane. Besides, I thought he was Mr. Tebaldi—how was I to know he was Fowler?"

I looked at the others. Steiner was sitting there like a stuffed owl at a tennis match, his head swinging at questions and answers. Lacy looked like he was ready to go bananas.

"I guess now we think about people who did know about Mr. Tebaldi/ Fowler," I said quietly.

"You were watchin' me th' whole time!" Sarah cried. "How in God's green earth could I have found him at the beach?"

"He could have blinked his headlamps!" Sparrow interjected, happy at the prospect of someone else in the hot seat.

"But he didn't! You were watching and would have seen that . . . an' you would have seen me go into his van!"

"This is incredible, Peete! What right have you to hold this kind of inquisition?" Steiner shouted with the chorus. "I was in South Carolina and have been dragged up here to listen to this drivel!"

"This is actionable, Peete!" Lacy shouted, no longer able to contain the cyclonic winds. "I don't mean in the civil sense—I mean it's criminal! You think you're so damned clever but you've crossed the wrong man this time! I saw Fowler once when Steiner brought him to my New York office. He was a nobody; I paid no attention to him. I could have passed him on the street a dozen times and never known who he was behind his beard. Withers—call Bernbaum now—on that phone. He won't dare stop you; if he so much as touches you, I'll have him up for assault!"

The Snow Queen, at last having something to do with her hands, rose and walked purposefully to Miz Charlotte's desk and lifted the French phone, her slim fingers efficiently spinning the dial. At last she had a machine to play with....

But this was the Grand Finale . . . Miz Charlotte played the final scene from Don Giovanni. You know the one when the Devil walks through the wall to take Juan to Hell. Opening the bookcase panel to the clean room didn't make a lot of noise but bright light flooded the aperture into the mutely lit library. Miss Benedict stood framed in the light, a darkened figure standing dramatically. You couldn't see her face. What she needed was one of those theatrical smoke machines . . . smoke should have been wafting around her....

Chapter XXX

It was still pretty good. It jarred the hell out of me and I knew what was coming. Her square chin was up and she glided like a wraith over to her desk in her long, cream colored dress. Hammerschmidt was nonplused. His mouth opened, dropping his fat cigar into his lap, bobbling it like a little league shortstop. But he recovered quickly, his face smoothing out into an admiring smile.

"Magnificent, my dear Charlotte," he chuckled.

"Thank you, Oskar, you always appreciated good theater."

Sergei, as usual, was a crab. "This is a charade! You have no intention of selling the Casket! You . . . Peete. . . ." he sputtered.

"Calm yourself, Sergei," Miz Charlotte said. "Have a brandy. You really should develop a better sense of proportion. You can't have everything, you know. . . . There's the Mona Lisa, the Pieta . . ."

"Bernbaum's on the line, Mr. Lacy," the Ice Carving said.

Lacy walked resolutely to the phone. "Bernbaum!" the great winds blew again. "I want you in my office at 11 A.M. tomorrow!"

"I suggest that he come here, to Gloucester County," Miz Charlotte said sweetly.

"What the hell are you talking about?" Lacy snarled.

"Mr. Bernbaum seems highly competent. If I were you I

should want him present while the police discuss these matters with you," Miss Benedict replied.

"That's ridiculous—I was in New York . . ."

Charlotte eyed Miss Withers still standing by the desk. "Was he, Miss Withers? If I were you I would be very careful right now. Mr. Lacy's movements haven't been subject to any real scrutiny . . . as yet."

"But why?" Miss Withers' eyes widened microscopically.

"Well you see, Miss Withers, Fowler's schedule speaks of an orderly mind . . . a meeting with Miss Grey at 11 P.M., with Mr. Kamaroff at 12 P.M., and with Mr. Sparrow at 12:30 A.M. What about 11:30 P.M.? Not with Professor Steiner; he couldn't compete financially. But you, Mr. Lacy, are a man of some means." She turned to face Lacy. "Why shouldn't Fowler see you as a potential buyer and call you in New York, as Dr. Peete did, to invite your bid? You could have gone early and knowing that you couldn't compete, killed him in a fit of your famous pique, to make sure that no one else got the Casket."

"I want everyone to remember this!" Lacy shouted. "This is actionable! You were watching the beach at 11:30 Sheriff—and I was nowhere to be found! I'll want you swearing to that in a court of law when I take this old bag for everything she's worth!"

"Really, Mr. Lacy," Charlotte said sweetly. "I wouldn't put too much reliance in that. I said that Fowler's mind bespoke orderliness—but it also bespoke avarice. He was arranging a deal that involved millions—he'd have no qualms in changing his original schedule from 11:30 to say . . . 9:30 for that kind of money." Charlotte's eyes again shifted to Miss Withers. "That's why you must be very careful, my dear. Mr. Lacy never, to my knowledge, receives phone calls directly . . . they come through you. Am I correct?"

"But I wasn't at the damned beach!" Lacy shouted.

"Someone came by boat at 9:30, Mr. Lacy." Again, Miz Charlotte looked calculatingly at Miss Winters. "Let's postulate that Mr. Lacy is guilty. There will be phone calls from Fowler to New York. I can't imagine that someone as efficient as yourself wouldn't log the date and time of such calls . . . somewhere. . . . Then the travel, probably by private plane but flight itineraries are required to be filed, I believe. There's the boat, probably rented or purchased second-hand. Again, there would be records; boats are licensed here, and it must be somewhere now. Finally, there's the purchase of the pistol . . . difficult, but not impossible for a determined law officer to pursue. I might advise you that, in my opinion, Sheriff Spooner is a *very* determined law officer. If, my dear Miss Withers, you should happen to know of these things and are not forthcoming, you could be an accessory after . . . possibly even before, the fact. I'm not a lawyer and courts are fickle."

Miss Withers sat in a vacant chair by the desk. She continued to look placidly at Miss Benedict. "There is nothing positive to indicate that Mr. Lacy did this thing even if it were established that he was here," she said. I was beginning to give her high marks for guts.

Lacy jumped at this. "That's right, Withers! You have no basis for this gross accusation, Benedict!"

"No? I wonder. It's interesting that you are the only person involved in this affair who didn't view the body of Mr. Fowler on the beach. Messrs. Hammerschmidt and Kamaroff did—as did Miss Grey. If, as you have just remarked, you haven't seen Mr. Fowler, who you say was a 'nobody,' since the day Professor Steiner brought him to your office in New York, how did you know that Fowler had *grown a full beard* since his return to the United States?"

"I never . . ."

"Ah but you did, Mr. Lacy. You said that you'd met him but once and could pass him a dozen times on the street and never know him with his beard. I'm afraid that was before witnesses and *on tape* . . . You heard, Miss Withers. I suspect that you have a very good memory. There was no newspaper reporting of Fowler's beard or any other details—we were very circumspect about that . . . again, I would be *very* careful."

Withers calculated for a moment and then spoke. There was no emotion—it was as if she was working out a complex mathematical problem. "I purchased a small, outboard motorboat from a Richard Debbs of Newport News. I used the name of Marian Kemp."

"Withers. . . !" Lacy sputtered.

"Where is it now?"

"In Bayside Marina in Mathew's. I paid the agent $35 and asked him to sell it. I gave him a fictitious address."

"At Mr. Lacy's direction?"

"Of course."

"And travel down here?"

"Mr. Lacy took the company jet from the Newburgh Airport in upstate New York to a small field north of Richmond."

* * *

Marv came and took over. After taking depositions from the Snow Maiden and the rest of us it was 3 A.M. before he carted Lacy and Winters off to the local bastille for further consultations. Oskar and Sergei knew the game was over and began to relax. Sergei skulked off into a corner for some serious drinking and Oskar got himself a snifter of Miz Charlotte's 30-year-old brandy, relit his cigar and draped his elegant form into an easy chair. He began to wax eloquent.

"A charming evening, my dear Charlotte. One that shall

warm me during those cold Alpine nights. Only made more delicious, I might add, by your dramatic return from beyond . . . (he chuckled again) . . . but the scrolls? I concede your superlative victory, my dear, but may not the vanquished even glimpse the prize?"

"Of course, Oskar . . . David?"

I carefully carried the scrolls to Miz Charlotte's desk. Even Sergei staggered over although at this point he might have been looking at hieroglyphics with little pink elephants.

Oskar sat at the desk, his pince-nez perched on his nose, breathing hard. After about twenty minutes he pointed an accusing finger at Aristotle's commentaries. "This iss not sepia!" he said, alarmed, "the ink . . ."

"The extract of some kind of berry, I think," Charlotte said. "and, of course, a forgery. As is the last scroll, the inane pact with Baalzebul. You'll also notice, Oskar they're both on an inferior quality of papyrus . . . Sicilian, I suspect."

"And the first scroll—the Iliad?"

"The ink is sepia and the papyrus is, I think, of excellent Egyptian quality. I'm not at all sure about that one. They're still quite interesting products of the medieval mind. Of course, Alexander was repugnant to the powers in being then; the man deifying himself, conquering the world, establishing a cult of personality—all very bad form to the medieval way of thinking. The whole business smacks of monks, burning tapers and chanted orisons. The Satanic pact was the *pièce de résistance*, the hackneyed method of discrediting people in the time of deLacy. This alone convinced me it was all a chimera."

"But the first scroll, the Iliad. . . ?"

Miz Charlotte was uncompromising. "It certainly is a rare example of a very ancient manuscript—but, I'm afraid, nothing more. After all, Oskar . . . when one looks at the thing dispassionately, what have we got? A battered old bronze box of indeterminate age that could have been used for storing old shoes ... an excellent and rare old scroll ... and two highly suspect articles that I, for one, have absolutely no faith in ... a lot of supposition and fairy tales from Ireland."

Oskar threw up his hands with a sardonic smile. "Thank God you are safe, Charlotte! What would we do without your cold, incisive logic to keep us up to the mark...." This proposition was seconded by a loud snort from Sergei who was by now snoring off in a chair in the corner. Later Miz Charlotte offered our guests breakfast but they were sated—both with food and wine and Avalon. They departed for their respective hotels.

So the Casket of Alexander was put to rest but I was disappointed deep down. It would have been fun if it had been the real thing. One small point kept bothering me though.

"What about the skeleton with the broken neck ... what do you make of that?" I asked Miz Charlotte.

She removed her glasses and polished the lenses. "I'm afraid that we'll never know...."

"Maybe she tried to cop the casket ... or maybe she was Odo's mistress and ..."

"How many times must I tell you, David—I can't stand mindless speculation!"

The Casket was packed a week or so later and forwarded to the proper authorities in Ireland but not before there was a "grand" to-do in the local and national press. Panels of experts would pore over the scrolls in the future but I don't have any question in my mind as to the outcome. Miz Charlotte didn't make mistakes in these kinds of things. In the weeks that followed the Casket began to fade into memory and we got back to the serious business of finding new and ingenious ways of needling each other.

Marv was able to dig up all kinds of stuff on Lacy. The boat was launched from the same ramp that our intruder used back in May and Lacy was identified by some local people. The airplane movements also checked out, but the icing on the cake was the gun. Marv found a dealer near Petersburg who sold the gun to Lacy. He remembered him because he was well-dressed and the dealer tried to sell him a fancy Browning. He couldn't figure out why anyone so prosperous would buy such a piece of junk.

Sarah Grey slithered off and I have no idea what the Irish Government did about her escapades but I, for one, was happy to see the back of her.

About three weeks later we got a bread and butter call from Oskar in Switzerland. After all, he had downed a bushel of prime oysters and about a gallon of booze. I listened on the extension while he renewed his suit for Miz Charlotte's hand in connubial bliss. Toward the end of the conversation he said, "By the way, you might be interested to know that I've engaged Miss Withers."

"Oh really, Oskar? I don't think she's at all your type."

"My dear Charlotte, this iss strictly business, I was impressed by her efficiency."

"But what about her loyalty, Oskar?"

"Only a fool depends on loyalty in underlings—look at your Dr. Peete. The only true guarantee of loyalty is satisfied self-interest and I'll make it worth her while."

Don't let her wander too close to those glaciers, Oskar . . . you'll never find her again. Imagine that—the Snow Queen working for Hammerschmidt! Oh well—like they say . . . everybody's got to be somewhere . . .

– The End –

Author's Note

The "Casket of Alexander" is one of those interesting footnotes in History. I first found it while perusing *The Dictionary of Phrase & Fable* by the Reverend E. Cobham Brewer giving the Derivation, Source, or Origin of Common Phrases, Allusions and Words that have a tale to tell; Copyright MCMLXXVIII (1978) by Crown Publishers, Inc., Library of Congress Catalog Card Number: 78-56842; Page 220:

Casket Homer. Alexander the Great's edition (of Homer), with Aristotle's corrections. After the Battle of Arbe'la a golden casket, studded with jewels, was found in the tent of Dari'us. Alexander, being asked to what purpose it should be applied, made answer, "There is but one production in the world worthy of so costly a repository," and placed therein his edition of Homer, which received from this circumstance the term *Casket Homer.*

The casket's finding its way to the Library of Alexandria and its donation to Caesar by Cleopatra are, as Dr. Peete would be the first to point out, pure moonshine.

The quote used by Dr. Peete and attributed to Robert E. Lee: "Duty is the sublimest word in our language. Do your duty in all things. You cannot do more. You should never wish to do less." may be found in *Bartlett's Familiar Quotations*. It is also inscribed beneath his bust in the Hall of Fame. It was purported to be extracted from a letter written by Lee to his son, Custus, then a cadet at West Point, dated 5 April 1852. The letter in fact is a forgery (see *Robert E. Lee, The Man and Soldier,* by Philip Van Doren Stern, Library of Congress Catalog Card Number 63-18544, page 88-89). It was first printed in the *New York Sun* on 26 November 1864 and then a few days later in Richmond. It was repudiated and exposed by Lee himself. I thought it appropriate to include the quote in the text as an example of the perniciousness of historical forgeries and frauds.

Lastly, nothing is known of the relationship of Alexander and Aristotle except what may be deduced from their known actions (i.e., Alexander was known to have continued to send examples of the natural world back to his old tutor during his campaigns). All references in the text to their personalities and personality conflicts are flights of fancy.